LITTLE
INFAMIES

STORIES

LITTLE INFAMIES

PANOS KARNEZIS

FARRAR, STRAUS AND GIROUX   NEW YORK

Farrar, Straus and Giroux
19 Union Square West, New York 10003

Copyright © 2002 by Panos Karnezis
All rights reserved
Distributed in Canada by Douglas & McIntyre Ltd.
Printed in the United States of America
Originally published in 2002 by Jonathan Cape, Great Britain
Published in the United States by Farrar, Straus and Giroux
First American edition, 2003

Grateful acknowledgment is made to *Granta* and to the *New Writing Anthology*,
where two of these pieces, "Whale on the Beach" and "Deus ex Machina,"
respectively, originally appeared.
Grateful acknowledgment is made to Princeton University Press for permission
to reprint lines from "Things Ended" by C.P. Cavafy, from *Collected Poems*,
copyright © 1975, 1992 by Edmund Keeley.

Library of Congress Control Number: 2002112478
ISBN: 0-374-18937-4

www.fsgbooks.com

1 3 5 7 9 10 8 6 4 2

Engulfed by fear and suspicion,
mind agitated, eyes alarmed,
we try desperately to invent ways out,
plan how to avoid
the obvious danger that threatens us so terribly.
Yet we're mistaken, that's not the danger ahead:
the news was wrong
(or we didn't hear it, or didn't get it right).
Another disaster, one we never imagined,
suddenly, violently, descends upon us,
and finding us unprepared – there's no time now –
sweeps us away.

— C.P. Cavafy

Contents

LITTLE
INFAMIES

A Funeral
of Stones

I

Since dawn the air had the sultriness of fermenting juices and later, just before lunch, the dog started barking for no reason and did not stop until Father Yerasimo chased her away with stones. He could not imagine then that the poor animal was only trying to warn him. Because no sooner had he washed his dish, fed the leftovers to the chickens, and sat on the veranda to drink a glass of wine, than a roar like the beating of an enormous vat echoed across the village. Father Yerasimo watched with fascination as his glass toppled, and the red wine spilled over the table.

'Shit!' he uttered. 'It's the Second Coming.'

On the trees the crows suddenly took flight as if a gun had been fired, and a herd of sheep not far away bunched together and started bleating. Father Yerasimo crossed himself. The first tremor was as imperceptible as the dynamite detonations that

3

reached the village from the penitentiary mines; it made the grid cables sway a little, and the canary banged its wings against the wires of its cage. The momentary shadow of a cloud that passed in front of the sun fell on Father Yerasimo's humble house, increasing his terror. And when the door to the veranda creaked on its hinges, he shivered like the time he had heard the hiss of a demon during one of his failed exorcisms. '*Kyrie eleison me,*' he whined, and touched the cross on his chest, remembering his pastoral failings. 'It's not my fault. I have tried my best. But those heathens have the heads of mules.'

He had hardly finished his penance when the concrete veranda started rocking, as if it were floating on water. The pair of rubber galoshes in the corner, which he wore in winter to walk the few yards from home to the church, jumped up and down, and the swinging storm lantern on the wall rained paraffin on his threadbare cassock, but such was his shock that he did not move.

Then, as suddenly as it had started, the earthquake stopped.

For a while there was silence except for the occasional shattering of loose tiles slipping off roofs. The birds returned to the trees, while inside its cage the canary shrunk on its perch. In the square, in front of the church, people started arriving from every direction like a hunted herd. With them they carried the things they had salvaged from their homes: dishes of fake china, a shotgun with its cleaning rod, a wall clock whose cuckoo had fallen off its spring mechanism, the money from under the mattress, a still smoking Russian samovar, a bride-to-be her hired tulle gown, the mayor the cast-iron typewriter he had paid for with municipal funds, and someone else was pushing the bed with his sick grandparents still in it.

'The battle of Armageddon has begun!' Father Yerasimo shouted malevolently from his veranda. 'Too late for you to repent now.' They looked at him, shamefaced. 'Don't say I didn't warn you,' the priest added.

They were still in the square debating what to do when the terror returned. The earthquake announced its second attack by tolling the church bells, and although the belfry endured the subterranean violence, shaking like a fishing rod, the delicate mechanism of its clock did not, and its iron hands stopped at that hour of misfortune. The villagers could only watch as the ground beneath their feet rippled and the cypresses dropped their cones. The plaster of the murals inside the church broke up, and a moment later the big blue letters above the door of the town hall fell off one by one. Soon after the balcony slipped off its cantilevers too, and landed on the ground in one piece: floor, railing, flagpole and the deckchair in which the mayor used to take his afternoon naps.

The destruction continued among the laments of the villagers. Houses that found themselves in the path of the earthquake surrendered to its force: roofs caved in, chimneys toppled and blocked the streets, and adobe sheds disintegrated to piles of dust and straw. But the villagers had little time to grieve the loss of their property. Suddenly there was a noise of cracking stone and masonry, then a cloud of dust arose and from the cloud emerged the horns of a bolting cattle herd.

The people sought refuge inside the church of St Timotheo. A family of Jehovah's Witnesses, whom Father Yerasimo did not let in, climbed as high as they could on the cypresses in the courtyard, held tight to the dense branches and said their prayers, while underneath the cattle rushed past, heading towards the other end of the village. When the herd had disappeared, Father Yerasimo held his breath and discovered that the earthquake was also gone. He then carefully opened the church doors, looked left and right, and said with a sigh: 'This village is drawn to misery like moths to a light.'

They had to count themselves three times to be sure that no one was missing and after that the people began work. The blacksmith assessed the damage to the church clock. He concluded that the only thing the mainspring and the wheels needed was straightening and the clock would be ticking again, but the village unanimously voted to leave it as it was, so that it would forever remind them of the disaster. Some men followed the barber to his shop, where they cleared the dust in the air with a pair of bellows from the smithy, stepped over the fallen crossbeams, moved the leather chair out of the way, and lifted the heavy panel with the carved cherubs that had come off the wall, already knowing what they would find underneath: of the exquisite mirror, which the barber had bought cheaply from a fading city beauty with an obsessive habit of counting her wrinkles, there remained only a heap of sharp, reflecting splinters. But nothing saddened the men more than the news they heard next: Sapphire's house on the edge of the village, the one with the whitewashed walls and the carmine shutters, the pots of basil and rosemary, and the half-open door with the horseshoe on, had turned into a pyramid of colourful rubble. Only Father Yerasimo was pleased: 'At last,' he said, 'the house of sin is cast into Hell.'

It was evening when the wind turned and they finally heard the shrieks of the peacocks that lived at the cemetery. When the crowd got there, lifted the twisted iron gate off its hinges and walked in, they discovered that the passing of the earthquake had not only split the ground into countless pits, broken the tombstones to pieces, and devastated the small glass shrines with the oil candles that had not been filled for years and the vases of dried-up amaranths that had never been watered, but also — and worst of all — had exhumed the coffins of their ancestors.

They tried to push the coffins back in but it was a vain effort, because as soon as they touched them the worm-eaten planks would crumble. So they decided to make new coffins. The men worked all night in the light of lanterns and all through the next day too, while the women were told to take out the bones, and mark them so they would not get mixed up. It was during this time that they chanced upon a coffin filled with books, and Father Yerasimo, embarrassed, hurried to explain that it was a pile of worthless paper filled with the lies of blasphemous and ignorant heretics. But they made other discoveries too: inside another coffin they found a complete telegraph system next to the remains of a man afraid of being buried alive, and in yet another they were puzzled to see a liver in perfect condition under the bleached bones of a notorious drunk; the doctor explained that it was the alcohol that had preserved it.

They had almost finished piling up the unearthed coffins when a particularly small one caught Father Yerasimo's eye. It was not its size that intrigued him, because he knew that death was often tempted by the helplessness of children in the village, but what its flaking coat of paint revealed underneath: it was in fact a box for packing salted fish. But his greatest surprise came when, after using his shovel to break the rusty nails in its lid, and going down on his knees, he saw that rather than a child's remains the cheap wooden box contained eighteen heavy stones, each chiselled and polished to the unmistakable shape of a human heart.

It took two days to make the new coffins, and on the third the villagers, wearing crape made from women's garters, heard mass for the repose of the souls of the dead to the sound of cicadas. No sooner had Father Yerasimo said 'Dust to dust' than they were all on the road home, leaving him alone in the cemetery but for the undertaker who started covering the graves. Standing in front of the box of stones the priest felt an overwhelming loneliness. No one could remember the exact location where it had been found – or they would not tell him. Father Yerasimo gave the box a frustrated kick. 'A sin has been committed,' he said. 'Some time ago I administered the last rites to a pile of stones.'

The cemetery was on top of a hill overlooking the village. The tombstones ruined by the earthquake had been made into a heap, and unadorned wooden crosses had taken their place. Father Yerasimo fed the corn and stale bread he had brought with him to the pair of peacocks before collecting their dropped feathers which he used to decorate the altarpiece. It was a day of clear and pleasant weather. Since the earthquake he had not been able to stop thinking about his mysterious discovery. During the two previous nights he had awoken with tears of mortal fear in his eyes, because he had dreamed of the destruction of Sodom and Gomorrah by a rain of brimstone and an earthquake, while on the morning of the mass he had heard noise coming from the closet where his vestments hung; holding his cross in his trembling hand and whispering a prayer of exorcism he had opened it, only for an enormous rat to jump out.

He had considered these the machinations of the Devil, and soon convinced himself that the very earthquake itself had been sent by God so that he would discover the box. Solving the mystery, therefore, would be the beginning of the long road of the village's penance, he thought. With that in mind, some time later he entered the civil guard station.

'You are wasting your time, Father,' the corporal said as soon as he saw him. 'And, more importantly, mine.'

'A sin has been committed,' Father Yerasimo said.

'That is your jurisdiction, Father, not mine.'

'There might be a crime involved, too. It is standard police procedure—'

'I'll look into it after I finish with these,' the civil guardsman said, and pressed his palm on a stack of criminal suits regarding the looting of private property after the earthquake. He added, ironically: 'In the meantime keep the stones safe, Father. They're crucial forensic evidence.'

Father Yerasimo blushed with anger. 'It was a sin,' he repeated stubbornly.

He was not a man to give up easily: he decided to do the inquiry himself. But he did not know where to start, and instead wandered the streets for hours, deep in thought. Whomever he came across he questioned about the extent of the damage to their property, but with such absent-mindedness that when their paths crossed again some time later he would ask the same thing and offer his sincere condolences anew.

Large parts of the village were in ruins. On his way to the square Father Yerasimo had to climb over the rubble of what was once a two-storey house with a fireplace on each floor and a broken jasmine shrub that used to reach all the way to its roof. Though the plant was now buried under many layers of brick, plaster and masonry, it still emitted the memory of its perfume. Not far away the earthquake had spared a stable. Donkeys and mules were tethered outside, and the owners had taken over their shelter. The priest stopped at the barber's shop, where the barber, on all fours, was piecing together the mirror.

'Don't step on the shards, Father,' the barber said, with a bottle of glue in his hand. 'Unless you are so light you can also walk on the sea.'

Father Yerasimo obeyed. He lifted a chair lying upside down on the floor, wiped the seat with the cuff of his cassock and sat down. The little shed was in a bad state. Deep cracks crossed the walls, and there was a big hole in the roof. In a corner the five-bulb chandelier lay on a pile of glass tears and dust. It reminded the priest of a dead swan.

He asked: 'Do you know anything about the stones in the box?'

'I have no idea, Father,' the barber replied immediately.

He was still bent over the mirror, but he had slowly turned so that he now had his back to the priest. Father Yerasimo observed him in silence. Out in the street women and children walked by carrying pails full of mortar. The barber started humming.

'Have you ever thought of losing your beard, Father?' he asked after a while. 'I'll do you a good price.'

The priest did not respond to the joke. He felt that it was an attempt to evade his questions.

'Strange,' Father Yerasimo persisted, stroking his beard. 'Because men tell their barber things they wouldn't even tell their wives.'

'Not me, Father. They say I am worse at keeping a secret than King Midas's barber.'

The priest did not believe him. But he knew that it would be bad tactics to show his suspicion at this early stage of his inquiry.

'Done,' said the barber after a moment. He stood up, and wiped his hands on his trousers. 'Will you give me a hand, Father?'

Father Yerasimo helped him hang the heavy mirror back on the wall. When they had finished, the barber asked: 'What do you think?'

Father Yerasimo looked at the mirror. It was like a mosaic made by an amateur. There were gaps between the shards and his reflection was so distorted that his face resembled that of a mule.

'This thing is only good for the House of Mirrors,' he said bitterly. And, unable to suppress his feelings any longer, he added: 'You're no better at repairing mirrors than telling lies, barber.'

That night his nightmares returned. Father Yerasimo cursed and sighed for a long time before admitting defeat in his efforts to fall asleep. He sat up in bed and looked out of the window. It was still several hours till dawn. His house had only one room: it was a bedroom, a study and a kitchen all in one. He put as much ground chicory – on account of his fragile finances – as coffee in the pot, a bit of sugar, and boiled the mixture over the spirit stove. He then wrapped himself in his cassock and sat in the same chair on the veranda from where he had watched the attack of the earthquake three days earlier. He drank the coffee while it was still burning and contemplated the horizon where the outline of the hills was barely visible. When he had finished his cup he made some more coffee and returned to the veranda, where he remained, deep in his thoughts, until the hills had taken on the colour of honey. Only when the cocks crowed did he remember that it was soon time for matins, and rushed to get dressed, saying: 'Forgive me, Lord. Even I have forsaken Thee.'

The service was so badly attended that it only increased his melancholy. In addition, he twice caught himself thinking about the irreverent burial while he consecrated the bread and wine. He offered Communion in a hurry and said the Our Father faster than usual. Then he woke up the old women who invariably fell asleep during the service, and when everyone was gone he removed his liturgical vestments and wore his dirty cassock again: he was now ready for another day of questioning.

He started with the coffee shop, where the waiter was surprised to see him so early. 'The only other time I remember you coming to the shop at this hour, Father,' he said from behind the counter, 'was when you ran out of Eucharist wine.'

Father Yerasimo liked him. The waiter was such a giant of a man that when he moved across the shop he reminded the priest of an ocean liner trying to dock without a tugboat. And his delicate manners had convinced Father Yerasimo that he was the most sincere, biggest-hearted man in the village. He brought the priest his coffee.

'That was some emergency,' said the priest, recollecting the event with both shame and childish mischievousness. 'I had to sneak out through the back, and even the psalmist didn't notice.' He checked his chuckle, and added, solemnly: 'I hope the Lord has since forgiven me for offering brandy that day.'

'I am sure he has, Father; it was one hundred and sixty proof, if you remember. I was saving it for my sister's wedding.'

'And I am grateful to you, my son,' Father Yerasimo said soberly.

He had taken a seat at a table near the counter. On the wall was a circle of dirt where the clock used to be. It was a clock in the shape of an enormous bottle cap with the logo of a popular beer brand on it, delivered free of charge to any retailer with an annual turnover of five thousand cases or over.

'Shame about the clock,' Father Yerasimo said.

The waiter looked at the mark on the wall with sadness.

'It was a good clock,' he said.

'Swiss?'

'The mechanism, yes. Seven rubies.'

Both men looked at the dirt mark on the wall in silence.

The waiter said: 'It only lost a minute a month.'

'Is that a fact?' Father Yerasimo shook his head, impressed, and quickly moved on. 'Today I need your help again, my son, but on another matter.'

Apart from the clock, the only other damage suffered by the shop during the earthquake was a piece of plaster falling from the ceiling on to the display refrigerator. Through the cracked glass of the refrigerator the priest watched the waiter washing dishes.

'My help, Father?'

'Yes. What can you tell me about the stones?'

'The stones?'

'The stones in the coffin.'

'The . . . coffin?'

Father Yerasimo studied the giant's hands with suspicion. That morning they had little of their familiar dexterity – in fact, they were shaking. Also, as soon as the waiter had washed all the dishes, and although they were clean, he moved them back into the lather, and started sponging them again.

'Weren't you at the cemetery when I found the fish box?' asked the priest.

The other wiped his forehead with the back of his hand.

'Oh, that coffin . . . yes,' he replied leaning over the sink. He had foam on his brow.

'Well?'

'I wish I could help you, Father. But when my customers talk in earnest they're so drunk I can't make out what they're saying. It's a problem.'

Father Yerasimo felt betrayed. A week earlier he had given this man a quick absolution for having cut the spirits with water. Now he was paying him back with a lie. His fury choked him, and he downed his coffee decisively. 'The real problem, my son,' he said, raising his finger, 'is that you have been fraternising with heathens for too long.' He neither waited to hear the other man's excuses nor did he pay for the drink.

That afternoon Father Yerasimo managed to sleep for an hour before the dog awakened him with her whining. After feeding her, he washed his face at the sink, dried his beard with the dishcloth and went to the railway station. The side wall of the ticket office had collapsed, and there were bricks and plaster on the furniture and the floor. Furthermore, the counter of the telegraph room had come off its hinges, while in the waiting room the windowpanes were broken. Father Yerasimo found the stationmaster sitting in a rocking chair on the platform. He was cleaning a stack of framed posters with a feather duster. He was in his uniform and had his cap tipped back. The priest greeted him.

'Good afternoon, Father,' the stationmaster replied without turning round. 'There won't be any services for a while.' He pulled his cap lower and started rocking in his chair.

'Why is that?'

'The rails are bent.' The stationmaster pointed to the track some distance away. 'Can't you see the broken sleepers?'

The priest nodded even though he could not see that far. 'Misfortune hits the rich with a gavel,' he said dispiritedly, 'and the poor with a sledgehammer.'

The stationmaster agreed. He was still dusting the old posters. He said: 'As soon as I fix the telegraph I will notify the company.'

'Shit,' murmured the priest, and immediately bit his lip.

'Were you planning a trip, Father?'

'Me?' the priest said nonchalantly. 'I haven't travelled in twenty-three years, son. Even if there were to be another Great Flood now I wouldn't be able to move.'

It was only half the truth. He had come to the station with the intention of sending telegrams to the civil guard headquarters, the prefect and the bishop regarding the box of stone hearts. He had also considered travelling to the county capital personally, but only by train – the coach journey he could not make on account of his senile need for frequent urination. Now that both plans had failed, Father Yerasimo felt the need to sit down. He carried out a chair from the waiting room.

'Sometimes I feel as if I'm carrying the sky on my shoulders,' he sighed.

The stationmaster finished dusting the posters and lit a cigarette.

'I should know,' he replied, staring idly at the horizon. 'I break my back carrying luggage.'

'At least if there was a moral reward . . .' Father Yerasimo pondered.

'Unloading luggage is not my job,' continued the stationmaster. 'But this station is undermanned.'

The priest was close to tears. 'And the loneliness of it all. Oh Lord, I can't stand the loneliness . . .'

'Sometimes one has to accept things the way they are, Father.'

It was these words that awakened Father Yerasimo from the stupor of his disappointment. All his life he had admired the voluntary suffering of Christian hermits; suddenly he realised that every defeat, every minute of loneliness and every drop of sweat on his forehead represented one further step towards Heaven.

'Never!' he said defiantly. And jumping from his seat, he grabbed the stationmaster by the collar.

'What the hell, priest!' The cigarette fell from the stationmaster's hand.

'Tell me what you know about the stones!'

The stationmaster tried to free himself, shouting: 'I am a civil servant. You cannot touch me!'

But Father Yerasimo tightened his grip with a strength that impressed even himself. His frustration, which had been building up since the discovery, had found its prey in the stationmaster who was conveniently a small enough man to overpower. After being held down for several minutes, and with his rocking chair in precarious balance, the stationmaster finally gave up.

'Ask my wife,' he whispered. 'She'll tell you.'

Father Yerasimo let him go. Trembling, the stationmaster searched for his cigarette on the floor.

He and his wife lived in the small house next to the crossing. Built by railway engineers, the house was modelled on an army lookout post. Thanks to its reinforced concrete walls and floors, it had endured the earthquake undamaged. In the stationmaster's absence his wife was responsible for lowering the road barrier when a train was approaching. More importantly, for many years she had been the village midwife. Father Yerasimo knocked at the door and entered without waiting for an answer. He found her at the table, reading a romantic novel with a woman in a tight dress and a low, revealing neckline on the cover. As soon as she saw him she hid the book in a drawer and blushed.

'I'm here on important business,' the priest announced.

She knew immediately what he wanted. She offered him a seat and was about to go and make coffee when he ordered her not to. The midwife was a small, plump, childless woman who wore a headscarf even indoors. Father Yerasimo remembered her as a beautiful and energetic child; now she had grown a moustache that was not much smaller than her husband's. He spread his hands on the table. She looked at them curiously: they were hairless and scrawny, with long fingers, uncut nails and purple lesions.

She said light-heartedly: 'Your hands look like crabs, Father.'

Father Yerasimo refused her the joke. Instead he asked: 'Who did it?'

'You shouldn't ask who but why, Father.'

'I will ask the culprit that.'

Father Yerasimo sat back and the chair creaked under his weight. A smell of garlic came from a wooden mortar and pestle on the cupboard. He crossed his hands over his chest and tapped his fingers on the table.

After a while the midwife said: 'The mother died immediately after birth. You officiated at the funeral.' She took a deep breath. 'And you were told it was a stillbirth. The baby was buried next to the mother – the box.'

'The box with the eighteen stone hearts,' the priest said.

'One for every year of her life.'

'So the baby lived.'

'Both. They were twins.'

'Was it the father who concocted the lie?'

'Of course,' the woman replied drily.

The priest pointed his finger at her. 'I want his name.'

She only had to look in his eyes to understand the futility of her resistance. She told him.

'I remember the burial now,' Father Yerasimo said, nodding. 'The two coffins, yes.' He recalled the small, cheap, freshly painted baby's coffin that had remained sealed throughout the ceremony. 'Tell me everything, woman,' he demanded. 'It's your last chance to save your soul.'

The sun was behind the hills, and the village was slowly sinking into a sullen darkness: during the earthquake the electricity substation had collapsed and all the equipment had been destroyed. When Father Yerasimo left home with the storm lantern in his hand he could only see the Dog Star, but after an hour's walk the sky was dark enough for him to recognise all the constellations. He sat on a rock on the side of the dust road and perused the stars. It was a habit he had maintained since childhood. Once he was satisfied with his celestial knowledge he lit the paraffin lantern and walked on.

He was not afraid of the dark; the dog he had taken along for company. He could hear her bell as she ran ahead of him, lagged behind, or left the road – possibly to chase a rabbit. Occasionally she would come and brush herself against the priest's leg, and he would let her lick his hand.

'If only people obeyed God the way dogs obey us,' Father Yerasimo mused.

His destination was a house on the other side of the village from the cemetery, where the widower lived. Father Yerasimo had not seen him in church for several years. In fact, the man almost never came to the village these days, and then only to buy provisions from the chandler. Father Yerasimo remembered the first time he had seen him after his wife's death. He had appeared at dusk, wearing his brimmed hat like a mask, an old army tunic without insignia, and a pair of riding boots he must have picked up from the flea market in the county capital. The furtiveness of his walk had almost convinced the priest that he was the ghost of a soldier killed in action.

Father Yerasimo saw the house in the distance. The earthquake had ravaged it. The outside walls were standing, but the roof and all the interior walls had collapsed; the rubble remained untouched where it had fallen. The moonlight shone through broken windows, and in the garden the monumental chimney had crashed on to the wooden privy. Father Yerasimo felt as if confronted by a rotting carcass – and not only because of the desolation; the smell of excrement was everywhere. Behind him the dog grunted. When Father Yerasimo reached the veranda and raised the lantern, the light unexpectedly shone upon a pair of yellow eyes. 'Lord Saviour!' he cried out. The lantern fell from his hand and the flame blew out.

In the dark a voice said wearily: 'I've been waiting for you, priest.'

The words sounded as if they were coming from the end of a tunnel. Father Yerasimo felt about for the storm lantern. When he lit it again and his eyes grew used to its glow, he saw the outline of a man. He was lying on a camp bed, covered with blankets to the neck, and from the blankets emerged the barrel of a shotgun. The priest raised the lantern and looked at where the roof had been. 'You're lucky to be alive.'

'I always sleep out in the summer. The afternoon of the earthquake, in fact, I slept through it all.'

Father Yerasimo nodded. 'You sleep well for a sinner, Nikiforo.'

'The only sin I know of is the death of my wife,' the other said.

He sounded angry. Father Yerasimo had only to glance at the shotgun to change his tactics immediately. A wild animal could be tamed with food, he thought; a dangerous man with the right words. He indicated the shotgun.

'What's that for?'

'Birds.'

'You should start work on the roof,' the priest said calmly. 'Before the rains.'

The man coughed, and stirred under the blankets. 'It can wait.'

Father Yerasimo climbed the steps and shone the lantern at the man. On the blankets was the bad news of consumption: the man had been coughing blood. The dog smelled the sickness and kept her distance. But Father Yerasimo's curiosity pushed him closer. There were rats under the bed and they ran away.

'You ought to be in a sanatorium, Nikiforo.'

'I'm fine here, priest. Those places are hotels for poets.'

Father Yerasimo leaned against the only standing pole of the trellis that once roofed the veranda, and put the lantern on the floor, where the snapped branches of a grapevine lay like dead snakes. Neither man could see the other's face from that distance. The priest spoke up.

'I've come across a buried fish box, Nikiforo.'

The man shifted under the covers.

'Yes, I've heard.'

Father Yerasimo was surprised. 'How come?'

'When the wind blows from the village I can even hear you playing with your string of beads.'

'I see . . . I believe you know what was inside that box.'

They were both silent while the man picked up a pack of cigarettes from the floor and an ancient flint-and-wick lighter. He lit up with slow movements. He said: 'I met my wife twenty years ago. I still love her.' He talked as if hypnotised. 'Our marriage wasn't arranged. We'd met at the market.'

He said that that day, sent by her mother, she had come to the open market to buy corn. It was the eve of her seventeenth birthday. She had raven plaits, and wore a dress with house martins printed on it. It was a day of little business and Nikiforo was stretched on a chair under the awning, oiling his shotgun and killing time.

'Mother!' he had exclaimed as soon as he had seen her. 'These martins brought spring earlier this year.'

It had indeed been love at first sight. Immediately he had come from behind his stall and run after her with an armful of fruit. 'Please have these peaches. They're my own produce,' he had said. 'Their stones are real rubies.'

She had ignored him mercilessly.

'Only my mother's cat claws the hand that tries to feed her,' Nikiforo had said, insulted. 'She thinks she's a leopard.'

His surprising directness had shattered the young woman's defences. She had stopped and blushed.

'I'm sorry, I didn't hear you,' she had apologised with a lie. 'Our house is next to the church, and the bell has damaged my eardrums.'

Nikiforo had responded gallantly. 'I'm the best shot in the valley,' he had boasted. His stall in the square stood not far from the church that day. 'For you I'll bring down the belfry.' He had raised his shotgun to prove it, but she had stopped him. The moment she had touched the barrel she had felt the sparks of love on her fingertips and had let out a cry.

'Don't be afraid,' Nikiforo had explained. 'It's static electricity from polishing it with the wool.'

She had not listened to him, choosing to believe instead that the minute jolts were a sign of their mutual and inescapable attraction.

Father Yerasimo yawned. He was a widower too, but during his married life he had been more tormented than exhilarated by the declarations and applications of love.

'I prefer the worship of God myself,' he said. 'But I understand how you must've felt.'

'You have no idea, priest.'

'Love is my chosen profession, Nikiforo.'

'Your love is even further away from what I mean than Sapphire's services.'

Father Yerasimo lost his temper. 'Blaspheme as much as you like. The fact is that your cauldron is boiling in Hell as we speak.'

The man started coughing. Father Yerasimo said: 'You always had my sympathy, Nikiforo. God knows, yours was a heavy cross to bear. But—'

'In the cellar,' the man said, wiping the blood from his mouth. 'That's where I used to keep them. Let me show you.'

He pushed the blankets aside and tried to stand with the help of his shotgun. He wore the same tunic Father Yerasimo remembered him in, but now a large part of it was eaten away by the rats.

II

His wife's pains had started during an afternoon of biblical rain, as soon as Nikiforo had sat down in the wicker chair by the window with the sports newspaper and a cup of sage tea. They were recovering from an imperial meal. The previous months one after the other all the hens had been slaughtered to satisfy Olympia's cravings, and Nikiforo could see no reason to tolerate any longer the broken-hearted crows of a lonely cock: that day he finally had him pot-roasted, with boiled potatoes on the side, ewe's cheese, freshly baked bread and resined wine.

'I feel as if I've been crushed by a tombstone,' his wife had said ominously, when they had finished. 'Help me to bed.'

Nikiforo carried Olympia to the bedroom, untied the hemp rope he had given her when her belly had grown too big for the tasselled cord of her dressing gown, and put what was left of the lunch in the meat safe that hung from the eaves on the veranda. He did this and other chores with perfunctory movements and somnolent eyes which not even the vapours of the brewing sage could revive. In fact, such was his stupor from that day's culinary adventure that when he heard Olympia's cries he assumed she had seen another rat in the bedroom. He was wrong.

'Stop running around with the broomstick like a fool and go fetch the midwife,' his wife instructed him.

Nikiforo took the bicycle but did not count on the rain. Less than a mile from home he fell into a pool of thick mud from which he could not pull out the wrought-iron bicycle and he had to continue on foot. Every time the wind turned and the rain beat against his face he would walk with his eyes closed. Then he would invariably step into another mud trap, and he would have to get his feet out of his galoshes and dig them out one by one. Finally, he arrived at the midwife's house. The stationmaster opened the door, rubbing his eyes: he had been asleep. Nikiforo explained the urgency of the situation.

'Why do I have to pay for other men's folly?' the stationmaster asked, surly. 'My respect for sleep was exactly the reason why I never wanted children.'

Soaked through, Nikiforo begged him to wake up his wife.

'There're more than enough souls in the world already,' the stationmaster continued. 'Why on earth do we keep breeding like rabbits?'

Nikiforo lost his patience and pushed him aside. The midwife was in bed in her hairnet and curlers; she had fallen asleep reading a novel about pirates. The moment she opened her eyes and saw above her head a man whose face was caked with mud, she mistook him for a Berber. It was several minutes before her husband calmed her down.

When Nikiforo returned home, a big surprise awaited him: Olympia was not in bed but in the kitchen warming the leftovers in the pan. Nikiforo and the midwife looked at the pregnant woman, speechless. In her tattered gown and a shawl wrapped round her inflated belly to keep it warm, she reminded Nikiforo of the balloon that had landed in a cornfield outside the village when an ignorant farmer had taken a shot at it.

'Have a seat,' Olympia said casually. 'Dinner is almost ready.'

But her body was only resting in the eye of its storm, because no sooner had the three of them sat at the table than the pains returned, and this time they were worse. Soon the contractions became so excruciating that Olympia, in a demented reaction, unscrewed the peppermill and threatened to swallow a deadly dose of peppercorns.

'First I'll kill your bastard and then I'll do you in too!' she shouted at her husband. 'This rat is crucifying my loins.'

While the midwife was cajoling her out of doing it, her

waters broke and Olympia collapsed on to the floor. It was the opportunity Nikiforo was waiting for: he rushed her to bed and tied her hands and legs to the iron posts with the straps of a mule harness before she regained her senses.

'I haven't seen anything like it,' he said in awe. 'She's possessed.'

'Nothing more than what women have had to suffer since time immemorial,' the midwife replied with composure. 'And for what? Speaking to a snake, and eating a damn fruit.'

But even she could not suppress a cry when blood started trickling from the mattress and on to the unsanded floorboards. 'Boil more water,' she ordered Nikiforo immediately. 'Then cut a clean bed sheet to strips and soak them in alcohol.'

The weather had worsened. The wind had changed to a petulant northern that slammed the shutters against the windows, chinked the plaster of the outside walls, sent the weathercock flying out into the valley, and drove the rain down the chimney with a force that almost killed the fire. Several times Nikiforo put down the scissors and sheet, and rushed to revive the embers with pieces of tow daubed with turpentine. At the same time, using the bedcovers to hide her actions from the worried husband, the midwife tried to stop the haemorrhage. She had not succeeded when the baby's head emerged.

'It's coming,' she said with trepidation. 'Let's hope your cake is fully baked, Nikiforo.' And turning to Olympia she urged her: 'Push, woman. As if you were a skyrocket set alight.'

It had been a girl. They had all cried when it was over and kissed each other, in what had soon proved to be a premature celebration; the midwife had only to take a quick look to find that out.

'Here we go again,' she said. 'You've got someone else's share too, Nikiforo.'

The second girl arrived with less pain. The midwife cut the

cords and cleaned the babies before wrapping them up in warm sheets. In the jubilation of the births even she had forgotten the lethal haemorrhage. When she finally turned her attention to Olympia she knew it was already too late. While Nikiforo was busy with the babies she checked the woman's pulse to make certain and then, whispering the words of a short prayer, gently covered the body with the blanket.

'They are beauties like their mother,' Nikiforo said with the twins in his arms. 'Don't let her go to sleep, midwife. I want to show them to her.'

The midwife took the babies from him, and placed one in the cot and the other in the fruit pallet Nikiforo had fetched in a hurry. 'I cannot do that, my poor friend,' she said with her back to him. 'Better you get the undertaker.'

The house had been a hostelry already abandoned for several years when Nikiforo bought it. It had been a brave purchase since he had paid for it with the money from the sale of his tractor, which meant that from then on he would have to plough with the mule. It had been the best house he could afford. He had turned down everything else, saying, 'I won't have my bride living in a barn where even the pigs would rather sleep outside.' The thick walls had survived the rages of nature and war many times over, but the rest of the building was true to its centenarian past. Downstairs were a modest-sized kitchen and a vast room where meals were served in the old days, with a stone fireplace in one corner large enough to fit a double bed inside. Upstairs were another two rooms: one was what used to be the hosteler's bedroom, while in the other the travellers would sleep together on bare mattresses pushed against the wall, which the couple found gutted by the rats when they moved in. Nikiforo had burned them in a big bonfire in the garden that same afternoon, along with the worm-eaten furniture. Apart from the stone fireplace, the house was also unique for its cavernous cellar – but that was a luxury a humble household did not need, and it had therefore been left to the rats and spiders without a second thought. And it remained that way until Nikiforo had finally found a use for it.

It was the day of Olympia's funeral. As soon as Nikiforo returned home he went to the kitchen, pushed aside the table, the cushions and the ottoman in the corner, and lifted the Arabian rug his late father-in-law had brought back from his pilgrimage to the Holy Land. Underneath was the forgotten trapdoor. With a candle in hand Nikiforo climbed down to the cellar. Having inspected every corner of the dark and airless catacomb he nodded with satisfaction.

'Perfect,' he said. 'A crime deserves a comparable punishment. And there's no crime more abominable than matricide.'

The spark of his eyes had been eclipsed for ever by an uncompromising hatred. The same day he also hired a woman who had given birth recently to feed the twins, but forbade her to teach them any words or indeed even to hum while the babies were within earshot. She asked why.

'Because dogs cannot talk,' Nikiforo replied.

He had conceived his plan only hours after Olympia's tragic death, on the long road to the village to notify the funeral director: for the rest of his life he was going to show his children no more affection than his livestock.

Indeed, he never once yielded to his paternal instincts. As soon as the girls stopped breastfeeding Nikiforo moved them from the kitchen to the cellar. There they had to get used to sleeping naked on the cobblestone floor, snuggling up to each other to keep warm, and to accept the futility of their cries: even when Nikiforo would hear them through the locked trapdoor he would ignore their pleading grunts as if they were the whines of a dog. Once a day he threw them his leftovers, filled their bowls with water and promptly birched them in order to teach them obedience from an early age.

Their existence was a sinister yet delicious secret shared by everyone in the village apart from the priest, the doctor and the civil guardsman. Almost every day someone would take the road to the old hostelry to bring the widower, who stubbornly refused to remarry, a leg of ham, a plate of home-made dumplings or a basket of eggs. The presents were obvious excuses; the real reason for the visits was the fascination of the villagers with the twins. Nikiforo would not disappoint his uninvited guests. He used to take the children out of the cellar in their collars and leads, and have them perform like monkeys. They never failed to please.

The visitors asked: 'How did they learn those acrobatics, Nikiforo?'

'We're all descendants of monkeys, friend,' the father would reply, and then tug the leads to encourage a more spirited act. 'You'd be surprised at what we could do if we weren't weighed down by clothes.'

They were on the veranda.

'Bring them round to the pen, Nikiforo. There's more space there.'

'No way. They'll scare the sheep.'

But Nikiforo had to be careful for another reason too. He had narrowly escaped once, when he had heard a knock on his door. He went to see who it was.

'Today every devil counts,' the stranger in the suit and with the black eye said cheerfully.

He was a government clerk. Nikiforo had forgotten all about the census. He quickly locked the trapdoor, rolled the rug over it, and invited the man in. He boiled coffee before sitting down to answer his questions.

'I'm grateful for your hospitality,' the clerk said. 'Most people tell me to get lost, and I often have to peep through closed shutters in order to do my job. That can lead to misunderstandings.' He pointed at his black eye under his *pince-nez* and sipped his coffee noisily. 'In any case, we add ten per cent to our numbers to account for those travelling during the census, et cetera.'

'I see.'

'And if a mayor can afford it,' he winked, 'we also have lists of dead people available for resurrection.'

'What for?'

The clerk raised his finger. 'There's strength in numbers, friend. Especially in small municipalities like yours. Wife?'

'Deceased,' replied Nikiforo solemnly.

'Dependants?'

'Only sheep, pigs and chickens.'

The clerk nodded. 'Please sign here.' He gave Nikiforo the biro. Suddenly a noise came from under the floorboards.

'It's nothing,' Nikiforo said immediately. 'There are rats in the cellar.'

If the twins could have talked his secret would have been revealed at that moment. The man had thanked him and left.

But it was another lapse of his prison-like routine that had brought about the end of his familial arrangement. One day when they were eleven years of age he had left the girls unattended, tied to the veranda rails, while he succumbed to a sudden attack of diarrhoea. When he returned from the privy he discovered with terror that the twins had chewed through their leather harnesses, stamped on his beloved pansies with meticulous spite, stolen the raw steaks from the meat safe and disappeared.

From the day of their tragic birth the girls had been denied the traits of humanity. No one had taught them the fundamentals of language, and, since they mostly lived in a world of silence, they had memorised only a few words. The only time they had listened to music was when a backfiring lorry full of gypsies had driven past on the dust road. It had been a brief incident, but enough to seduce them. They had turned their ears to the wind and tried in vain to repeat the melody.

'Fools,' their father had said, laughing. 'You sound like a worn-out drill.'

They had been kept away from the pleasures of sweets and toys too. Every time they would come across a little sugar spill on the kitchen table, they would lick it with such desperate pleasure that their tongues bled on the splintered wood. And the only toy they could find was the ball of twine they had to fight the cat for. But nothing showed their misery more than when Nikiforo, not being able to bear the suffocating stench they had contracted from loitering with the pigs, gave them their first and only bath at the age of ten. The moment they saw the steaming tub they must have assumed they were going to be boiled like potatoes, because they put up such a fight that Nikiforo had to tie stones to their hands and feet to keep them in the water.

In that world of demons the twins had developed an attachment to each other that could not be explained simply by the sharing of the same blood. They communicated neither with sound nor gestures but with an almost undetectable shift of the eyes, and when one sprained an ankle or burned a finger the other felt it too; it was a supernatural ability.

'I'll find them even if I have to travel to the ends of the world,' Nikiforo vowed in the empty house when he discovered them missing. He sat by the stove with his shotgun on his lap and started taking it apart. On the kitchen table were the oiling can, the cleaning rod with the wire brush in one end and the felt brush in the other, a box of empty paper cartridges, a large pouch of gunpowder and the biscuit tin where he kept the lead shot. The shotgun was of the double-barrelled type. It was the same shotgun he held in his hands the day he first met his wife. He had inherited it from his father who only used it once – enough to discover that he had more respect for life than appetite for game meat.

Nikiforo worked with the concentration of a clockmaker, and his movements affirmed that unlike his father he himself was not only a veteran hunter but also a cruel, stubborn man. When he finished cleaning the shotgun he made several cartridges. Outside it was getting dark. He did not worry; he would start the following morning from the village where someone would have noticed something. He regretted not having a dog, but if he could get some help he was confident he would soon find his daughters. Before turning in for the night he lit the lamp in the bedroom shrine and prayed. He looked at his wife's photograph which stood among the icons of saints.

'Trust me, my love,' he said, 'there're not enough holes in the earth for those rats to hide.'

Considering the severity of the situation Nikiforo slept very well. He woke neither from the soliloquy of the valley winds, nor from the cold. It was a deceiving October and Nikiforo had not lit the wood stove next to his bed, so when he opened his eyes in the morning he was not surprised to hear the chatter of his teeth.

'A treacherous month,' he said. 'Much like those two seeds of Satan.'

The freezing room did not change the good mood he always felt before a hunt. An hour later, after filling his cartridge belt and drinking a cup of burning coffee, he slung his shotgun over his shoulder and left for the village, whistling. Soon he came across a man pulling a mule.

'Good morning, Fanourio.'

The old man returned the greeting by raising his dusty fedora, while trying to catch his breath.

'The road to your house gets longer every day, Nikiforo,' he said.

'Why aren't you riding, Fanourio?'

The mule had a straw hat on with holes cut for the ears. The old man caressed the lock on its forehead, and the animal looked at him with doleful eyes.

'Matilda has lumbago, friend. These days I really take her along only for company.'

'Were you coming to see me, Fanourio?'

The old man nodded. 'Yes. I wanted to bring you some pumpkin pie. And, given the opportunity, show Matilda the twins.'

Nikiforo broke the news to them. The mule looked down and let out a short neigh.

'This is bad. Matilda is very disappointed,' the man said and shrugged. 'I hope you get them back soon.'

'I'd find them even if they've grown wings,' Nikiforo declared. 'I just need a little help.'

The old man coughed. 'I'd be glad to. But Matilda, like I said . . .'

Nikiforo refused the pie and walked on. He kept his eyes open for any signs of his daughters' passing through, but discovered none. When he arrived at the village he went straight to the coffee shop. It was empty but for the waiter and Dr Panteleon who was doing the crossword in the newspaper.

'Want to hear a good one?' the waiter said. 'Father Yerasimo ran out of wine today.'

Nikiforo put his shotgun against the wall, took off his cartridge belt, and sat at a table with a sigh.

'How do you know?' he asked. 'Even Lucifer goes to mass more often than you.'

'Lu-ci-fer,' pondered the doctor at the other table, and slowly pencilled it in the crossword. 'But of course.'

The waiter said: 'I know, because he asked me to lend him some brandy.' He looked at the shotgun and the full belt with curiosity. 'You're late, Nikiforo. By the time you get to the hills the rain will have driven the rabbits underground.'

'Not the ones I'm hunting, friend.'

The doctor looked up from his newspaper. Nikiforo bit his lip. For a brief moment he had forgotten that the doctor did not know about the twins – he would definitely have informed the civil guard. Nikiforo winked at the waiter conspiratorially and joined him behind the counter.

'I've lost them,' he whispered.

The waiter felt as if a punch had taken him unawares. He brought his hand to his cheek in a reflex response. 'What are you going to do?' he whispered back.

Nikiforo waved him to be quiet. He asked: 'What's the latest news?'

The waiter tried to think. There was the fracture of the pipe from the aqueduct which had left the village without running water for two days now, there were the nominations for sepulchre bearers at St Timotheo's procession, and of course there was the news of the arrival that morning of the first bus from the county capital following the extension of its route.

'It costs twice as much as the train,' the waiter said. 'But it takes half the time, because for some reason it doesn't stop to take on water.'

Nothing with regard to the twins. Nikiforo leaned closer. 'I could use someone's help,' he said softly. 'Two or three of us might—'

The waiter hid his hands inside his apron and looked away.

'Impossible to shut the shop,' he said. 'I have to honour three promissory notes by the end of the year.'

Nikiforo ordered a beer and returned to his table, disappointed. Across the shop the doctor had gone back to his crossword. The autumnal wind shook the leaves of the plane tree in the square and a quiet, sad drizzle started. Against the corrugated iron roof of the coffee shop it sounded like the dripping of a tap. Slowly a smell of wet clay spread everywhere. For the first time since the disappearance of the girls Nikiforo felt miserable. But not for long. No sooner had he brought the beer than the waiter snapped his finger in the air.

'Oh, yes,' he said. 'And earlier today the midwife reported some petty theft.'

Ten minutes later Nikiforo was knocking at her door. When the stationmaster answered Nikiforo was surprised to see he had been crying. 'It's a disaster, friend,' the stationmaster said.

A towel was tied round his neck and his breath smelled of onion. Although he was an older man, the short sleeves of his uniform, the holes in the armpits and stained collar gave him the air of a mischievous schoolboy. Nikiforo and he had become friends because the stationmaster – unbeknown to his wife – visited the old hostelry at least once a week to watch the animal tricks of the twins. Nikiforo was surprised that the news had travelled so fast.

'How do you know about it?' he asked.

The stationmaster wiped his eyes with the back of his hand.

'I've seen it with my own eyes,' he said. 'The speedometer goes up to fifty; it has a radio; the windows have blinds; the seats have springs underneath . . .' He sighed. 'The fate of the stagecoach awaits the train too, my friend. Soon everyone will be travelling by bus.'

Nikiforo patted him on the back. 'Don't worry,' he said. 'People will always need an excuse for being late. Where's your wife?'

The midwife appeared before her husband had even turned

round, and eyed the widower with evil energy; she had been standing behind the door all along. Although she was one of the few people in the village who disapproved of his behaviour, she, like the others, had bowed to the rule of silence without challenge. On her apron were stuck the remains of a chopped onion and she held a knife.

'What do you want, Devil?' she asked him.

Nikiforo curled his lip. 'You reported a theft.'

The woman frowned. 'It's none of your business.'

The stationmaster intervened. 'Two dresses from the clothes line, friend. Why?'

Nikiforo told him. While he talked the stationmaster turned red and started shaking. He said: 'I've never stopped warning all you young men. And in your case, Nikiforo . . .' He paused for emphasis. 'Twin birth, double the trouble!'

On the contrary, his wife reacted to the news by clasping her hands and raising them to the sky theatrically. 'Blessed be the Lord,' she said. 'At last the slaves have broken their shackles!'

Nikiforo told the stationmaster: 'With a little help I'll have them back by sunset.'

The midwife gave her husband a reproachful look.

'Good luck,' the stationmaster said timidly. 'But you shouldn't waste your time waiting for help. There're not many laws in this country, but there's still one that could put heads in the noose for a crime like yours.'

And before Nikiforo could reply, the midwife had pulled her husband back inside and shut the door in his face.

Indeed, everywhere he went Nikiforo encountered palisades of refusal and even blame. In the end he set off on foot, all alone. He spent a week crossing the valley from north to south, and then east to west. He searched every path and almost every briar for tracks, but he came across only a group of lost tourists suffering from sunstroke. Nikiforo took pity on them and showed them the way to the village before carrying on. On the evening of the seventh day of his search he sat on a rock and wiped his neck with his handkerchief. Of the twins he had seen, heard and smelled absolutely nothing. A day earlier he had also run out of food. Now he drank the last drops of water in his flask. The autumnal sun rolled behind the hills and the valley changed colour from green to yellow to red. For a moment Nikiforo admired the view and the strange patterns of a swarm of birds flying south. He then stood up with the help of his shotgun, slung it over his shoulder and cleared his throat, which was already dry again. He said: 'Maybe those bitches did grow wings after all.' And: 'The hell with them. I'll leave the job to the jackals.' After that he took the narrow trail back to the village, whistling and having nothing on his conscience at all.

When they had finally eaten through the leather of their harnesses and freed themselves, the girls listened to their father's agonising cries from the privy and knew they had little time. Their captivity had caused them great suffering, but fortunately also granted them a bestial instinct they could rely upon at that very moment. They found the food in the meat safe by sniffing the air, drank water from the well, then quickly left not on the road but across the fields and in the direction of the village. They were naked. Since his wife's death Nikiforo had banished all clothes to a seaman's trunk with iron padlocks in the attic but for a mourner's suit he wore every day. The twins made it to the village noticed only by the dogs, and they silenced them easily with the meat they carried. There they spotted the washing on the line at a concrete house by the railway line.

They were fortunate that the woman at the kitchen window who raised her head absent-mindedly and met their eyes was the midwife. She was surprised but bit her lip so as not to scream and alert her husband. And although she did manage to remain silent while the runaways dressed in her clothes in a desperate hurry, she could not suppress her tears of joy, and after the girls were gone and she sat opposite her husband at the table he only had to look up from his newspaper to see that she had been crying. He frowned behind his glasses.

'What now, woman?' he asked wearily.

She quickly conjured one of her incredible excuses, which never failed to get on her husband's nerves: 'How many times do I have to tell you not to buy onions from that peddler. He grows them in the old battlefield and they're full of tears.'

But luck would run one more errand for the twins that afternoon.

Even from far away it was clear that the lorry they saw had been resurrected from the scrapyard several times already. The cabin was missing both its doors, more smoke was coming from the engine than dust from the potholed road, the roof was made from dried cane and straw, and there was even the national flag raised on a tall pipe fitted through the rear bumper. On closer inspection one could see that the bonnet was a crude replacement made from tin dustbins cut, shaped and welded together, while instead of seats there was a gutted sofa bolted on to the floor. The driver was a fearless woman with a stevedore's tattooed arms, strange rings with precious stones on every finger, and untamed hair with long locks that coiled themselves round her neck. She had been travelling for more than seven hours and was just dozing off when she saw the two girls in the middle of the road. Immediately she hit the brakes. When the dust settled the girls were in exactly the same place, looking at her. She leaned out of the doorless cabin.

'Get off the road, fools!' she shouted.

The twins stood in silence, barefooted.

'Get lost, do you hear?'

But still they did not move. The woman jumped down from the lorry, fuming.

'I said go away. Shoo! Home!'

'Home,' said the twins together, suddenly coming alive. It was one of the few words they had learned on their own. 'No home.'

The woman took a step back and slowly rubbed her hairy chin. Slowly she lost her fury. 'Do you mean that you are of no fixed abode, ladies?' she asked politely.

The girls pointed at the flapping rag of a flag. 'Clothes!'

The woman looked up, puzzled. 'That's our national flag, children. It's there so that they won't confuse me with the gypsies.'

'Gypsies,' the girls repeated.

The woman now looked at them in disbelief.

'Yes, gypsies,' she explained slowly. 'Like us, people, but with hoofs instead of toes.'

'Hoo-oofs!'

The woman shook her head from side to side, and then looked at the sky.

'It serves me right, Lord,' she sighed. 'I pray for help and all you send this sinner is two village idiots.' She spat on the ground and studied the girls in silence. Their hair had neither been washed nor had a comb passed through it for weeks, one had somebody else's cheap dress on and the other a nightgown, and also, intriguingly, both wore thick leather dog collars round their necks. 'At least you aren't male,' she said in the end. 'Which is better than being descended from the finest pedigree.'

'Ped—'

'Oh, shut up.'

She waved them to follow her and climbed back on to the lorry. The twins obeyed like faithful pets. No sooner had they taken their seats next to her than the engine stalled and they could hear a pandemonium of warbling. Their jaws dropped with delighted astonishment.

'Don't worry about them,' the woman said. 'After a while you stop noticing.'

The lorry was loaded with cages masked with thick tarpaulin under which birds of rare colours fluttered, sang and bit the wire bars. The girls were fascinated.

'Watch your step. Those devils shit more than cows,' said the woman. 'Now, let's go.'

The twins shook their heads in refusal.

'All right, but only another minute,' the woman said, looking up and down the road. 'Any longer and they'll start suffering from stage fright.'

She was a bird-fancier. Among the cages were several with exotic birds she had bought cheaply from zoological parks and the aviaries of botanical gardens, because they would either not sing at all or not stop singing, peck at children's fingers or have an uninhibited amorous disposition which embarrassed the keepers.

The girls returned to their seats while the bird-fancier cranked the engine. When she sat at the wheel again, the twins said: 'Travel.'

'Yes,' said the bird-fancier, and she pointed her armoured forefinger with the three rings at a swarm of birds in the sky. 'We follow the larks.'

The first thing she taught them was how to start the engine without the crank bruising their wrists. Then she showed them how to build traps from fishnet and cardboard box, how to keep the string still and taut as the larks walked into the trap baited with sesame seeds, and how to hold down the desperate birds in their cupped hands so that they did not crush their wings. 'Remember, their bones are made of glass, girls,' she kept repeating. 'Treat the poor things with love.'

Their destination was a southern shore with endless sand dunes, a strange landscape resembling a desert where the birds of the north came every year to pass the winter. When they arrived the bird-fancier shielded her eyes and surveyed the landscape. It was carpeted with thousands of birds, and she said with satisfaction: 'This is like stealing a blind man's wallet.' The birds perched on the sand, recovering from the rigours of their long journey. The bird-fancier noticed the grief in the girls' eyes.

'Don't be too sentimental,' she said, already setting up traps. 'They don't mind being caged. Listen.'

The birds in the lorry chirped.

'In fact,' the bird-fancier continued, 'they're like any artist. They sing better in the cage.'

She never convinced the twins that hers was an honest and necessary trade, but they nevertheless stayed with her not only because they had nowhere else to go, but also because of her talent: she could sing even better than the birds. Under the only tree for miles – a large pine with branches charred by lightning and a twisted trunk fossilised by the salt of the sea winds – the twins had listened, night after night, to melodies in unknown languages and tempos of a mathematical complexity before surrendering themselves to sleep.

'There's life in the old siren yet,' the bird-fancier would say, feeding the fire.

In fact she had been a professional singer until her voice, wounded by the punishment of her daily performances, had finally cracked. She felt no bitterness about it, because she loved her new business. 'Besides,' she would say, 'birds are like singers. But without as much ego.'

It did not take her long to discover that the twins were not weak-minded but simply illiterate. Then she drove to the

nearest town, where she bought grammar books and antholo-
gies from schoolchildren in return for robins and canaries, and
held daily lessons with the twins. It was a slow process but the
twins saw it through with a convert's passion. Whenever they
would manage a full sentence she would reward them with a
song. In fact the first question they had asked when they knew
how was: 'Where did you sing?' The bird-fancier had sighed.
'In my day, my dears, a woman would get money for songs
either at the opera or in the *bordello*. Unfortunately, my voice
could never reach the high notes of the arias.'

Fascinated, the girls demanded to learn how to sing too, with
such a mule-like persistence that the bird-fancier had no choice
but to agree. Luckily, she remembered having used sheet music
once to line some cages, and the next morning the twins started
solfeggio with the additional difficulty of deciding whether the
markings on the staffs were notes or dried bird dung. Soon they
could tell the difference between a folk song and a waltz, and
switch mid-song from a madrigal through a barcarole to a
canzone. In return, they showed their gratitude to their teacher
by trapping the rarest birds that wintered on the shore, and by
not forgetting to fumigate the pair of peacocks which were
constantly tormented by ticks.

Years passed in the company of books and songs, and
following the same routine: in autumn the bird-fancier and her
assistants would drive to the warm shores of the south, where
they caught as many birds as they could load on the ancient
lorry, while in spring, when the birds returned north, the
women would dig out the wheels the wind had buried in the
sand, and get back on the road again. All summer they travelled
from town to town, hawking the most beautiful and melodious
merchandise in the world with the help of an electronic
megaphone.

With a mother's authority but not her inevitable cavils the

bird-fancier was the perfect guardian. The first evening they spent in a town and not by the side of the road she had advised them before letting them go out for a walk on their own: 'Do with men whatever takes your fancy. But don't show any of those roosters that you're enjoying yourselves. If they knew we like it as much as they do, they'd go back to doing it only with the sheep.'

She did not have to warn them. The tribulations of their childhood had caused the twins irreparable damage: their love was exhausted on the bird-fancier, and they treated everyone else with the fear and mistrust of wounded animals. The bird-fancier approved.

'Not everyone wants to tie cans on your tails,' she would say, 'but it's good practice to think they do.'

Travelling through a desolate and unhappy country where natural and handmade disasters were more frequent than rain, they had come to accept their own misfortune as a severe yet unsurprising verdict of destiny. Until the day they killed the snake.

They had stopped at a well by the side of the road to top up the radiator. It was an ugly well—built with cement and left unpainted, and round it motorists had left their signs: stubbed cigarettes, fruit rinds, old newspapers. The well had a windlass but there was no bucket at the end of its rope. A slow, intermittent wind pushed its heavy steel crank, and it swung with a creaking sound.

'Use the cans,' the woman said.

She was at the wheel, fanning herself with a piece of cardboard and fighting off the flies that had smelled the bird dung. Two jerrycans were strapped on the side of the lorry and the girls took them down. Dressed in skirts and men's shoes without socks they had picked up from a street market, they went to the well, whistling.

'Make a double knot,' the bird-fancier instructed from her seat. 'You don't want to lose the cans.'

They obeyed. The jerrycans hit the water with an echoing noise. While they filled up the twins played with a bent hubcap, and then they lifted the cans out, turning the crank together. But they only realised how heavy they had become when they released the pulley and the jerrycans landed on the ground, making the concrete shake and disturbing a grey adder with pearl eyes that had hidden in the shade. It instantly uncoiled itself, shot its arrow body between one girl's feet with impressive speed, and bit the other right above the ankle.

The twins reacted instinctively. They used the jerrycans to trap the snake against the well, and then hit it with them until the bird-fancier snatched the cans from their hands. She looked with sadness at the lifeless skin with the splendid black stripes. 'This venom won't kill you,' she said. 'Only teach you to watch your step.' She then washed the wound with soap, poured brandy on it from a cut-glass decanter she pulled from underneath the driver's seat, and ripped one of her clean undergarments to use as a bandage.

The incident was a turning point in the twins' behaviour, for they had finally discovered the thoroughly human emotion they had until then missed: the pure pleasure of revenge. It was inevitable that their newly found feeling would reveal to them its most deserving victim. Indeed that afternoon, over the dead adder, the twins swore not to rest until they had punished their father. But they had to find the opportunity first.

An endless day in August with a profane sunshine and a desert wind that covered trucks, farmhouses and animals with a sparkling layer of sand, the lorry was driving slowly on an empty road through dried cornfields. Every now and then it would stop, and one of the twins jump out with a jerrycan and refill the leaking radiator. At the back, among the birdcages, the bird-fancier snored louder than the engine. The day before they had been to a miners' town one hundred miles away, where they sold all the canaries. They were exhausted. It was not until midday that the bird-fancier finally awoke and asked them to stop; as soon as they pulled over the engine died with a gurgling noise. The twins listened to the cicadas outside, and those few birds in the lorry that did not suffer from the heat. They turned round, and at the far end of the dark lorry saw the woman with a handkerchief over her mouth.

She raised the straw roof of the lorry and looked out at the cornfield where rooks squabbled about a rat carcass. She shook her head with silent sadness.

'Girls,' she announced, 'I feel as if I've eaten a cupful of broken glass.' She coughed with strain. 'I think I know what it is.'

It was consumption.

'You're wrong,' said the twins, mixing their tears with sweat. 'It's the flu from sleeping out in the open.'

The bird-fancier almost smiled. 'It's August,' she said. 'The only thing one gets this time of the year from lying under the sun is dehydration.'

The girls started crying.

'I wish I could tell you there was hope,' the woman said. 'But it'd be easier to escape my own shadow than shake off this curse.'

That night they camped in a field not far from the road, between the haycocks and a rusting harvester with burned tyres. No one was hungry. The twins switched on the lorry's headlights as the bird-fancier made her bed at some distance from where they were preparing to lie – it was a necessary precaution with her disease. 'Switch off the lights,' she said. 'The last thing we need out here is a flat battery.' The truth was that she did not want them to see her tremble from fear at the pain that was certain to come. They spent the night under the stars and in the morning the bird-fancier opened her eyes to see the girls sitting cross-legged next to her.

'I told you: not too close, you stubborn mules!' She cursed them, and covered herself with the blanket. 'You want to keep me company in Hell?'

They had been waiting for her to wake up.

'We need to ask you a favour, Mother,' they said timidly.

It was the first time they had called her that, and she was moved to tears.

'My business will be yours, of course,' she said, knowing very well that that was not what they wanted.

'We thank you. Not that.'

'Then what? Tell me, children,' she said, burning more with curiosity than pain. 'Before I kick the bucket.'

That morning in August they finally told her the painful secret of their past. About the cruel man who they grew up to realise was their father, about the cellar without windows, and about the harnesses. She listened to the story with more tears.

'Poor babies,' she said. 'I wish I could hold you in my arms. But my disease is more deadly than leprosy.'

The twins looked at her with beady eyes. 'That's what we want to talk to you about, Mother,' they said.

The barber had a customer that morning.

'. . . And trim back the sideburns two centimetres, barber,' the man on the chair demanded. 'Precisely.'

The barber took out a wooden ruler from his back pocket and pressed it on his customer's cheeks. 'What's that in imperial, friend?' he asked.

It was while using the clippers on the man's nape that he heard the lorry. 'The gypsies are coming,' he announced indifferently. But when he looked up he saw the flag. 'No,' he corrected himself, 'it's that itinerant man-hater of a bird-fancier.'

'It's been a long time,' said his customer while reading the news.

In fact, it had been seven years. The bird-fancier had not returned to the village since she had come across the twins, in case someone was looking for them.

The day she had acknowledged her mortal sickness she had insisted that they should raise the yellow flag with the black spot on the lorry's mast, in order to protect everyone on their route from contagion. But when the village came into view, they had stopped and replaced it with the national flag again; it was part of their plan.

As soon as they parked in the square, the barber abandoned his customer and hurried towards the lorry. But he stopped short when, instead of the old bird-fancier, he saw two young women on the seats. A voice called him from the back of the lorry, where he found the old woman sitting on the floor. She explained that she suffered from vertigo, and that the girls were her assistants.

'They are very beautiful,' the barber said, and spied on them through the hatch of the cabin. 'I wouldn't be surprised if they had wings under those dresses. They look like angels.'

The twins were a far cry from the naked beasts with the sharp nails, the greasy hair, the skin spattered with excrement. They were women now who smelled of tallow soap and rosewater, whose long hair was pomaded, and who wore ivory muslin dresses they could have only bought in the capital. There was no way anyone in the village could recognise them.

'They're too young for you, barber,' the bird-fancier replied. 'What do you want?'

The barber gave the twins another look. They had inherited

the abundant looks and conqueror's walk of their mother. And furthermore, they were her exact age when she had died.

'Somehow, they look familiar,' said the barber.

The bird-fancier turned away and coughed inside her handkerchief.

'Naturally. You see them in your dreams every night.'

The barber bit his lip. 'The swan you sold me died last winter. I wonder whether—'

He was an unapologetic bird lover. The bird-fancier found her torch in the dark. 'Have a look,' she said impatiently. She was struggling to hold back her pain, while pretending she had come to the village on business. The barber put his clippers in his pocket and started lifting cages. 'The swan had a hose of a neck but the only time I heard him sing was on his deathbed,' he complained. Finally, he chose a black bird with a yellow beak. 'Can this sing?' he asked.

'Better: it talks. In fact, it has given lectures at the National Academy.'

The barber was fascinated with the mynah. He searched his pockets for his wallet and counted out the money on the floor of the lorry. Before handing over the banknotes he looked at them one last time, as if they were family photographs. He said: 'With the money I spend on birds I could have had singing lessons myself.'

In order to find their old house, the twins had to retrace the course of their flight years earlier. But they could still not remember, until all of a sudden they recognised the cement house by the railway with the small windows. The door opened and someone spoke up.

'Show me your faces.'

It was the midwife – but to the twins she was a stranger. They stepped back, like ambushed animals.

'Don't be afraid,' the woman said. 'I'm the one who tied your belly buttons.'

But still they did not trust her.

'What are you doing here?' The midwife received no reply. 'I see,' she said after a while, understanding the reason for their visit. 'Let me tell you what you should know, and then I'll show you where he lives.'

They heard all about their mother, her tragic end, and were shown her grave. In return they told the midwife how they had escaped and had found good fortune following the bird-fancier. Then they revealed their plan to her. She nodded with satisfaction, before pointing them in the direction of the old hostelry. She wished them luck, and touched their faces, saying with pride: 'I can hardly believe it. There's nothing in you any more of the animals you once were.'

First the enormous chimney rising above the flat valley caught their eye, and then the rest of the house: the tiled roof with the attic windows, the stone walls with the resolute buttresses, the cement veranda taken over by the unpruned grapevine, where the twins used to perform for the visitors. When the lorry came closer, the bird-fancier saw to her surprise that the windowpanes were covered with black paint.

'They were always like that,' the twins told her.

They stopped outside the gate and in the back of the lorry the woman opened her suitcase. Inside were a handheld mirror, a tin of petrified talcum powder, a hardened brush, several dried lipsticks and a moth-eaten bag of kohl. 'I can hardly remember how to use these,' she admitted, scratching her head. But she did her best to hide the signs of her malady behind the perfumed creams and mixtures, and then swigged down a bottle of laudanum, crossed herself and stepped down from the lorry.

She passed the gate and walked towards the house feeling as if she were on a ship's deck. She had climbed the steps to the veranda when she suddenly lost her balance, and would have fallen had there not been the railing. She had been overwhelmed not by the vertigo of her disease, but by the horrific sight that awaited her there: the concrete floor was covered with decomposing bodies of house martins. She felt more pain than if cut by a blade.

A man had planted himself resolutely outside the door. The bird-fancier tried to speak, but the macabre surprise had robbed her voice of its consonants. The widower sized her up for some time.

'They are my demons,' he finally said about the dead birds.

He explained that ever since he had discovered the house martins had an insatiable appetite for grapes, he had started spraying the vine with poison. 'You wouldn't believe how much they chirp,' he said. 'Enough to drill a hole through one's brain.'

He went inside and returned with the broom. 'What can I do for you, madam?' he asked, sweeping the dead martins from the veranda.

Slowly the bird-fancier regained her composure. She opened her bag with hands trembling from fury. 'Do you recognise these?'

She was holding the dog collars the twins had been wearing years earlier when she had come across them on the side of the road. The widower had only to take a quick look to see through the cobwebs of the past.

'Where did you find them?' he demanded.

'Give me a drink.'

The widower did not move, but narrowed his eyes. 'How long have you had those?'

'Seven years. I'd forgotten about them, but then I heard someone in your village tell a story.'

The man hit his fist on the door. 'Fools,' he said. 'They can't control their mouths any more than their arseholes.'

He led her inside, where she needed two glasses of water to quench her cough. Lit candles were everywhere: no light passed through the blackened windowpanes. She asked the widower the reason for it. He replied, hastily: 'There's nothing to interest me out there. Now, tell me about the collars.'

The plan had worked; the bird-fancier sat close to him, and every time she opened her mouth she pushed him a step closer to his destiny: her voice carried the death of her lungs with it; hopefully it would have infected him.

'I found their bodies on the hillside; eaten by the jackals.'

The widower rubbed his hands together with bliss. 'I knew it. What did you do with them?'

'Buried them out there – I can't now remember exactly where.'

'You should have left them to the ravens, woman.'

It was his hatred that was making her want to vomit, not the blood in her lungs. She said quietly: 'Yours is a strange disease.'

'No one has loved the way I have, woman.'

She tried to contain herself, but could not. 'The problem was that you bet it all on a single throw of the dice.' She wanted to say more, but felt her cough returning. She used her handkerchief, kept on her lap under the table, to hide the blood from him. 'I'm leaving now,' she said. She stood up and leaned over the widower. 'Remember: there's still time to repent before you go.'

'I'm not planning any trips, woman.'

Back in the lorry the twins waited.

'Let's go,' the woman said, exhausted. 'God alone will make the decision. I just hope that he'll agree with me.'

He must have, because within weeks the widower started coughing, waking up every morning in bedsheets soaked in his sweat. He lost so much weight he was convinced his bones were shrinking, and he was burning constantly with a high fever. The bird-fancier heard the news while lying in a small bed in the village *pension*. She smiled for the first and last time in months. 'You can be happy now, my darlings,' she told the twins, convinced their father would die. 'It's the blood of your sadness he'll drown in.'

Less than a month later the girls sold the lorry to pay for her funeral, and buried her close to the mother they had never met. Then, coming back from the service, they chanced upon a band that had played at a wedding the day before. The musicians were still dressed in their dusty black suits and patched shirts, and were on their way to the railway station.

'We want to come with you,' the girls said.

The bandleader looked at them from head to toe, and misunderstood their confidence.

'You'll be wasting your time, girls. We don't go past many barracks.'

They blushed with anger. 'We're singers,' they said proudly.

The man immediately showed his teeth in an impertinent smile.

'I apologise, ladies. We've been on the road for so long that we can't even tell a ewe from a ram any more. Please sing something.'

The bandleader produced an accordion from his case and accompanied their song with professional ease. The rest of the band listened and nodded in approval.

'Ladies,' the bandleader said when they finished, 'come along as long as you can afford the fare.'

But there was one final matter the twins had to settle. That afternoon they let the birds go: the barn owl that had never lived in a barn, the rare parakeets that were so used to their prison they bit the hands that freed them, the larks which set off south almost immediately because it was already autumn. Later, while they were breaking the wire cages to pieces, the girls came up with the idea of taking the pair of peacocks to the cemetery. There they lived ever since, brushing their iridescent trains against the tombstones, the adobe crosses and the trunks of the tall cypresses.

It was evening when the twins kissed the midwife on both cheeks and boarded the train with the musicians. And when the locomotive finally whistled and a blast of steam spread across the platform, they rolled down their window screens and vowed never to set eyes on the village of their misery again.

III

Sitting on the widower's veranda, Father Yerasimo blew his nose in his handkerchief and craned his neck towards the stars.

'You'll definitely burn in Hell, Nikiforo,' he said. 'My only sadness is that I won't be there to see it.'

'If it's any consolation to you, priest, my lungs feel like lit coals.'

'Your wife's death was a God-sent misfortune. You should have accepted it with a penance. Instead—'

'It was their punishment; they killed her.'

'They're children of God.'

'No. They were an abomination,' the widower hissed. 'I tried selling them to the circus once, but the ringmaster brought them back when he discovered they had a bigger appetite than the tigers.'

Father Yerasimo took off his cap and scratched his head. 'It's a sinister miracle how the civil guard never found out.'

'They couldn't tell the moon from the stars, priest,' Nikiforo

said. He crossed his arms under the blankets and waited for
another attack of coughing to pass. He smacked his lips. 'Well,
there is nothing you can do now, priest. The jackals had them.'

Without getting up, Father Yerasimo used a stick to catch the
sick man's packet of cigarettes. He lit one with the storm
lantern, then sat on the veranda steps again. He had not smoked
since his seminary days. In his pockets were his neatly folded
stole, a silver-and-sandalwood cross, a Bible bound in leather. It
was his duty to say a few words for Nikiforo's soul when his
time came – but he would not give that man absolution even if
he paid him. He was about to tell Nikiforo what he had learned
from the midwife when the widower spoke up again.

'I won't need your services soon, priest. In fact, I plan to cry
at your funeral. Dr Panteleon says the worst is over.'

Father Yerasimo squeezed his cigarette nervously. 'I admire
your spirit, Nikiforo. It is good that you don't surrender to your
pain.'

'No. It's the new drug.' He paused and rubbed his chin trying
to remember. 'The antibiotic.'

Father Yerasimo felt a mounting disappointment. 'Nonsense,'
he uttered.

'I'm telling you, priest, I'm getting better.'

The priest felt as if his faith was a dog he had fed for years
only to see it run away. He had several puffs at his cigarette,
struggling to suppress his doubts. 'Science,' he finally said. 'Why
does it have to interfere in God's business?'

The widower paid no attention to that. There was something
else on his mind.

'I always wondered, priest.'

'What?'

'Demons.'

Father Yerasimo curled his lip. 'What about them?'

'What do they look like?'

The priest scratched his head; he could not remember whether any of the ecumenical synods had ever addressed that question.

'Because my demons have wings, priest,' said the widower. 'I dream about them all the time.'

'Normally they resemble two-legged goats with arrowhead tails,' the priest replied. 'But Evil can come in many guises, of course.'

'Are you afraid of them, priest?'

'Me? Of course not. God is omnipotent. It's the agnostics and the sinners who should worry.'

Nikiforo coughed again. The dog came and sat at Father Yerasimo's feet. He cuddled her and started smoking another cigarette. Perched on the rubble of the collapsed chimney an owl shrieked, and flew off silently into the valley. The priest snuffed out his cigarette, put it in his pocket and hugged himself. Suddenly it was cold.

Another Day
on Pegasus

She wore a yellow dress that promised to come apart at the seams – but it was not going to happen that day. The driver kept looking in the mirror above his head, and his patience slowly turned into misery. He was so lost in the mist of his amorous thoughts that the coach veered off the tarmac and was only yards away from a deep irrigation ditch when the passengers' cries brought him back to reality. He put both hands on the steering wheel and turned the coach round at the very last moment. Curses came from the back.

'Sorry, friends,' the driver said coolly. 'I was just testing the suspension.'

For two years he had been driving the coach twice daily between the county capital and the countryside. The old coach had thirty-two seats, a rear-mounted diesel engine which left a continuous trail of oil on the dust road, and a body round like an ageing cetacean's, quietly rusting under the green livery of the Regional Transit Services Co-operative. In the folding seat next to the driver sat the conductor. He wore a wrinkled uniform, a limp cap with the badge of the Co-operative pinned on it, and on his lap he had his money safe: a metallic box with several compartments for banknotes and coins. When the driver had performed the sudden manoeuvre the conductor had clenched his teeth, goggled his eyes and said nothing. Once the coach was on the road again, he took out a handful of change from his pocket – the fare collected at the last stopover – opened the money box, and started loading coins into compartments according to their denomination.

'Fool,' he murmured. 'You could have bent the shaft.'

It was eleven o'clock on a cloudless morning. The journey had begun five hours earlier from the depot. The coach was travelling east, calling at towns and villages. The conductor threw the money box on the dashboard with a sullen gesture, lowered the windscreen visor and took out the ticket book from his breast pocket. He thumbed the stubs of the concessionary tickets and frowned.

'I didn't know there were so many minors in the world,' he said. 'Until I became a conductor.' The driver rubbed his eyes under his dark glasses and drank more coffee from his flask. 'And in any case why do their mothers have to take them along?' the conductor continued. The driver paid him no attention. He looked at the woman in yellow in the mirror and then straight ahead again. He wiped off the sweat on his forehead and hung the flask from his backrest without taking his eyes from the road. The conductor was his brother-in-law. 'They're bad for business,' said the conductor again, and puffed his cheeks. 'And we've only just started.'

Only months earlier the two of them had bought the coach from their employer who was retiring. Since then they had stencilled their names on the door, the word PEGASUS above the radiator grille at the front, and the conductor had drawn all by himself what was possibly a winged horse on the spare-wheel cover at the rear. In addition, they had changed the worn mudflaps and installed a sign inside the back window which every time the coach braked flashed BE CAREFUL, FRIEND in red. The interior they had also decorated with gusto: a Virgin Mary vase with plastic flowers on the dashboard, a garland running across the windscreen and the best months of a Pirelli calendar on the ceiling. Finally, what money was left they had spent on a horn that could play as many as five different tunes.

The conductor asked: 'Have you changed the silencer yet?'

Instead of replying the driver hit the accelerator, the coach jumped forward and a loud noise came from the exhaust.

'In the name of God!' shouted a passenger. 'You aren't delivering cattle.'

The driver looked in the mirror rudely, before slowing down. He turned up the radio. 'Did you at least weld the oil sump?' asked the conductor, raising his voice.

The driver did not reply this time either. He put his arm out of the open window and knocked with his knuckles on the metal to the rhythm of the song on the radio. He looked in the mirror again, but this time his eyes had a confident expression.

'My name's Theofilo,' he said, scratching his chest under his gold cross with the thick chain. 'What's yours?'

The woman in the yellow dress had boarded the coach an hour earlier, and that was also when the troubles had started: before veering off the road the coach had on previous occasions hit a deep pothole, nearly run over a stray dog, skidded sideways when the driver braked for no reason over the gravel that had fallen from a tipper, and not stopped when a man in black at a lonely crossroads had flagged it down.

She did not tell him her name. Instead she asked: 'Didn't you see the man back there?'

'There was no one,' said the driver. 'It was a mirage from the heat.'

She was sitting in the window seat behind him, and next to her was a buckskin bag she regularly rummaged through for a watch with a broken strap, her lipstick and make-up mirror, or her purse. On the rack above her head was a lace parasol and a small suitcase held together by a belt.

She bent down and asked again: 'Do you own this coach?'

The driver looked in the mirror: her dress had a deep *décolletage*. 'I call it Pegasus.'

'Pegasus,' she concurred, and sat back. 'How nice.'

A backfiring motorcycle overtook them as they entered another town. There was no depot there; the coach stopped on the side of the main square outside a closed *patisserie*. In the middle of the square was an empty fountain. A little wind scattered newspaper sheets across the street and pigeons perched in the shade of balconies. The conductor jumped out and climbed on the roof of the coach, while the disembarking passengers pointed out their luggage. A taxi circled the square and the driver looked at them, waiting for a signal.

'Careful with that one,' ordered a woman. 'It has a porcelain dinner service inside.'

The conductor untied the cheap suitcase from the rack and threw it with no more care. 'There's no way you could even afford a porcelain thimble, woman,' he said. 'Besides, we are late.'

The coach set off again. Soon they reached a crossroads with tin arrow signs where the names could not be read because of the rust. The driver took the route of countless hairpins that descended towards a valley.

'One of these days,' he said aloud, 'I might take the wrong turn.'

The woman leaned forward again. 'What about us – your passengers?' she asked playfully.

'You can come along,' he said, and winked. 'The rest I'll throw out.' He took his hand off the wheel. He wore a gold bracelet with his name engraved on it and a cheap watch. He pointed at the conductor. 'Starting with him.' The woman let out a little chuckle and the conductor bit his moustache. 'You, Pegasus and me,' continued the driver. 'What could go wrong?'

The conductor said: 'You might run out of petrol.' When the woman laughed, he felt encouraged. 'Or get a puncture.'

The driver looked at the steep hill, then the next hairpin, then in the mirror again. 'He went to Sunday school,' he said. 'Can you tell?'

The woman eyed the conductor for a moment and he blushed. 'I went to Sunday school too,' she announced.

The conductor's face beamed with pleasure. The driver shifted into lower gear and the coach slowed down further. He looked in the mirror. 'Of course, it's all right for girls,' he said. 'Like lessons in home economics.'

The woman in the yellow dress looked out. It was a barren landscape of dried briers and carob trees; the only thing that moved was a herd of goats far away. Inside the coach most of the passengers were asleep. A pair of live chickens, strung from their legs, hung upside down from the rack and were letting out low guttural sounds. The conductor turned to the woman.

'He didn't know what Pegasus was,' he whispered to her, and indicated the driver with a nod. 'It was my idea.'

The other man saw him out of the corner of his eye. 'I didn't have the benefit of your education, my friend. When my parents died I had to look after my sisters.'

The woman felt tired. She took a magazine from her bag and leafed through it.

'You never met your mother. Until last year you thought she was that mongrel bitch sleeping under Pegasus in the depot.'

The driver shook his hand in a dismissive gesture. 'That's because I believe in reincarnation.' He looked in the mirror again. The woman was reading – but he said it anyway: 'A hard youth I had but I've made it. I wish my poor mother could see me now.'

The conductor said: 'Easy; drive by the whorehouse and blow the horn.'

They had reached the bottom of the valley. Smoke was rising from a plot of land not far from the road: an abandoned bed of embers kept alight by the wind.

'What's that?' asked the woman, putting down her magazine.

The conductor looked that way. 'Yesterday's fire-walking feast,' he explained. 'It's some sight to see. The fire-walkers work themselves up into a holy ecstasy before—'

'It's easier than it sounds,' the driver interrupted him. 'Anyone can do it.'

'Not you,' the conductor said. 'St Constantino only protects the soles of true Christians.'

'I would like to see it some time,' the woman said, and returned to her magazine.

'St Constantino,' said the driver. 'Patron saint of soles.'

It was past one o'clock now. Through the holes on the lowered blinds the sun burned the plastic of the seats and the faces of the passengers. No one could sleep any more. They made hats from newspapers for the children and opened the baskets with the food. The smell of garlic mixed with that of sweat. The conductor shook his head.

'I gave you my sister,' he told the driver, unprovoked.

'I let you into the business,' the other retorted.

'I let you into my house. Whenever you'd walk under our

balcony my sister would lock the door so that our mother wouldn't crack your head with one of the basil pots.'

'Before me, my friend,' said the driver, 'you were picking up cigarette ends.'

'You were eating pap three times a day.'

'Anyone can give out a ticket.'

'Not you. You can't count to ten.' He turned and looked at the woman, but she was paying them no attention; she had a handkerchief over her nose and was looking out. The conductor turned back. 'At least I have a school-leaver's certificate.'

'And I a driving licence.'

The driver looked in the mirror. The woman's lips formed the words on the page. Disappointed, he took his hands off the wheel to light his cigarette.

The next stop was in a village that had just been added to their route after countless petitions. On the roof the coach carried the morning papers, a crate packed with jars of glazed fruit for the coffee shop, and provisions for the taverna and the chandlery. At the entrance to the village there was a cloth tied from lamp-posts on either side of the road that read WELCOME, PROGRESS. When the coach appeared, dogs started barking, and a group of children ran after it, shouting and waving. The driver blew three different tunes on the horn to impress them. Beside him the conductor buttoned up, fixed his tie and removed his cap to comb his hair with his fingers. The driver took a last draw at his cigarette, shot it out of the window and assumed a serious expression. In the square a crowd waited.

'Stay in your seats until we've come to a stop,' he shouted in the mirror.

The passengers crammed the aisle and took down their luggage from the racks. When the coach stopped, the conductor said: 'Don't push, and watch your step at disembarkation.'

The woman in the yellow dress looked up from her magazine, where she had just finished reading a story with more sarcasm than meaning, and scrutinised the crowd that had already circled the coach. Suddenly, not from far away, came the arriving whistle of the train. She leaned out of the window.

'Which way to the station?' she asked a villager.

He showed her. She marked the page and put her magazine back in her buckskin bag. Then she called to the driver. 'Could you help me with my luggage?'

The conductor had heard her too. One man carried her important parasol, the other the small suitcase held together by the trouser belt, and they stepped down from the coach ahead of her. A crowd of villagers immediately surrounded the two men and started patting them on the back. It was some time before they saw the woman in the yellow dress again, still inside the coach. The driver and the conductor shouted at the crowd to let her through. She took her luggage from them, thanked them, and slipped through the villagers who paid no attention to her: they all wanted to touch the coach. The mayor came forward.

'Stay for a drink, friends.'

'We can't,' said the conductor. 'We're running late.'

But they did drink a coffee and two brandies each on their feet, while listening to the sound of the departing train with nostalgia. She had taken the secret of her name with her. The mayor insisted on giving a little speech, some more passengers boarded the coach, the door was shut, the driver revved up the engine and twenty minutes later they were on their way again. It was a further ten minutes before the conductor stood up to collect the fares and discovered that the money box on the dashboard was completely empty.

Deus ex Machina

She came on the morning train, on Monday. She had been loaded on the cargo car together with a bale of hay and the bottom half of a worn-out boiler which had been hastily cut with an oxyacetylene torch to make a watering trough. A king-size mattress was nailed on each of the wooden walls to protect her from the sharp bends of the track. She had a canvas bag roped to her croup between her legs to collect her dung, but by flipping her tail to swat the flies she had displaced it and it had served no purpose at all during the trip. The stationmaster became aware of the smell immediately he opened the door, even before his eyes had time to get used to the dark interior of the car. She came at 14.07 on the 11.03, and no one knew about her until then.

An hour earlier, the stationmaster finished reading yesterday's paper, cut it into square pieces several pages at a time and walked to the small shack across the track. Pinching his nose he hung the pieces from a nail next to the toilet bowl and quickly

63

got out again, closing the door behind him. Back on the platform, a young man in a suit sat on a bench and put his cardboard valise next to him.

'Are you sure I haven't missed my train?' he asked.

'Yes.'

The big clock above their heads showed 13.10.

'But it's over two hours late.'

'That clock is running fast.'

Pretending to check his watch, the stationmaster climbed on the bench and turned the hands back three hours. There was a whistle in the distance and the young man stood, straightened his jacket and picked up his suitcase. A minute later a train passed through the station at full speed and threw him off balance. From the concrete floor he watched the open freight cars leaving the station in a cloud of air and gravel.

'It's iron ore,' the stationmaster explained. 'From the mines of the penitentiary.'

The stationmaster sat on the bench and took off his cap. He took a collapsed cigarette packet out from under the lining and offered one to the other man.

'What do you sell?' he asked, after lighting their cigarettes.

'Encyclopaedias.'

'What sort?'

'Medical.'

The stationmaster shook his head.

'People don't get sick much around here. Maybe it's the fresh air. Or maybe because they die young, while they're still healthy.'

'Why do they die, if they're so healthy?'

The stationmaster took a draw on his cigarette and swallowed the smoke. 'I haven't thought about it before.'

They watched the train disappear over the horizon, bumping up and down on the uneven tracks, and there was silence again.

A brief wind turned the blades of a water pump and brought over the smell of the shack from the other side of the track. The young man spat, disgusted.

'Virgin Mary! What's that smell?'

'Sanitary facilities.'

They carried on smoking.

'Our station is at the top of the Public Works list of repairs,' said the stationmaster after a while. The salesman did not reply. Above their heads, the carousels of gears ticked the minutes inside the old clock. The stationmaster listened to it with attention and pride: it never missed a minute. 'But the customer's always right,' he thought, amused. A fresh cloud of smoke emerged from the hills and soon another train approached. This was a passenger train and was slowing down. The salesman combed his hair and picked up his valise, but put it down again when the train stopped at the water tower outside the station.

'This isn't your train either,' said the stationmaster, stretching his legs. 'How much are the books?'

The salesman fell back on the bench.

'Much less than you'd expect. And you can have one volume free. Either the anatomy atlas or the digestive system.'

While the train was taking on water a woman climbed down and ran to the shack. But as soon as she opened the toilet door she closed it again. She covered her nose with her handkerchief and returned to the train. She wore a dress with a print of roses and a hat.

'How about the reproductive system?'

'That will cost you extra.'

They fetched the plank they had for unloading barrels but it was no good. When she put a hoof down, the wooden board sagged and oscillated and made a hollow sound, and she backed into the car, neighing and refusing to walk down again. In the end, they took stones from the collapsed wall of the yard and built a solid ramp under the board, from car to platform, strong enough to support an ox. But she did not trust them any more.

Passengers got off the train, made suggestions as to how to get the horse out of the car and then started eating what remained of their provisions. They carried straw baskets, a pair of cackling hens hung upside down, a demijohn of wine, a braid of garlic. A man in a white hat and a summer suit with a leather briefcase also climbed down from the train and wandered among the crowd. The stationmaster assumed he wanted to use the facilities.

'I'm afraid the toilet's broken, sir.'

'I don't understand.'

'Better wait until the next station, sir.'

When the horse neighed to greet him, the small circle of people stepped aside with respect and he said that he was a solicitor from the capital on business.

He suggested feeding the horse sugar and they did. But only after she had eaten the whole stock of sugar cubes from the village chandlery did she listen to their commands. Finally, when she stood on the platform, they were all so impressed they forgot that they had missed lunch, they could not smell her dung any more, and they ignored the fact that they would be drinking their coffee bitter for at least a week. For what they saw was a racehorse, an Arabian mare from Damascus which had won thirty-two races in her youth – although they did not know that then – and she still had a perfect set of teeth. She stood naked but for the halter and a rubber-stamped luggage tag tied around her neck with the name of the village on it, and her flanks were such a glorious sight that the men cheered, the women sighed and the children wanted to touch. The encyclopaedia salesman compared her mane to the tassels of the

velvet curtain of the National Theatre, but no one acknowledged his simile because they had never been to the capital city.

'What's her name?' the stationmaster asked.

'History,' said the solicitor.

'Hell!' said a boy. 'They called her after a book!'

As if it were the beginning of a religious procession, the
crowd started down the street with the mare in front. The
solicitor was on one side holding her halter and on the other
were the encyclopaedia salesman and the stationmaster, who
had forgotten in the commotion to semaphore the train out of
the station. The train engineer was there behind him, determined to see who the lucky owner of the mare was. Further
back walked the train's passengers, both those who were
returning home and others whose destination was some other
place along the line. The crowd took a shortcut through the
forest of listing crosses in the cemetery, turned left at the
ramshackle telegraph office where the wasps had made their
nests in the chinks in the plaster, and made a brief stop at the
civil guard station with the withered flag. The corporal checked
the papers of the solicitor and joined the procession.

When they arrived at the house, the solicitor knocked at the
door. Silence. He knocked again. The door opened and a
young woman with hands covered in dough squinted at the
sunlight, then looked at the solicitor, annoyed. Then she looked
at the horse and finally at the crowd.

'Where's your husband?' asked the stationmaster.

'He's not in. Some people work for a living.'

A boy found Isidoro in his plot and told him they were looking
for him. The young man stopped working and leaned against
his hoe. The words PROPERTY OF were painted on its handle, but
the name had been ground away with emery paper. He had a
brief look at his land. It was small and on such a steep slope that

now he had worked the earth deep, the soil had rolled to the bottom of the hill and he would have to carry it back up bucket by bucket.

'Isn't that old Marko's hoe?' asked the boy.

'No, it isn't.'

'It must be. The blade's broken at the corner just like Marko's, and—'

Isidoro put his foot on the blade and pushed it into the earth.

'What's this about?' he asked.

'The horse.'

'What horse?'

'The horse that's so important it travels by train.'

Behind the bar of the coffee shop the landowner sat on a low stool. His eyes just came above the counter in front of him. He watched the door, every man that walked in, the traffic outside, and his eyes shone in the shadows like a swimming crocodile's. He wiped his forehead with his handkerchief and put his fingers deep into the brine of an open tin. When the waiter came he caught him eating the olives.

'Why don't you sit at a table like everybody else?'

The landowner wiped his fingers on his trousers.

'The doctor said I should stay out of the sun. And in any case, I've saved you a table.'

The waiter took up the bucket and mop while the landowner searched the shelf for newspapers.

'Where's today's?'

'The train hasn't come yet.'

A customer walked in, leaving the door open. The wind blew into the shop from the direction of the station.

'Close that damn door,' shouted the landowner. 'My clothes will smell of shit.'

The customer obeyed silently.

'They should demolish that toilet at the station,' continued the landowner, addressing no one in particular. 'In fact, they should demolish the lot. It's a public danger.'

'It's required by law to have sanitary facilities in public places,' the customer offered.

'Why do I waste my life in this shithole?'

'You're the richest man for miles.'

'What's the point when all I can smell is shit and I can't get my newspaper on time?'

He leaned against the wall and rested his legs on the gas cylinder of the stove. The waiter finished mopping and the sun on the wet floor made the round tables look like lilies in a pond. The landowner gazed beyond them to the square glow of a window where a cat was licking its paw. Suddenly the cat jumped off and the face of a horse looked at him from the other side of the glass. Then a crowd of human faces covered the windows and it became dark inside the shop. A well-dressed man walked in.'Send a boy to find him,' he said to the crowd who had stayed outside and watched quietly. 'I'll wait here.'

The landowner turned to the waiter.

'Who is he looking for?'

'The man you sold that useless patch of land to. Up in the hills.'

Later, when Isidoro came, the solicitor told the crowd about the mare. How she used to belong to a retired army general, a relative of Isidoro so distant he was not sure whether he was from his mother's side of the family or his father's, God rest their souls. In fact, he was the cousin of Isidoro's wife's aunt, an eternal bachelor, a major during the war, a pagan repenter who had been told on his deathbed that the pearly gates would remain shut like a constipated arse unless he demonstrated humility and the altruism of love. The general donated his fortune to the benevolent fund of his local parish, but it was not enough. He scratched his head. Son of a bitch, he thought, those priests are worse than politicians.

Finally he remembered he had once had a family: a father, a mother who had a sister, yes, who had three children he used to play War of Independence with when he was a little boy until he had almost impaled one of his cousins in an attempt to re-enact one of the most moving pages in the history of the Revolution. He called his solicitor then, and gave him orders to trace his closest relative.

'I have to put him in my will.'

'Who, sir?'

'Any bastard you can find as long as he's a man, because only a man can care for my beloved History, the only female I loved in this life.'

He signed the inheritance papers and two days later peacefully passed on.

'And now she's yours,' the solicitor said to Isidoro. He opened his briefcase and took out a typed page and a pen. 'Please sign here.'

'I know nothing about horses,' said Isidoro.

'You are twice lucky today,' the encyclopaedia salesman said. 'I have everything you need here.'

'You sell human anatomy books,' said the stationmaster.

'It's the same thing.'

The wasps appeared at sunrise, after the horse had spent a few days in the house. They found her from her smell, methodically searching for a crack in the shutters until their persistence had paid off. Then, encouraged by the warmth, they explored the rest of the house. It was a small rubble house with only two rooms, a bedroom and a kitchen, where they eventually made a banquet from the food shelves and the meat safe. The cobwebs on the lintel caught a dozen of them, but that was merely an inconvenience because of the strength of their numbers. Diamanda was aroused by the sound of their wings and, under the delusion of sleep, she believed it was the noise of a radio. But only for a moment, because soon she was awake enough to remember they could not possibly afford one.

She tiptoed to the kitchen door, opened it, and her eyes had only a few seconds to take it all in: there were wasps on the leg of lamb, on the bread, sucking the oil and bathing in the jar of molasses, licking the sugar and sipping the drops of lemonade on the table. Taken by surprise, the thick cloud of insects took flight and tried to escape not through the open window but through Isidoro's shaving mirror. Diamanda quickly closed the kitchen door and woke up her husband.

'What is it, woman?'

'I don't know why I ever agreed to marry you, but I know now why I should divorce you.'

It took Isidoro several hours to calm her down. Every time they heard steps or the hammering of donkey hoofs on the cobblestone path outside their house, they stopped until the sound had faded away and then carried on arguing.

'Fine feathers make fine birds,' said Isidoro, and killed a wasp that had escaped through the kitchen window only to re-enter the house through the bedroom. 'People used to pity me for what that cheat the landowner did to us.'

'A plot on a slope we need ropes to get to!' exclaimed Diamanda.

'Anyway,' said Isidoro, regretting he had brought up that matter. 'Now with the mare, I get free drinks and snacks, and people talk to me like old friends.'

'All they want to talk about is the horse.'

'It's talk, isn't it?'

Diamanda closed the bedroom window. The wasps had

managed to escape from the kitchen and were circling the house. In the garden the cat clawed the air.

'What are you going to do about the tools?' she asked.

'That horse was a God-sent gift. It will help us buy our own. Then I'll put them back in Marko's shed.'

'How's the horse going to help you do that?'

'I'm thinking of racing her.'

'You know nothing about horse racing!'

Before Isidoro could continue there was a knock on the door. It was the landowner. He walked in without waiting to be invited, shaking his handkerchief to get rid of the wasps.

'What do you want?' Diamanda asked.

'I have business to talk to your husband about.'

'The last time you talked business with my husband we almost ended up in the poorhouse.'

The landowner turned to Isidoro.

'I understand your uncle, son.'

'My uncle?'

'The general. I'm a widower. I can use some company too.'

'You should remarry,' said Diamanda.

The landowner made an expression of displeasure.

'I want to buy the mare,' he continued. 'I will look after her well.'

Isidoro stood up. He was still in his woollen long johns and looked more stout than he really was. He felt as if a dream had come true. He felt lucky, like the time he had won his necktie in the church raffle, and proud.

'She's not for sale.'

The landowner looked at him for a moment. He then left without saying another word.

Diamanda sighed. 'We'll live to regret another of your decisions.' She opened the kitchen door a crack; at least the wasps had gone.

★

That same evening the landowner sat with the priest in the coffee shop. They started by drinking coffee, then had a beer each, then the landowner suggested they had a couple of brandies.

'Why not?' said the priest.

'Will you be all right for matins, Father?'

'If you'd ever been you'd know it's only old women who come these days, and they're all deaf. I could recite the Cup results and they wouldn't know the difference.'

They drank the brandy. A group of loud children were playing in the street. Then a woman came and sent them home, cursing and throwing stones at them as if they were stray dogs. After they were gone, the men in the coffee shop could hear the music on the radio and the women sitting at the doorsteps could chat in peace.

'The man who couldn't afford a donkey now owns a racehorse,' said the landowner.

Father Yerasimo nodded in agreement. 'Who would believe it?'

'This country is on course for disaster, Father. The poor are too proud for their own good.'

The priest ordered another round of drinks.

'There's a lot to be said about the evils of pride.'

'By the way, Father, do you know about Marko's tools?'

For the rest of the week the wasps would come every day at dawn and circle the house for a way in, but they could not find one because Diamanda had put mosquito nets in the windows, Isidoro had blocked every crack in the walls with plaster, and the cooking fire was kept alight day and night so that they could not get in through the chimney either.

On Sunday the rooster crowed earlier than usual. In bed

Diamanda thought, This means a clear, sunny day. Just what the wasps love. It had rained the night before and soon the humidity added misery to the heat. Inside the house the smell of horse manure and urine from the cellar had taken over. Isidoro got dressed standing at the window, looking towards the hill where his plot was. Money was running out, spent on hay for the mare and the encyclopaedia payments. But he was not worried. Even though it was a warm day he put on his only coat and did up all the buttons. He opened the door and jumped out. Before the wasps had time to attack him, he hid his head inside his coat. 'This is the siege of Constantinople!' he said and started walking fast, while the wasps fell on the coat like rain.

Half a mile down the road he took off the coat, hid it in the bushes while watching for neighbours, and in his short-sleeved shirt got back on the road and headed towards the square. There was plenty of time until the meeting. On a wall a lizard basked in the sun's rays and he clapped his hands to watch it run away. 'Fast, but not as fast as my horse, lizard,' he said. He looked up and, although he was far away, immediately recognised the priest from his black cassock. 'Damn,' he whispered and crossed himself. 'It's bad luck to see a priest early in the morning.'

'I didn't see you today at church, Isidoro.'

Isidoro kicked a stone.

'Well, I'm busy these days, Father.'

'Lay not up for yourselves treasures upon earth, where moth and rust doth corrupt, and where thieves break through and steal.'

Isidoro shrugged his shoulders.

'I'm poorer now than I ever was, Father.'

Father Yerasimo stroked his beard.

'You know, old Marko's lost his set of tools.'

Isidoro avoided the priest's eyes.

'I know nothing about that, Father.'

'But if you ever do, you'll make sure Marko gets back his hoes.'

'Why is Marko bothered? He's old. He doesn't work the fields any more.'

'A sin's a sin, my son.'

'Yes, Father.'

'You used to be a good Christian, my son.'

'I am, Father.'

'I'll investigate that.'

After the priest had gone, Isidoro spat on the ground. 'Priests aren't happy unless they see you in a pine box,' he told himself. 'I'm not a thief. All I need is one race, one win. And I'll buy Marko and everyone else ten hoes each.'

In the coffee shop he greeted the other customers and took a seat to wait. It was 10.30 and the 07.35 was due at any time. He ordered coffee and then decided to buy everyone else a drink with the last of his savings. When he turned to give his order, he saw the landowner's eyes fixed on him from behind the counter. That bastard crocodile is everywhere, Isidoro thought calmly. But today's my day.

The other men asked him questions about the horse and he answered them all until the train whistle interrupted them. A few minutes later the first passengers crossed the square. Isidoro watched, trying to determine who was his man. Soon the square was empty again but for a boy playing with the stray dogs. Isidoro grew impatient. He won't come, he thought. What a jinx, that priest.

The boy was the first to see the little figure walking from the road that led to the station. He was dressed in dark clothes, patent-leather boots and a hat. Isidoro walked out to meet the stranger and led him to the coffee shop. When the visitor entered, everybody stood as if he were a guest of honour.

'Thank you for coming,' Isidoro told him.

'I'm afraid I don't have much time. The train's leaving soon.'

'As I said in the telegram,' started Isidoro, 'I have a horse. A racehorse. I would like to get into partnership with someone who knows about racing.'

'I was surprised to hear that someone owned a racehorse in this—'

But he did not finish his sentence.

'Yes, History is a great horse.'

'Did you say History?'

'Maybe you've heard about her. She's a champion.'

'Everyone in the business knows about History. She was a champion indeed. A very rare mare.'

'Well, I own her now. Inheritance, I won't bore you with the details. I'm thinking of racing her.'

'Racing her?'

'Racing her, yes.'

The man had some brandy and smiled. 'The fact is,' he said, 'that horse has no racetrack value any more. She's too old.'

Isidoro and everyone in the coffee shop went silent.

'And she's not a workhorse either,' the man added. He stood and checked his watch. 'I guess she's only good for walks now. I hope you'll enjoy riding her.'

Suddenly, a laugh began from behind the counter like the cackle of a hen. It was the landowner, sitting on his low stool and holding the folds of his belly like an accordion, spitting olive stones with every breath. Everybody else was silent. The waiter collected the empties and returned to the kitchen to wash them in the sink. He turned on the tap all the way in order for the running water to cover the laugh, but it was quite unstoppable now, louder than the wind on Isidoro's land where only rock grew, or the drone of the wasp cloud and the sound of Diamanda's insecticide bomb. It was worse than the smell from the station every time it blew towards the village, and worse than the pestilent air inside Isidoro's house.

The moment Isidoro picked up the knife from the table, the laughter became the sound of dynamite in his ears, and he could already see himself in the iron mines of the penitentiary, shovel in hand and a civil guard behind his back with a rifle, lazily smoking and keeping an eye on him. But the image did not discourage him and he slowly walked towards the man behind the counter. The landowner fell off his stool as he tried to back off. He had nowhere to hide. The only way out was past the young man who shuffled his feet, still coming.

He would have killed him then if it were not for Diamanda, who walked into the coffee shop that very moment and, seeing what was happening, stood between them.

'Isidoro,' she said. 'You are about to sign another contract without having read the small print first.'

Isidoro stopped. His face was red. He looked at his wife and finally dropped the knife, ashamed.

Father Yerasimo sat at his desk with a cup of coffee, a plate of meat and the oil lamp next to his notebook. He did not have much to do for the next day: a one-page sermon, a few lines for a lamentation and a letter to the bishop in the county capital. It had been a strange few days. But now old Marko's tools had been returned and he had given Isidoro absolution and a promise not to notify the civil guard – but only after the foolish young man had agreed to the donation. As far as Father Yerasimo was concerned it was a fair punishment.

He started the sermon. Writing about the rich, the poor and those in between, he became so absorbed that at some point he imagined he was Archangel Michael and his pen was his mighty sword. He had to stop then, because he realised he was committing the deadly sin of pride. To get his mind off it, he picked a slice of the cured meat he had kept for himself before sending the rest to the poorhouse. He tasted it. 'Sweet!' he exclaimed. 'A God-sent gift. That horse saved Isidoro's soul and will feed the poor too.' And he proceeded to eat everything on his plate, stuffing his mouth as if he had not had anything for days.

Jeremiad

That morning Mr Jeremias, a retired carpenter and master stonecutter, left the village on the early coach to the county capital. Two hours later he was pressing the stop button above his seat, not knowing at that moment that the small switch was the trigger of his fate. Having disembarked two stops too soon, his plan to be at the front of the queue in the Pensions Office had collapsed, even though he ran an impressive mile for a man of his age and superfluous physique.

He made it to the office only in time to take the last available seat in the waiting room. He was sweating profusely, breathing heavily, was disappointed and hungry. Had he been first in line, he could have sorted out his pension within the hour. But now he could only put his dog-eared stamp books in the tray on the counter, sit back to get his mind off his misfortune, and hope he would be seen before closing time. It was what he had been hoping for twice a week for the past two months.

He closed his eyes and listened to his heart, which beat at a tempo he had never managed to follow on the recorder whenever he played with the village band. Only a few moments later Mr Jeremias, a bachelor aged sixty-five, opened his eyes as if someone had called his name and peacefully passed away from exhaustion in the familiar surroundings of the Pensions Office.

And no one noticed. No one heard the silence of his dead man's nostrils, or noticed that his collar remained buttoned up – if he were alive he would have undone it no later than nine thirty, when the heat, the cigarette smoke and the sun through the stuck windows always made him sweat and complain. In addition, he had his hands clasped on his lap instead of playing with his string of beads while repeating the speech he had prepared for the branch manager, and, even though he did have his legs crossed, he did not once cross them the other way around in order to avoid pins and needles, as he would invariably do, or scratch his ankles, which always itched under his polyester socks.

With his head leaning slightly back, resting on the dusty wall, and his eyes open, he seemed as if he were staring at the laminated poster of a paradise island on the opposite wall. His freshly shaven cheeks were still red and his face had a pleasant expression – in fact, he was almost smiling, maybe a little puzzled, as if someone had just told him a humorous anecdote he had not understood but was polite enough not to show it.

Some time later the retired brigadier and decorated hero of the war who was sitting opposite, spat on the floor. He said: 'This place is more crowded than any dugout I've been in in my time.' He proceeded to roll up his trousers, and unfastened the straps of the wooden leg he had lived with ever since his release from hospital. He then produced a gouge and explained to the other claimants that he had recently taken up woodcarving. 'It is a great hobby for pensioners,' he said, and started work on a mermaid relief on his artificial limb.

A woman next to Mr Jeremias, encouraged by his honest smile, talked about the living and dead members of her family tree, which went back seven generations to a lady-in-waiting of the first German queen.

'You're the best listener I've ever come across,' she told Mr Jeremias an hour later.

She had not caught his name, but, embarrassed to admit she was also a little deaf, she decided not to ask him again. Besides, it was her turn. At the counter she demanded a disability allowance in her pension, on the grounds of severe back pain from kneeling at mass for over fifty years. The clerk listened patiently, and replied: 'Sue the bishop. Next claim.'

Her case started a discussion among the claimants. A former sexton with a toupee had to agree that, indeed, there were several dangers lurking inside a church.

'It's worse than a battlefield,' the retired brigadier said.

He listed the danger of fire from the wax and oil candles, the fact that one could slip on the marble steps of the altar or stumble over the brass legs of the candelabra, and also the chance of contracting an infectious disease through the sharing of the Communion cup.

The time passed with the claimants walking between rooms in order to get a signature on their forms, buy tax stamps from the cashier and use the mimeograph. The discussion moved to the matter of death.

A schoolmistress said: 'Resurrection is the greatest advertising campaign ever launched by the Church.'

'And paradise is a private club,' added a man with dyed hair, gold rings and a medallion. 'But, even though you pay membership fees for a lifetime, you may still be refused admission at the door.'

The brigadier shook his gouge in disagreement.

'I believe we come back as flies for three reasons,' he said.

'First, there are enough for there to be one for every soul on Earth since the beginning of time. Second, aren't they often flying around corpses? And third, they like living in houses – old habits die hard.'

The woman next to Mr Jeremias asked: 'Yes, but they eat—'

The brigadier shrugged. 'In the next life we reap what we sow.'

Annoyed, the sexton left the waiting room and lost his place in the queue. When he returned he realised his mistake and decided to come back another day. A moment later, the waiter from the corner café came in holding an electric fan.

'Who ordered this?'

'I did.'

It was the widow of the herbalist who had made a fortune selling bitter concoctions that cured cancer and other terminal diseases. He was finally arrested, his fortune was confiscated and he was left to die in prison. His wife, who had become addicted to infusions of the medicinal herbs from the unsold produce, was left with nothing.

'Poverty is killing me little by little,' she said.

The clerk pressed the REFUSED stamp on her documents.

'Don't worry. You drink enough philtre to live for ever.'

By midday, Mr Jeremias's putrefaction was producing a detectable smell. Yet no one suspected it was coming from that respectable gentleman. His tight collar squeezed his bloodless Adam's apple, and the rubber ends of the chairlegs, pushed by his weight, gave another half an inch. As time went by, his muscles hardened and his face became paler. But the sun had moved beyond the skylight, and Mr Jeremias was now sitting in a shade that hid his body's transformations. Six hours had passed since he had expired, during which no one had looked at his strangely amused face for more than a second, or laid a concerned hand on his sinking shoulder.

It was an ignominious end for the man who had almost single-handedly built the village. Many years before, he was crossing the valley on foot when he noticed some tin and adobe shacks, and headed towards them. The moment the people saw the man in the maroon leotard, the big tattoos and the ripped boots enter their village, they felt as if a dog had wandered into their house.

'Who the hell are you?' they asked.

'I am Jeremias,' the man replied, blushing. 'I used to be the strongest man in the world.'

He explained that once he could pull a steam locomotive plus eleven wagons with his teeth, hew a marble boulder into a Virgin Mary with the sharp edge of his hand, and crush a concrete block with a single knock of his forehead. The villagers looked at him, unimpressed.

'I'm looking for a job,' the strongman finally said.

The mayor came forward.

'Can you build walls?' he asked.

Because the houses had no foundations, the village was prey to the winds that blew across the valley, lifting whole shacks in the air and dropping them miles away. Within two years, Mr Jeremias had built stone houses for every family, a town hall and also a church with a belfry.

'We cannot pay you,' the mayor said. 'But I can sign the papers to claim a state pension.'

'A pension?'

'It's like a salary,' explained the mayor. 'The difference is that you get a raise only before the elections.'

In the Pensions Office it was now an hour before closing. Only the brigadier and the man with the medallion were in the queue in front of Mr Jeremias. The door opened and a woman in a tight dress walked in. She looked around with distaste. In the end she walked to Mr Jeremias and pulled down the neckline of her dress.

'For you,' she said, 'only ten drachmas.'

The brigadier turned to the medallion man.

'What does she sell?'

'Miracles.'

She looked at the dead man for a moment. Then she asked the other two: 'What's wrong with him? He smells like expensive cheese.'

'You are wasting your time. He's from a village so poor it doesn't have a name.'

The woman turned to the brigadier.

'How about you, old man?'

'I haven't been with a woman for years,' he replied. 'But I'm a fighter.'

Half an hour later in a hotel not far away, and leaning over his wooden leg on the floor next to the bed, the brigadier counted the banknotes in his wallet, and decided to stay where he was for some time more, thus surrendering his place in the queue to Mr Jeremias.

Ten minutes before closing, the clerk finally took Mr Jeremias's forms from the tray, but did not notice the dog that walked in, attracted by the smell of rotting flesh. While the man was studying the forms, the dog bit Mr Jeremias's shoe and started pulling it with desperation. The clerk stood up and, scratching his head, went to see his supervisor.

When the branch manager approached Mr Jeremias, the dog was already gone. He looked at the old man without a shoe, whose hair was messed up, and who had a half-smile on his ash-grey face, and could not suppress an irreverent laugh before saying: 'This is your lucky day, Mr—' He put on his glasses to read the name on the documents in his hands. 'Je-re-mias, yes. I am happy to inform you, Mr Jeremias, that your situation has finally been resolved.'

Whale on
the Beach

Whale arrived at work a little after seven with black circles round his eyes. All night his stomach ulcer had kept him running back and forth between his bedroom and the kitchen, searching every drawer and cupboard for his ammonium carbonate tablets. In desperation, not being able to endure the firecrackers going off inside his stomach, he was about to down a bottle of Mercurochrome he had found under the sink when his sister walked in. 'Don't do it, fool!' she cried. 'Or the doctors will turn you inside out and scrub you with a steel brush.' She found his tablets in less than a minute; but by the time they had taken effect it was time for Whale to get to work.

He unlocked the padlock and raised the rolling shutters in a well-executed clean-and-jerk lift learned from his amateur weightlifting days. For a few months now the shutters had become heavier and, thinking that maybe the rains had corroded the bearings, he promised himself to grease them. Puffing and sweating he opened the glass door and immediately felt like he was stepping into the mouth of a sewer pipe: it smelled of rotting cabbage and alcohol. He turned round and spat in the street. The boy had not taken the rubbish out last night.

Whale sighed. He had to clean the place himself before the first customers arrived. He collected the rubbish and, because the dustman had already passed, left the bins in the back. After washing the ashtrays and the glasses, he climbed on an empty beer case and lit the oil lamp next to the picture of St Varnavas. From there he inspected the shop. All in all, there was a refrigerator with a glass front, a cupboard built in the wall where his sporting cups and medals were, and seven tin tables with wooden legs he had made himself. Their legs were standing at such random angles it was as if they were walking towards the door.

The case swayed a little, and Whale's hair brushed against the dusty fan blades above his head. Climbing down, he caught himself in the mirror: the dust on his hair and last night's insomnia made him look older. My mother was right, he thought. I do look like my father, after all.

That moment the door opened and a woman came in. Whale turned round, and the woman looked at his hair and raised an eyebrow.

'Good morning,' he said.

The woman, who had only one shoe on, limped towards a seat. She sat down and breathed with relief. 'I've been walking like a cripple for a mile,' she said. She held her other shoe in her hand along with a small handbag and put both on the table. The shoe was black patent leather and its enormous heel had come off.

'I can fix that for you, Sapphire,' said Whale.

'Don't bother,' she replied, but gave him the shoe.

Still out of breath, she cut every word short. She lit a cigarette and smoked it in long draws. Before she had put it out Whale had fixed the shoe.

'It's easier to roller-skate than walk in these,' he commented, giving the shoe back. 'Here. It'll last for ever.'

Sapphire sighed. 'Thanks. But the only thing that lasts for ever is my callus.'

The morning coach drove past outside. It was the Feast of the Assumption and the village was empty: most people were on the beach. A cloud of hot dust blew into the shop and Whale rushed to close the door. 'This weather is only fit for camels,' he said, switching on the fan; but the blades did not move. He flicked the switch a couple more times but still nothing happened. Scratching his head he opened the fuse box on the wall. The fuse for the fan had blown and there was no spare. Whale took a bottle of lemonade from the refrigerator.

'Apologies for the discomfort,' he said. 'Drinks are on the house.'

The woman took a sip.

'I'm hungry, Whale.'

'I can make you eggs. They're good for you.'

He returned behind the counter without waiting for a reply. While he fried the eggs, he whistled and hummed. 'With this heat,' he joked, talking over the sizzling, 'I could probably fry them faster on your table top.' With the fan out of order, Whale slowly disappeared behind the smoke coming from the pan. Sapphire could hear but not see him.

'I'd give anything to be at the beach now.'

'What?' asked Whale.

'I said,' said the woman, raising her voice, 'don't cook them for too long.'

Whale finally appeared with a plate and another bottle of lemonade. The woman ate avidly. Whale observed her for a while, as he would have observed a child.

'A day like this,' he said, 'one should be at the beach.'

'I thought the same thing, you know.'

Whale shrugged his mountainous shoulders and for a second he looked out the window in silence.

'You seem to be the only customer today,' he mused, wiping his forehead with his apron. 'We might as well lock up and take the afternoon coach to the beach.'

'Do you mean that?'

'Sure.'

The woman put down her fork and tugged her hair behind her ear.

'Where do you want to go?' asked Whale.

'The beach next to the fairground. The tickets are on me.'

'Fair enough. We can hire an umbrella there − in this heat.'

'Deckchairs.'

'And two deckchairs,' agreed Whale.

The woman ate some more from her plate and took another swig of her lemonade.

'Why not visit the rides too?' suggested Whale. 'They advertise the roller-coaster as the scariest ride next to taking a taxi in the capital.'

'And the house of horrors.'

'Sure. And the shooting gallery.'

Suddenly the woman changed her expression and put down the bottle.

'Maybe I should ask Retsina first. I haven't seen him for days.'

Whale lowered his head. His hair was still covered in dust.

'I wouldn't have anything to do with a man who calls himself after a wine,' he said lightly.

The woman looked at him quizzically.

'You're named after a fish.'

Whale blushed.

'Not fish. Mammal,' he corrected her. 'And I didn't choose it.'

They said nothing for a while. On the plate, there was still one egg left. The woman picked up her fork and played with its yolk. The door opened and a young man came in with a small radio in his hand. He was nearly half as tall as Whale, with narrow, sloping shoulders and a face with puckered lips as if he were in agony from constipation.

'Damn! It's as hot as a kiln in here,' he said. He sat next to the woman and placed the radio on the table. He switched it on and fiddled with the aerial.

'Get me a double brandy, fat man,' Retsina said, still concentrating on the radio.

Whale went to the counter and brought him the drink.

'What is this?' asked Retsina after he had tasted it.

'Brandy.'

Retsina smiled with contempt and turned to the woman.

'He'll soon be selling us shit for cheese,' he said.

He picked up the fork and tasted the egg. He then produced a small comb from his back pocket. Turning round, he brought his face close to the window.

'Where were you?' he asked, watching his reflection and combing his hair.

There was silence.

'I buy you everything you ask for,' he said again, still combing his hair. 'Even the shoes you wear. And then you disappear for days.'

'I was in the capital, seeing my sister,' Sapphire murmured. And added: 'Besides, it's my money.'

'What?'

'I earn that money myself.'

The man turned round and looked at her. She looked down.

'You earn that money yourself,' he said. 'I see. She earns that money herself.' He drank some brandy. 'Never mind me staying up all night, walking round the house like a dog, making sure you don't get knifed by a stupid farmer. You earn your money all by yourself.'

Sapphire picked up her fork, but the man grabbed her hand. 'Let's go.'

Whale came from behind the counter.

'She has plans for today.'

'Plans?'

'We're going to the beach.'

The man let go of the woman. 'Well, well,' he said. He sat back in his chair, turned the radio down and tapped his comb against the table. 'Listen to that! Whale is going to the beach today!'

'Cut it out,' said Sapphire.

'He's going to play on the sand with his friends, the seal and the dolphin.'

The woman stood up.

'Leave him alone, Retsina.'

'Whale is going to go to the beach with my woman to sun his love handles.'

'Nothing wrong with that,' said Whale.

Retsina sat back in his chair and stretched his legs. Next to him, the woman chewed her nails. Inside his stomach, Whale felt his ulcer getting inflamed and bit his lip. Retsina tapped his little comb again on the tin surface of his table. His eyes fell on the framed pictures on the wall and the dusty cups on the shelf.

'Whale the weightlifter will go to the beach and eat an ice and tell my woman all about his weightlifting days. About his medals and his cups that brought him all this fame and glory.'

He spread his arms to show that he meant the coffee shop. Whale's pain spread to his kidney. He dug his nails in the soft cushions of his palms and cold sweat appeared on his temples.

He tried to forget about the pain. He thought of his sister in the kitchen. Every day at lunchtime she would bring the pan and they would eat in silence behind the counter.

'I'm a decent person,' he said.

'You'll miss the coach if you don't hurry, fat man,' said Retsina again. 'Why don't you come and take my woman by the hand and rush?'

'Retsina—'

'Shut up,' Retsina cut the woman off. 'Whale is going to take you to the beach.'

'I'm a decent man,' said Whale again. 'There's nothing wrong with going to the beach.'

Retsina looked him in the eye. Whale stood there as if his shoes were nailed to the floor, his face turning white from the pain in his stomach.

'Look at your decent boyfriend,' said Retsina finally. 'His face's whiter than his apron.'

'He's not my boyfriend.' Sapphire pushed Retsina timidly. 'Let's go.' She looked down and added: 'He misunderstood.'

Retsina looked at her.

'Are you sure?'

'I want to go. Now.'

'To the beach?'

'Home.'

Retsina stood up. He put his comb in his back pocket, took his radio and turned to leave. But then he stopped and came back to finish the food. 'Forget the beach, fat man,' he said, with his mouth full. 'And other men's women. Learn to cook instead.'

Sapphire was waiting outside.

'And get some decent brandy,' said Retsina, and left without paying, leaving the door open.

Whale stared at the door for several minutes. Then he went

and locked it twice from inside. Walking with difficulty because of the pain, he began looking everywhere for his tablets. He could not find any. He thought of sending for his sister, but changed his mind and went and sat in a chair behind the counter. Gradually the pain became intolerable. But there he sat, with his plump hands on his stained apron, shivering despite the heat. Every now and then a customer knocked at the door, but Whale did not move. At lunchtime his sister came with the steaming pan but he did not let her in either.

The Day of
the Beast

The maestro raised his baton and immediately the funeral march started. Moving down the unpaved road towards the cemetery, with their blue tunics held together with safety pins, their torn cardboard epaulettes, their caps with plucked aigrettes and their battered instruments, the musicians resembled a retreating army. Behind them walked the four pallbearers with the hastily made coffin still smelling of lacquer on their shoulders, after them the priest swinging a smoking censer, then the rest of the people dressed in black. All the children were also dragged along, herded together by sheepdogs, and last of all, struggling to catch up, Zacharias the lawyer and Dr Panteleon in his tailcoat whose empty left sleeve was pinned on to the breast pocket. It was a solemn procession.

Earlier the crowd had heard the most splendid mass in the church of St Timotheo, under the dome whose Pantocrator fresco had collapsed during the earthquake and in front of the cheap altarpiece made from laminated wood with the portraits of the Apostles. Only half of the village could fit inside the church. The rest remained in the yard with the cypresses, where they listened to the eulogy in silence before moving aside to let the coffin pass, while the bell-ringer tolled the bell with a mallet because it had no clapper. It was a warm spring day of little wind, which carried the cadence of death beyond the empty village houses, as far as the barns of the estate that spread across the valley. Those buildings were also empty of people, and no one could be seen in the ploughed plots either. Everyone was at the funeral: the previous day the landowner had died on the mosaic floor of the church under the eyes of his villeins.

He had descended into Hell crying futilely for help, and had left behind him, floating in pools of blood, his remains in heaps of limbs and viscera, and the mauled carcass of his beloved pointer.

He had brought the village more misery than any winter or drought, because he had a burning predilection for indiscriminate punishment. Not only would he treat petty and serious crime with equal severity, but also he would pick at random ten villagers and have them flogged each time too, because he had read somewhere that it was society that was truly responsible for crime and that the criminal was only the tip of the iceberg. He had always enjoyed his evil reputation, but it was not until he met the love of his life that he also discovered his penchant for murder.

They had met in another town where the landowner had been invited to judge a beauty contest. He decided to pursue her the moment he measured her hips with the tape and found them perfect for yielding his heir, and in turn she let him succeed after seeing the money pouch under his shirt, the contents of which he offered to spend on champagne. They were married after a week and a year-long honeymoon in the capital ensued, where the bride satisfied her omnivorous desire for the theatre: she liked everything from ancient tragedy to the marionettes. During that time their relationship developed the first hints of affection, which could well have grown into true love, had the couple not come to live in the village on the groom's insistence. The bride had a change of heart the moment she stepped into a cowpat left on the platform, after having fought her way through a group of villagers carrying strung chickens and pushing to board the train.

The farmhouse was an even greater disappointment to her. Before her arrival the only work ever done to it was to repair the roof – whenever there were no pots left to cook in because they were all being used for the leaks. No sooner had the landowner carried his bride in his arms over the threshold according to a foreign custom, than she saw their bed. It was the same bed he had been born in, and the one in which both the landowner's parents lay when they had crossed, one after the other only six months apart, the Rubicon to the underworld. The bed had once been a wooden carriage from which the shafts and wheels had been removed and a mattress filled with old newspapers placed over it. The woodworm had left more holes than were in a piece of sponge, and it creaked so much that the couple could not make love without the servants postulating the details of their intimacy. The bride looked at the bed, where the maid had placed a white lily.

'This is a fine joke,' she said, and started laughing heartily.

But when the woman realised that she was actually looking at the eternal matrimonial symbol itself, and that it was not a prank played on her by her husband, she said coldly: 'This manger is only worthy of your scabby cattle.'

She would have thought twice before saying it, if she had known that the lettuces in the field outside the window were regularly fertilised by the blood of men who would voice lesser insults. But the landowner, clenching his teeth, simply replied:

'I forgive you, my love, but only because you are the mother of my son.'

The baby they both knew she already carried inside her not only saved her from punishment on that occasion, but also made the groom promise that he would buy a better bed as soon as possible. The opportunity came a week later, when an exiled king and his entourage stopped at the village to fix the leaking radiator of his Packard, and the bride noticed the four-poster in the back of one of the lorries that carried the regal belongings saved by the aides when the ousted court fled the palace. The landowner went to the coffee shop to raise the issue with the deposed king. It was easier than he thought.

'You can have it for free,' said the king. 'But I should warn you that this bed causes one to have nightmares.'

The landowner bought drinks for the monarch and his retinue.

'Majesty, there are always remedies for those. My father, who founded this farm, was tormented for years by the recurring nightmare of having gone bankrupt.'

The king leaned closer to the villager. 'Did he cure himself by hypnosis?' he asked.

'No, Your Majesty. By poisoning his creditors.'

The king sighed. 'In my case I would have to poison a whole nation.'

The matter of the bed had been settled. There remained the question of the baby's sex: the landowner was determined that his offspring would be a boy.

He would have consulted Dr Panteleon, the only physician in the valley, had they not been mortal enemies. Many years before, when the war that annexed that very province to the motherland was declared, the idealistic doctor had instantly dropped his studies and joined the infantry. He was a good soldier, but his youthful heroism had cost him dearly: in the last desperate counter-attack of the enemy, a cavalryman's sabre had severed his left arm from the shoulder. It was a misfortune that condemned him to more than the hardships of disability, because on his left pinkie he wore the future of his studies: a gold ring with a thirty-seven-carat ruby he had inherited from his grandfather. Immediately on his discharge from hospital he returned to the village, where he discovered that the liberated land had been already auctioned off. He visited the landowner to request permission to search his land for the ring that should still have been attached to his severed arm.

'This way, my son,' said the landowner, and waved the doctor to follow.

In the cellar the young man was confronted by a macabre smell the likes of which he had never encountered in his anatomy class. As his eyes adapted to the cavernous darkness, lit only by a single torch on the wall, he made out shelves listing under the weight of innumerable shoeboxes which, when he came closer, pinching his nose, he saw were marked FINGERS, TOES, GENITALIA ETC. On the wine rack on the opposite wall, instead of bottles he saw human limbs of assorted sizes, still covered with shreds of tunic, congealed blood and putrefied matter. By that moment his eyes had filled with tears and he stumbled over a hemp sack, from which a severed head wearing the distinctive handlebar moustache of his commanding officer rolled out and disappeared into a dark corner of the manmade underworld.

'You are fortunate,' the landowner said behind his back. 'I meant to give them a decent burial but I haven't got round to it yet.'

The doctor had only had to go through a few boxes to realise the reason for the amassing of such a gruesome booty: there were no rings on the fingers, no gold teeth inside the mouths, not even a single watch strapped on any wrist. He confronted the landowner about it.

'Not only have our soldiers died so you could buy this land for peanuts,' he accused him, 'but you also robbed them of those personal possessions which now rightfully belong to their families!'

The landowner did not flinch. 'I had to pay somehow for the memorial I volunteered to erect in honour of the dead,' he apologised.

It was an insult to the heroes. Dr Panteleon left, believing that he would never set eyes on the landowner again. Without the ring he was forced not only to drop his dream of specialising in anaesthesiology, but even graduating from the medical school itself. That was why he returned to the village, a place where no one could tell the difference between the fishing competition certificate he ended up hanging on the wall and the scroll of a university degree. Then one day he saw his ring round the landowner's finger.

'It's an ancient heirloom of ours, doctor,' said the landowner slyly.

Dr Panteleon lost his temper.

'One day you will die screaming for help,' he replied. 'But unless my arm has grown back by then you won't receive a helping hand from me.'

The landowner would never visit the doctor again. He would consult instead an itinerant herbalist. The latter was the man the landowner went to see when the matter of the baby arose.

'Was the conceiving intercourse during a full moon?' asked the expert.

The landowner scratched his head. The truth was that his infatuation had prevented him from recollecting anything but his bride's body from their honeymoon days. Besides, during that year in the capital the couple's lovemaking was interrupted only to attend a play or when, overtaken by coital fatigue, they would both pass out in each other's arms.

'I'm not sure about the moon,' replied the landowner with a dreamy expression, 'but I certainly remember stars.'

The calendar confirmed that there was little chance of it having been a full moon.

'It is going to be difficult,' admitted the herbalist. 'Our only hope now is the science of drugs.'

He was signing the death warrant of the unborn baby. Over the following months the landowner forced his wife to drink so many mandrake infusions that she miscarried. The dead foetus was indeed male. It was a disaster the landowner had caused all by himself, and one which would have made another man repent and start a new life of humility and penance, but it made him waive for ever his right of loving another human being. As he was throwing the last shovelful over the small grave in the cemetery, he had already decided to make his wife pay for his son's death.

'An eye for an eye,' he murmured, taking the road back to the farmhouse.

There was a lawyer in the village who could have saved the woman, but he was a drunk who shook from fear at the sight of the landowner's shadow. Even so, the woman had secretly gone to see him.

'I want to file for a divorce.'

Zacharias the lawyer had just returned from a nearby town, where he had represented a pharmacist in his long dispute with a neighbour over the ownership of a mule born from the casual mating of the former party's mare with the latter's jackass. The lawyer had managed to obtain a court order in favour of his client, and was at that moment quietly celebrating his victory, for which he had been paid by the pharmacist with a demijohn of ethanol and a set of laboratory glassware of assorted sizes.

He asked: 'On what grounds?'

'He's planning to kill me.'

Zacharias was already drunk. The graduated beaker in his hand was shaking.

'How?'

'I don't know yet. But I can see it in his eyes.'

The lawyer put his feet back on the desk and relaxed. He took another swig at the beaker.

'Come back when you have admissible evidence.'

The woman curled her lip.

'I will send you a copy of my death certificate.'

'So long as it's notarised,' he replied.

Zacharias the lawyer was not always a coward. In contrast to the doctor, his framed certificate was an authentic licence conferred with honours by a French university. But his career had not fulfilled the promise of his academic credentials, and these days he lived in a state of permanent amnesia, sustained by ever increasing amounts of alcohol.

He had once said in the taverna, after his fifteenth shot of ouzo, that what had caused his downfall and brought him to the village had been losing a straightforward case. Someone had asked him how he had failed to win in that instance and he had poignantly replied before passing out: 'Because that poor devil of a client was innocent.'

He had made his home and office in an abandoned windmill on the edge of the village, whose blades had been charred by lightning. Pieces of its conical roof were carried away every time the manure-smelling wind swept across the valley. There he lived a hermit's life compromised only once a month, when he visited the taverna to stock up with wine and read the papers. On the door to the windmill and under the ATTORNEY AT LAW sign hung a metallic plaque embossed with the image of a pair of compasses over a coiled snake biting its tail, a symbol the villagers could not explain but which meant a lot to the lawyer. He had espoused Freemasonry while a student in France and had been an active member of his lodge until he had left for the country. When the landowner's wife left his office in tears, Zacharias was not drunk enough not to recognise that he was betraying the humanitarian principles of his fraternity.

'At my age I need a conscience as much as the fly needs the spider,' he mumbled.

The woman collapsed suddenly one afternoon at the citrus orchard. It was the only place where the fragrance of oranges and lemons softened the smell of the farm beasts, the place to take refuge from the dog-day afternoon heat and the intrusive stares of the farmhands, and somewhere to rehearse the roles she would play on stage once she had figured out how to cut the leash her husband held her on. The maid found her mistress later the same evening, and she mistook her for a ghost. She immediately ran back to the farmhouse where she locked herself in the kitchen, until the landowner ordered her to open up and tell him what was the matter. At once, he took a group of men and went to the orchard himself, and only then did they understand the maid's reaction. The unfortunate wife was dressed in her favourite theatrical costume, a Renaissance dress made from white muslin. Her head was bowed forward, but the rest of her body was still standing straight, supported by the stiff corset and the iron stays hidden under her skirt, which the blacksmith had made for her because she could not find any baleen in the whole county. She was dead. On the ground next to her was an old paperback edition of Molière's plays. The landowner pushed the torso with his finger, and as the dead woman swayed on the skirt-stays to and fro, he commented: 'My poor sweetheart always looked like a doll.'

It was Dr Panteleon who figured out how her husband had slowly poisoned her, after chancing months later upon one of her silk handkerchiefs daubed with *eau-de-Cologne*: it was sprinkled with arsenic. But it was too late to reopen the case, as the doctor discovered after going to meet the civil guard chief in the county capital.

'I'm afraid the details of the case have been lost,' the chief said, embarrassed.

'But how?'

'Let me show you.'

He took the doctor to the basement of the civil guard headquarters. The archive was a labyrinth of dungeons where paper folders were stacked up to the moulded ceiling, and the only sound heard was the echo of dripping water and of rats chewing criminal evidence. Standing in the near dark the chief raised his arms in desperation.

'Someone has filed them,' he said.

That day the doctor decided to kill the landowner. But he needed help. When Zacharias agreed, the two men started devising their plan.

The Pandora's box which the landowner unlocked after the miscarriage of his heir was thrown wide open with the unpunished murder of his wife. Terror descended upon the village, as the landowner started behaving like an absolute monarch. The local civil guard station was manned only by a corrupt corporal, whom the landowner had in his pocket. Not even the repeated attacks of gout, which soon confined him to bed, made him ease his grip on villeins and freemen alike. He conducted his affairs from his four-poster with the help of his snitches and an antique brass telescope, and administered justice according to his mood. He had a farmhand nailed to a tree for cutting crooked furrows even though the poor man had warned him that the ploughshare was bent. When the priest came to free him three days later in the name of leniency the landowner sent him away, saying: 'Leave him alone, priest. You wouldn't have a job now if someone had saved your god.'

Other typical punishments were the regular burying of slaughterers in the hogwash with only their heads above ground in order to cure their sluggish performance, the forcing of mowers with dull scythes to walk barefoot over hot coals, and the hurling of naked housemaids into the cesspool every time a woman's hair was found on the carpet.

The landowner's orders were obeyed as if given by a hypnotist, but that did not make him lower his guard. He demanded that his cook tasted the food first, and even then he would not eat unless there were on his table a jar of baking soda as an antidote for acid and one of cathartic Epsom salts for lead, a piece of charcoal to counteract the effects of hemlock and strychnine, and a bottle of olive oil in case someone should try to poison him with ammonia. For his more daring enemies he always carried a double-barrelled shotgun loaded with buckshot, as well as a short but sharp knife hidden inside his right boot.

The first thing the landowner did after waking up on that day of his destiny was to reach for the bell pull. When the maid appeared at the door, he pointed to the closed window where the noise of the farm was coming through and ordered: 'Find that rooster and fricassee him with potatoes and shallots – for lunch.'

He was by then of a geologic age and had grown to like his confinement to bed, so that even when the attacks of gout subsided – as was the case that week – he preferred the feathers of his pillows to the leather of his saddle: he seldom rode across the farm any more. Above everything else he liked to dress up in his calico gown embroidered with a coat of arms of his own invention, and read until mealtime the books he received by post from a second-hand shop in the capital. That day he was gripped by a history of the French monarchy the bookseller had recommended for containing good descriptions of human torture, when he was interrupted by the foreman who entered the bedroom pulling a man along by the reins of a fitted bridle.

'This scoundrel has been stealing from the warehouse for over a year, boss,' he announced.

The culprit was shaking with fear. His elongated, bridled head with its large ears and glimmering eyes reminded one of a stray mule. The landowner put down his book and reached for his whip, which he always kept under the bed. He gave it to the thief and ordered: 'Give the foreman fifty-one lashes.'

He may had been reduced to an old man who needed the support of his cane if he were to walk beyond the privy, but the landowner had lost none of his talent for unpredictable decisions.

'That will teach you to keep your men on a short leash,' he told the foreman when the punishment had been completed. 'Now you do that rat anything you wish to.'

It was the last time he would administer justice.

He dismissed them at once because he had to get ready for church. For weeks the priest had been pestering him with invitations to Eucharist which he always turned down.

'You should receive the body and blood of Christ,' insisted the priest in his letters. 'It would be beneficial to your health.'

'Priest, only drinking the blood of my enemies makes me feel good,' the landowner had written back.

Finally, he had agreed to attend under two conditions: that the service would take place in the afternoon because he would not rise from his bed before lunch even if God Himself were to knock at his door, and that the priest would drink from the chalice first in case the Communion wine was poisoned.

At five past three the landowner entered the church of St Timotheo ahead of his twelve foremen, stooping from the weight of his hunting jacket, the full cartridge belt and the heavy shotgun slung over his shoulder. For the first time the village realised that he had become a mere allegory of their hatred, with his cane bent to breaking point, the bald head where only the eyes had not rotted yet and the neck that resembled a vulture's. There was silence as he looked round. On the walls and the dome only pieces of the murals remained: the landowner had refused to help restore the damage of the earthquake.

'So,' he said. 'Let's get this over with.'

At his side he had his hunting dog. The pointer, with the smooth white coat with liver-coloured spots, raised its square muzzle, sniffed the air and started growling.

'She's nervous,' the landowner said, and patted her head. 'She's never seen so many good-for-nothings in one place before.'

He walked down the red carpet that lined the nave and sat on the bishop's throne, six of his foremen standing on either side, and the service started. It was a ceremony during which the priest read the wrong passage from the Bible, delivered a sermon that no one understood because he jumped from one subject to another mid-sentence, and annoyed the psalmist by singing off-key. Near the end he almost turned the ceremony into a farce when, having disappeared behind the altarpiece, he came back carrying instead of the chalice the half-empty bottle of red wine he had used for the sacrament, and he did not realise until he raised it and pronounced: 'Drink ye all of it.'

It was most unlike him. Still, the service went on. Finally, after the priest had tasted the sacrament himself first, the landowner stood up to receive it. His lips had barely touched the chalice when he heard the doors creak. He turned and saw the silhouettes of Dr Panteleon and Zacharias the lawyer against the afternoon light. He must have heard then the clock of his destiny tick its final minute, because he turned to the priest for an answer, and indeed, the priest had only to whisper, 'May God have mercy upon your soul,' for the landowner to know that this was the end.

The pointer jumped to her feet and started barking, and then the wolf came through the door. It was the doctor's revenge on behalf of the village for all the landowner's crimes, and it was taken with the lawyer's help: an enormous yellow-grey wolf with black patches the two men had raised from a pup to commit a murder no man could attempt alone. The beast ran straight towards the altar and first attacked the dog on the steps, biting her neck at the root and letting her bleed to death on the red carpet, before the landowner's turn came. The old man took a step towards the throne: but his shotgun, which he had left behind when he stood to receive the sacrament, was not there any more.

'Bastards,' he said, smiling.

He had just pulled out the knife from his boot when the beast clamped its jaws on to his arm. Neither the people in the wings nor his twelve foremen or the civil guard corporal helped him. Not even when, after the great beast had cut the thread of his life, it was digging into his belly to pacify its hunger. Instead, they waited for it to finish its gruesome feast and, when the wolf finally left with a last piece of meat in its teeth, they formed a line and one by one they all walked past the altar and spat on the human remains. Later that evening, the corporal urgently wired his superiors in the county capital and informed them that a horrific incident had just occurred.

A Circus
Attraction

The lorries were loaded and the caravan was ready to go, but when Vassili the gypsy looked for him he could not find him. He walked back to the camp where they had spent the last two months, calling his name, but he only came across a boy from the village trying to sneak into Cassandra the tattooed lady's trailer. 'If I catch you here again, little rat, I'll feed you to the crocodile,' he said, pinching the boy's ear. A crow pecking at the rubbish took flight and sat on the roof of a shack made from wood and oilcloth. In a battered oil drum in the middle of the camp smoked the remains of their fire. Vassili looked at the drum, then kicked it. The dull sound echoed across the camp pitched in the abandoned quarry. 'Hell,' he murmured. 'Here we go again.'

He took the narrow path that led to the river and soon discovered him sitting by the bank, throwing stones in the water. The river went by quietly, carrying along briars and branches fallen from the pines. Trees were on either side of the river. One of the steel towers of the quarry's conveyor belt had collapsed into the river, and the driftwood caught in it over the years had built up a small waterfall. Over the sound of the water Vassili called: 'Friend, it's time we go.'

The centaur, with his back to the gypsy, threw another stone in the river.

'I'm not coming.'

He had receding hair, a dirty white tail and the narrow eyes of someone staring straight at the sun. His legs were scratched and his hoofs shoeless. When Vassili laid his hand on his shoulder he shook it off with a jerk, like a frightened animal. His breath smelled; he had been drinking.

'I'm not coming,' he insisted. 'I've made up my mind.'

The man sighed. 'We can only offer ten per cent.'

The river ran over the fallen tower, and went round a shallow bend, where smooth rocks showed above the surface like tortoiseshells. Vassili sat next to the centaur and searched his pockets. He found a cigarette but no matches. He put the cigarette in his mouth just the same.

'Listen,' he said. 'Sign for another year, and we'll talk again.'

The centaur said nothing. Both he and the gypsy faced the river. The sun made little diamonds on its surface and the tortoiseshells at the bend shone. Sitting on the riverbank, stock-still, the centaur looked much like a marble statue. His receding hair and the beard made him look older than he really was. Vassili chewed the filter of his cigarette.

'You come with us, and we'll find you a mare,' he said. 'How about that?'

'How many times do I have to tell you: I am not a horse.'

Vassili changed the subject.

'Who'll take care of you?'

'I can look after myself.'

A year earlier the caravan was crossing the valley, and they had heard in the village that Dionysio the cattle farmer had an item for sale.

'You're selling,' they said.

Beyond the veranda, the tilled land extended as far as the gypsies could see. Tracks made by the hoofs of mules cut across the fields in random directions. Dionysio rocked in his chair.

He said: 'You won't believe your eyes.'

It was a man dressed in a centaur suit. He was drunk. The gypsies inspected the centaur suit.

'Amazing,' they said. 'He almost looks real. How much?'

Dionysio shrugged.

'He would be priceless if he didn't eat too much and curse so badly when drunk.'

The gypsies looked again at his teeth, smelled his breath and finally shook hands with the farmer.

'We'll make more than the travelling show of exotic birds,' they said.

It had been a success. But now at the river the centaur said firmly: 'You are wasting your time.'

The unlit cigarette on Vassili's lips had started to soften.

'You have no idea,' he retorted.

'I am immortal,' the centaur said proudly. 'I can remember when your forefathers first arrived from India.'

'Times have changed,' the gypsy said. 'You'd be lucky now if you ended up pulling a cart.'

The centaur dug his hoofs in the ground, vexed.

'To them you're only a horse who can talk,' Vassili continued.

They sat in silence.

'Listen, you drunken freak,' Vassili suddenly said. 'We paid good money for you. You'd better change your mind – or else!'

The centaur looked at him with his haughty stare, until the gypsy threw his cigarette away and took the path back to where the lorries waited with the engines running. All the lorries were in a bad state: one was missing a door, another a windscreen, and in all of them the rust had opened so many holes that pieces of metal were falling off from the engine vibrations. Medusa and the girls had already taken their seats in the family van. Medusa still wore the costume with the golden scales and the snakes for hair. Vassili said: 'He's not coming.'

'We can't leave him behind,' Medusa protested. 'Harness him.'

'What's the point? He'll run away at the first chance.'

'We can't leave him.'

The girls stared at their parents blankly. Medusa climbed down from the van.

'I'll talk to him,' she said.

She found the centaur where her husband had told her. He was now lying on his side, with his hand under his head and his hoofs in the water. He was chewing a straw. He had guessed who was coming. Medusa fixed a snake behind her ear.

'Look at me,' she said.

'I'm not stupid,' the centaur replied. 'As soon as I look at you I'll turn to stone.'

'I've brought you something.'

The centaur squinted carefully at the woman's hand above him and took the sugar cubes. They were laced with brandy. He licked them slowly, keeping his eyes closed. His hoofs stirred the mud under the river surface, and the water turned brown like his skin. Medusa searched the pockets of her costume and found a deck of cards. She shuffled it.

'Cut.'

The centaur obeyed, and Medusa studied the cards with a serious expression. In the river, a wooden pallet drifted slowly downstream.

'Too many spades,' the woman commented.

The birds chirped in the pines, and the river ran over the fallen tower of the conveyor belt. Medusa dealt out more cards.

'You're going on a journey,' she said cunningly, and pointed to a card. 'The knave of hearts – that's you.'

The centaur looked at it. She continued: 'And this queen of clubs is a she-centaur.'

The centaur lay back on his side with his hand under his head and his legs stretched out, the way he was when the woman first came.

'Listen,' he said slowly. 'I'm immortal. I was around when they built the Parthenon. Don't try to fool me, stupid gorgon.'

'You're a man in a suit. Will you get this into your thick head?'

The centaur turned his back to her.

The lorries were still waiting with their engines running and a cloud of smoke surrounded the caravan. A pack of stray dogs circled the vehicles, wagging their tails. Every time an engine backfired they ran away scared, but a moment later they returned. The travellers were their only hope for a meal.

'Well?' Vassili asked.

Medusa raised her arms.

'I told you,' said Vassili. 'Let's go.'

In another lorry a door opened and a man jumped out.

'Well?' he asked.

'He's not coming,' Vassili said.

'He's not coming?'

'No.'

'But we play the village tomorrow.'

'I know,' said Vassili.

'We paid good money. We can't just go.'

Vassili rubbed his chin, then said: 'Let's tell the old man.'

The old man lived in an ambulance without an engine. One

of the lorries towed it when they travelled. They knocked at the door.

'Old man,' they called, 'we have a problem.'

'Go away,' came a voice from the other side. 'I'm listening to my music.'

They knocked at the door again, and when there was no reply, they opened it. The old ringmaster was in his armchair, with his head inside the bell of his gramophone.

'What the hell,' he said.

On the wall hung a heavy harquebus, next to the daguerre-otype of a young acrobat doing a handstand on a chair balancing on a leather ball.

'That's me,' the old man said. 'You knew that?'

He had never left the ambulance. On Sundays he opened the double doors in the back, sat in his armchair wrapped in a dragoon's tunic, and watched the acrobats practise.

'Sorry, boss,' they told him. 'But we have a problem.'

When the old ringmaster came to the riverbank he was breathing heavily. He had walked down the steep path to get there. He sat down next to the centaur and let out a sigh. The centaur scattered the horseflies with his tail.

'Not much of a river,' the ringmaster said after a while. He wiped his forehead with a handkerchief.

'I want my own trailer,' said the centaur. 'I'm tired of sleeping in the horsebox.'

The ringmaster curled his lip. 'Done.'

'With my name written on it.'

A crow flew on to the conveyor tower. The ringmaster again nodded in agreement.

'And I want a twenty-five per cent cut.'

The old man turned and looked at the path he had come down. It was very steep. It will be a devil on the way back, he thought. He was still out of breath.

'Twelve and a half.'

The centaur dismissed the offer. 'I have studied art, philosophy and mathematics,' he said.

'Right.'

'I can play the lyre.'

The ringmaster said: 'You are our main attraction. But if the circus with the sphinx comes this way, they'll put us out of business. Have you seen the size of her breasts?'

'That bitch,' the centaur said, and spat.

'And they make a killing by selling her riddles,' the old man added. 'The devil can't solve those.'

The centaur thought for a moment.

'Twenty per cent,' he said. 'Final offer.'

'No.'

'I'm immortal! I was there when—'

The ringmaster pretended to leave. In actual truth, the sight of the steep path was making his legs shake. He took some deep breaths. Suddenly, the centaur stood up.

'I'll accept fifteen,' he said quietly. 'Not a drachma less.'

The old man smiled, and offered his hand.

'Fifteen it is,' he agreed.

The sun was bright. The centaur crushed a fly with his tail, then the two shook hands, before the old man spoke again.

'A real centaur should be able to give me a ride back to the caravan without breaking sweat.'

The centaur made an expression of displeasure and slowly went down on his knees.

Stella the Spinster's Afternoon Dreams

The first person to notice him was the barber after the stranger must have been there for over an hour. He was a young man in a dark suit and shapeless hat, with a short moustache underlining his pointed nose, and, although he was sitting upright with his hands resting on his walking stick, he was so still that he had either mastered the skill of sleeping with his eyes open or was, simply, dead.

He was perching on the low whitewashed wall that ran round the plane tree in the middle of the square, sheltering himself from the evils of the afternoon sun, and, because his enormous arms did not comply with the proportions of the rest of his body, the barber thought that he rather resembled a moored rowing boat with its oars still in their rowlocks. Next to the stranger were a box made of lacquered wood, what must have been his personal effects wrapped in an antiquarian tablecloth, and a folded table with red legs.

It was afternoon in early summer and the barber would have

been in bed if it had not been for the shearing of the sheep. He had accepted the job with reluctance when his fellow villagers had asked him.

'Why me? I don't even like animals.'

'You are the only man in the valley with a pair of clippers.'

No one in the village owned more than five sheep each, most of which were mutton-type bred for the Easter feast. The rest were less than a dozen merinos, which the government had distributed for free to encourage farming diversification, but, ever since their owners discovered that the animals produced little milk, they treated them with more contempt than they showed the gypsies.

When the sheep were first brought to the barber, he had taken a look at them outside his shop and said over the bleating: 'They look like beggars in mink coats.' It was true: they were flea-ridden, underfed, sickly, and they would have soon been sent to the slaughterhouse had their fleeces – despite the maltreatment – not been of the finest quality. It was their wool that year after year earned the animals clemency.

The barber finished the shearing and the sheep were driven away. He had filled the cologne atomiser with insecticide and was spraying in the air to kill the fleas when he chanced to see the young man. He watched him from inside his shop for a while and then went next door where the chandler was trying to puncture an abscess in his toe with a sewing needle.

'Do you know the man out there?' the barber asked.

The chandler was also awake that afternoon, having found it impossible to sleep on account of the merciless pain in his foot. Rows of compote tins stacked on the windowsill stopped the light from coming in. On the floor next to the camp bed where he sat lay a rubber ice pack and a heap of compresses daubed with camomile infusion. Nothing had worked. The chandler cleaned his glasses and squinted through the open door.

'I thought it was a scarecrow,' he replied indifferently, holding his sockless foot. 'He must have come on the morning train.'

As soon as he said it he drove the needle into the swelling and twisted it until the pus spurted out. The barber watched the operation nervously, and for a moment he forgot the man under the plane tree.

'You should see the doctor,' he suggested. 'That needle might be infected.'

The chandler dismissed his neighbour's fears with a shake of his head.

'I held it under a candle until red-hot and then threw it into the icebox for thirty minutes. It's the pasteurisation process,' he said expertly. 'I read about it in the medical encyclopaedia.'

'That book kills more people than the brigands,' the barber said. 'They ought to put a price on the head of the man who wrote it.'

The chandler cleaned his toe with alcohol and carefully wrapped it in a clean bandage. Then the two men started an argument about hygiene, which was suddenly interrupted by a knock on the door. They looked up. It was the stranger.

'Excuse me,' he said, pinching his felt hat. 'I require lodgings.'

His voice had the nasal resonance of an influenza sufferer. He was standing at the steps, and at first the barber thought he had a dog with him. But when his eyes adjusted to the light from the open door, he realised that the dark mass at the stranger's feet was his wooden box. It was a natural mistake, because not only did the man hold the box from its shoulder strap like an animal's lead, but also he constantly looked at it with affection.

'What?' the chandler asked.

'Is there a hotel in the village?'

'There is a *pension*.'

'Will there be vacancies?'

The chandler guffawed.

'Don't worry. You'll be lonelier there than in your grave.'

The stranger frowned – but not because of the indelicate comment.

'You should rub it with vinegar,' he offered, pointing at the septic toe.

Before the chandler could reply there came from the square the barking of a pair of dogs brawling. The barber put his hand in his pocket.

'Ten drachmas on Colossus, chandler.'

'Two tins of apricot compote on Zeus.'

They shook hands. The dogs started moving in circles, eyeing each other, calculating their attack.

'Start opening those tins, chandler,' the barber said.

'Rubbish.'

'Yes? Look at the size of Colossus' tooth.'

The dog showed its sole tooth and it prepared to pounce. But suddenly a short whistle stopped it. It was the stranger. He whistled again and the two animals, wagging their tails, came straight to the chandlery and quietly sat down.

'Shit!' exclaimed the barber. 'Not even a tiger-tamer could separate them!'

'I promised them a bone earlier on,' said the stranger casually. 'Now, tell me how to get to the *pension*.'

They told him. But no sooner had he stepped through the door with his box over his shoulder, his folding table and the rest of his mortal belongings wrapped in the tablecloth, than the two men stopped him.

'Wait,' they said. 'Stella refuses a room to anyone who interrupts her afternoon nap.'

'Why?'

'Because in the afternoons she dreams.'

The young man scratched his head.

'And what does she dream of?'

'No one knows.'

The two villagers explained that Stella was an indecipherable spinster, who since the death of her parents lived alone in the *pension* she had come into after a relative had escaped overnight from poverty to Australia. The business provided her with a modest income, which she supplemented by selling vegetables from her garden. She used her profits to buy jewellery, which she hid in a biscuit tin and the tin in her dressing table. Over her spinster years she had amassed a small treasure of brooches, earrings, bracelets and pearl necklaces. But she never wore any of it; they were her dowry.

She was a woman of strange habits. After lunch she would unpin her formidable bun held together by a pair of thick knitting needles, in order to comb her silver curls not with an ordinary comb but with the set of grooming tools she had bought cheaply from Isidoro, the man who once owned a racehorse. First she would rub her head with the rubber curry-comb to untie the hard knots she had the habit of making when deep in thought, then would use the steel dandy brush to remove loose hair and dirt, and finally she would take out the soft brush which gave her locks an ambitious shine. Then she would go to bed for her afternoon nap. Attending to her hair was a duty she carried out daily and with religious devotion: as a child Stella had heard her mother say that a woman's hair ought to be regularly caressed by a male hand so as not to harden like a bramble, and had taken those words at their face value.

The *pension* was an unassuming house with unplastered walls and a pot of bougainvillaea on its cement veranda, while the first thing the traveller would notice inside was the smell of boiled cauliflower. There were also a grand piano, heaps of photo romances, which the newsagent in the county capital sent Stella once a week by coach, and a withered but still decorated fir tree, which would be thrown away only when its replacement arrived the following Christmas. The piano had been given in return for the brief accommodation provided for an exiled king when he had passed through the village. Stella had accepted it gracefully, before taking off its strings to let her cats sleep in it.

The moment Stella opened the door and saw the young man at her threshold, she blushed: she had been wearing her net and curlers.

'Good afternoon,' the young man said. He put down his luggage and wiped his forehead with his handkerchief before adding: 'I require lodgings.'

'What's the matter with you?' Stella snapped at him. 'Only Bible salesmen and city idlers are so rude as to knock at someone's door at this time of day.'

'I apologise.'

The dogs had followed him. They also lowered their muzzles to the ground.

'I could have been asleep,' Stella said sullenly, patting them on the head.

The young man looked around. The *pension* stood in the middle of a vegetable garden of modest size of which not an inch of soil had been wasted: there were tomatoes planted against the courtyard wall, gourd stalks twisted round the winch of the well, there were dill, mint and basil potted in rusty motor-oil canisters under the grapevine that roofed the veranda and among the enormous cabbages there was even a midget palm with ripe dates.

'Congratulations, Madame,' he swiftly flattered Stella. 'You have created the Hanging Gardens of Babylon!'

She did not change her expression, but his words had pierced her armour. '*Mademoiselle*,' she corrected him. 'Come in.'

Stella noticed the box the moment the man stepped into the

house. She was instantly intrigued by its polished wood, its copper hinges, its heavy padlock. But she said nothing. Instead, she showed the man to his room, brought him a fresh set of linen and towels, and warned him with a teacher's voice that breakfast was served before seven thirty. Only after he had taken his bath in the galvanised washtub he had discovered under his bed and had appeared, smelling of lavender, in her kitchen to return the clay ewer, did she ask the question, casually.

'And what was that box you were carrying?'

He replied with a hint of seduction. 'Take a guess.'

Once again, she resisted the allure of his smile. 'The commode for your chamber pot.'

Without another word he ran to his room and returned with the box and the table. He unfolded the table and set the box on it.

'Wrong,' he announced. 'It's a barrel organ.'

It was not until he raised the heavy lid that she lost her breath.

'It's more complicated than an automobile engine!' she exclaimed, looking at the antique mechanism.

The man explained the operation of the various parts.

'The music is produced by the staples and pins of the revolving barrel. They open the valves to admit wind to the pipes. The bellows that feeds the pipes with air is also worked by the barrel.'

She was fascinated. But suddenly the young man lost interest in his instrument. He sat at the kitchen table and reflected with melancholy: 'I used to play in restaurants, music halls and carousels; until the damn jukebox took away my music.' He sighed. 'All that was left for me to do was to take to the roads like the Wandering Jew or throw myself off a cliff.'

Stella touched his hand compassionately. But he barely noticed.

'You are fortunate, Mademoiselle. At least, no one can take away your dreams.'

Stella, feeling responsible for reminding him of his misfortune, tried everything to alleviate his sadness. But neither the laudanum, which she fed him by the ladle, nor the agaric infusion which the herbalist sold her, nor even the drops for pacifying teething infants which she found in the back of a cupboard were of any help. She had to cook a rabbit ragout with shallots and rosemary for him to recover his composure.

It was while serving him his third helping that she confided her secret to him.

'I wish what you said earlier were true.'

The man immediately put down his fork.

'I was a first-rate afternoon dreamer,' Stella continued. 'But ever since the garden grew into that ruthless jungle, I haven't had a moment's peace.'

'Why?'

'Because the garden is infested with moths.'

The man looked at her, puzzled.

'Everyone knows that moths carry nightmares,' she explained impatiently.

Only then did the man notice that the windows were masked with marquisette. Stella asked him to follow her to her bedroom, and there he saw the mosquito net as big as a sail that hung from the ceiling and veiled her bed, its edges nailed to the floor but for a narrow flap to let oneself in and out of bed.

'I have tried everything,' she said. 'Even if I brick up the windows one of those harpies will find a way in.'

It was the young man's turn to appease the landlady. But instead of alcohol, food or medicine, he offered her his professional services.

'My music can help you,' he said.

Stella replied with a bitter chuckle.

'Oh, I've never believed in the power of songs.'

She regretted her comment the moment she saw the young man's ears burn with exasperation.

'I am talking science proper,' he protested. 'Bugs cannot stand the harmonics of the barrel organ.'

She agreed only in order to please him. She took off her shawl, lay in bed in her nightgown, and then called him in. He entered carrying the barrel organ. Stella closed her eyes, pretending. The last thing she could remember before falling asleep was a music of sea-like rhythm and the creaking of the organ's rotating crank.

That afternoon not only did she dream again after many years, but her dreams were even deeper and wiser than the visions of biblical prophets. In fact, she had slept for less than an hour when the draught from the open window awakened her. The moment she pushed the bedcovers aside, from the folds of the mosquito net above her bed, the windowsill, the floor, the furniture, even from her muslin sheets, hundreds of moths of every kind took flight and started circling her bedroom. They were the proof that Stella had defeated her insomnia.

'Bless the stranger!' she cried. 'I'm cured!'

Only after she had wiped away her tears did she realise that the young man was gone. Then she saw the torn window screen, which explained the presence of the moths in her room, and finally her eyes fell on the open drawer of her baroque dressing table where she found the biscuit tin for her jewels empty but for a pair of mating butterflies. Stella the dreamer said nothing. Instead she returned to bed, where, to the sound of a cicada on the ceiling and the echoes of her apparitional dreams, she slept hungrily through the rest of the afternoon and well into the evening.

Cassandra
Is Gone

'Show me again, Cassandra.'

'What?'

'Show me your tattoos.'

I unveil my arms and he sees the crimson arabesques embroidered by the artisans of Alhambra, the intricate floral patterns that disappear under my callused fingertips, the Indian-ink bracelets that squeeze my sailor's wrists, and on my palms the stars of the universe copied from Copernicus's maps. I bow my head to let him touch the gold tattoo on my shaven crown (an exact copy of Helen of Troy's diadem), the black pearls drawn on my earlobes by the needle, the collar of thorns that pricks my pale jugulars.

He dips his finger in the warm blood.

'Does it hurt?'

'It's only a tattoo, child.'

I let him kiss my hypertrophic shoulders that rest on the colonnade painted on my back, caress my shoulder-blades (each the size of a crusader's shield, I have been told), and tighten the meandering pattern that girds my waist. I then turn round so he can also trace my other tattoos: the green spirals that resemble the blind snails that live on the bottom of the sea, the fading scales under my armpits from when I used to be the singing mermaid in a variety show, the dolphins on my belly which are from a ravaged palace in Crete, the blind eye (whose pupil is my navel) which belongs to the Cyclops Polyphemus, son of Poseidon and victim of Odysseus the sailor.

'I've never seen the sea, Cassandra.'

'Me neither, child. When I was a mermaid they kept me in a tank.'

He thinks the tattoos are the work of a master. There is more detail than his eyes will ever discover, there are colours he did not know existed, so he tells me that the closest he has come to such artistry is his mother's embroidery of the Annunciation on the wall above his parents' bed, but even that is a worthless piece of chintz compared to these tattoos – God forgive me, he says – despite the beautiful lily made from bleached white crewel, despite Gabriel's gold-threaded halo and plump wings with their real chicken feathers, despite Mary's blue stole, despite the fact it had taken his mother three months to finish it, during which time his father had almost starved.

'They must have cost you a fortune, Cassandra.'

'I paid no money, child.'

I show him the caterpillar scar low on my belly, stitched by an unskilled hand, and explain it was also done by the hand that did the tattoos. He asks me again why he had stabbed me. I shrug.

'He wanted my appendix for a memento.'

'If I ever come across him, Cassandra, I'll flay him!'

I laugh: 'You can't even swat a fly, child.'

And for the first time I touch his cheek and throw my flaxen

dress on to the floor, so that he will see again the feet of a
vaudevillian (they arch like Turkish slippers), the thick calves of
a trapeze artist, my shins that are sharp like Damascene sabres
and the round knees of a woman who kneels for no one. But he
ignores all this and rests his eyes instead on the shadow between
my thighs. There he discovers the inscription.

He spells out: ' "Φαρ-μα-κον νη-πεν-θες." What does it
mean, Cassandra?'

'Don't they teach you anything at school?'

'There's no school in the village, Cassandra.'

'It means "A remedy for grief", child.'

He does not understand.

'Tell me more, Cassandra.'

'More what?'

'Tell me more stories.'

I laugh, and he says my laughter is like the noise of the river. I
speak of having come across prehistoric hens without feathers
that lay pebbles instead of eggs, of beautiful arums which smell
like armpits, of men with flour-coloured skin and pink eyes
called albinos, of marble statues that have wings but cannot fly,
of having caught a glimpse of my guardian angel once.

'But a guardian angel is invisible, Cassandra.'

'No, he's simply too fast on his feet. You have to pretend
you're asleep, and suddenly open your eyes and look behind
you. Then you might see him.'

He tries several times, but sees nobody. Instead he gets dizzy.

'What does a guardian angel look like, Cassandra?'

'Bored – like someone waiting for the coach.'

'Stop teasing me, Cassandra.'

'I swear to God.'

'Father Yerasimo says, "Thou shalt not take the name of the
Lord thy God in vain," Cassandra.'

'Father Yerasimo should know. He drinks his God's blood for breakfast.'

'He also says the circus is the invention of pagans, Cassandra.'

From the round window of my trailer he watches the circus hands herd together the dromedaries from the Canaries, scrub the zebras with their steel brushes before loading them into the lorry, feed the dancing bear sitting on a stool with her arms crossed and sulking, fasten together with adhesive tape the jaws of Nefertiti the Egyptian crocodile which can break a hickory stick in a single snap, and finally they start to dismantle the tarpaulin of the ring.

'Where do you come from, Cassandra?'

Today I am the daughter of an unfortunate fire-walker barbecued to death when seized with cramp during a performance, the niece of a ferocious bare-knuckle-boxing aunt who used to go straight for the heart of her male opponents because that was where those big dolts hurt, and the widow of seven husbands who all told me that my twenty-cheroot-a-day habit would soon kill me.

'Where are you going next, Cassandra?'

I show him on the map towns marked with red crosses, but their names mean nothing to him. Then we both hear the gallop of the centaur outside. I jump to my feet and look out of the window; I smile, I wave, I fix my hair. He blushes with envy. He protests.

'But he's an animal from the waist down, Cassandra!'

I sigh: 'If only every man was, child.'

The caravan is ready to leave.

'I love you, Cassandra.'

'Go home, child. Your mama will be looking.'

'Let me come with you, Cassandra.'

'Go home.'

He tramples down my priceless Chinese velvet cushions, he

threatens to strangle himself with my feather boa once he has burned my wigs, he attempts to swallow my lapis lazuli necklace but the gemstones are too big for his throat, so he downs instead the gold potion from the vial he finds on my dressing table. It is only thinned thyme honey.

'Don't cry, child.'

'At least show me your tattoos, Cassandra. One last time.'

But I do not answer.

'Please, let me touch them, Cassandra.'

But Cassandra the Famous, the Great, the Divine is gone.

Wilt Thou Be Made Whole?

On Sunday morning Father Yerasimo announced from the pulpit that vespers would not be held that day because of the meeting, and that those who felt the need to worship the Lord could do it equally well from home. He then left the church ahead of everyone, and hurried to finish the erection of the platform in the middle of the square, with a sense of panic. Tomorrow His Right Reverence the bishop was passing through the village for the first time ever, and Father Yerasimo had to promise that there would be a platform ready if the motorcade were to make the unscheduled detour.

'It was a difficult negotiation, my brethren,' the priest said with pride, after telling them the joyous news. 'But with the help of God I succeeded.'

For months Father Yerasimo had reiterated his request to the bishop's secretary over the telephone. The man at the other end of the line would caress his silver moustache and pause to think. But not about the request: the priest always seemed to catch him in the middle of a backgammon game with the deacon on secondment to the offices of the diocese.

'Forget it, priest,' the secretary had said once, and kissed the dice for good luck before throwing a decisive twelve. 'As I said, those pens you lot live in like goats are not part of our tour.'

'We need His Right Reverence's blessing. Or, according to my calculations, our village is doomed!'

'The road through the valley is not fit for cars,' the secretary said. 'His Reverence is not driving a tractor, priest.'

Father Yerasimo fondled his beard.

'The coach driver has found that reciting the prayers of St Timotheo helps in avoiding the potholes,' he suggested.

He had persuaded the secretary on the sixteenth telephone call. The following Sunday he had announced the news to the congregation and had asked his parishioners to help him prepare a welcoming ceremony fit for a bishop. They had shrugged.

'Why should we help, Father?'

The priest raised his hand and pointed to the dome.

'Because I am certain He is going to appreciate it.'

'It's not enough, Father.'

'What more do you want?' he asked firmly.

'We want things done to the village, Father.'

'It is out of the question.'

'Then you will be waving the flag in the square alone, Father.'

The priest soon realised he had no choice.

'Do you promise us, Father?'

Father Yerasimo raised his eyes to the Pantocrator.

'Forgive me,' he said with a sigh of defeat. 'I've become a peddler for your Glory.' He then looked down at the congregation again. 'Yes. I promise.'

The church faced the square in the middle of the village. The day before, all houses had been whitewashed in anticipation of the visit. The moment Father Yerasimo came into the churchyard, he was ambushed by a group of children waving a tin pipe. He gave them an austere look, and carried on. In the middle of the square a hastily made platform stood on listing props. Immediately, something struck Father Yerasimo as strange. He came closer and only then did he notice that the pipe on the stove on the platform was missing. It was his own cast-iron stove he had carried all by himself from home, because he had been told that His Right Reverence was particularly sensitive to the cold. As a result, the night before he had slept wearing his alb, his stole and his cope to keep himself warm in the freezing house. He folded his cassock and stuck it under his belt before climbing on to the platform. He puffed, and said: 'If only I could get my hands on those rats.' He stroked his long white beard where he frequently discovered bits of food he had no recollection of having eaten. 'I definitely need a stovepipe,' he added. 'A puff of smoke on His Right Reverence's face, and everyone who sees him tomorrow will think he's the Bishop of Abyssinia.'

He started work without wasting any time. He had decided to paint the platform the colours of the national flag: the floor and railing white, the rest blue. He patiently flattened the nails sticking out, sanded off the boards and filled the holes of the cheap wood with stucco, before opening the paint tins he had bought in the county capital. That moment he discovered that instead of white and blue, he had bought seven gallons of glossy red.

'One of these days, ironmonger,' he said aloud, 'you and your communist friends will stew in the cauldrons of Hell.'

But there was nothing he could do. The bishop was coming in the morning. He dipped the brush in the tub, and started painting.

He had been born in the village and had lived there all his life apart from the years in the seminary. And in the valley cemetery he expected to be buried, in a plot next to his wife, with whom he had shared twenty years of a loving but childless existence. He was now surviving on bread, wine and kidney beans whose explosive action had condemned him to solitude. This loneliness was only equalled by his frustration at watching his village's slow journey towards damnation.

He had tried in vain to make good Christians out of his parishioners. He preached with fervency, and he maintained that the recent earthquake that had hit the village was merely a warning from God, which, if they continued to ignore, would be followed by a much greater catastrophe. But no sooner would he look down from the pulpit than he would see the congregation nod off, waiting for the sermon to end. Mass was said only on Sundays, and even then almost no one would have shown up if it were not for Father Yerasimo's idea to hold a raffle immediately after Holy Communion.

At home he kept jars with the names of his parishioners written on them – men, women and children – where he would add a number of beans according to the seriousness of the sins they would commit. Most of them – even the children's – were full to the brim; his was empty. After the earthquake, he had locked himself at home with the Bible, a textbook of geodesy, a pair of compasses and an abacus, and was not seen in public for a whole week.

'According to my calculations,' he had warned his parishioners when he had re-emerged, 'this village will cease to exist in two years, five months and eleven days from today. Unless you start repenting immediately.'

Then he had nailed on the church door a sign that read, THE WORLD WILL END IN —— DAYS, and every morning from then on he updated the number with a despairing nod. His people's last hope was the bishop's visit.

Father Yerasimo finished painting and, rubbing his back, inspected his work. The red platform gleamed in the twilight and he belatedly questioned his decision to use the red paint. With a dismissive gesture he took the road home as the sun set behind the hills and the street lights came on. Progress had arrived in the village in small doses. Electricity had been brought by the Corps of Engineers, and now every house had a socket and the square had lamp-posts all round it. A high-voltage cable snaked out of the village, and ended behind the wire fence of an electricity substation in the valley. A telephone line had been installed in the town hall. Then the television arrived, ordered by the owner of the coffee shop, who had also bought the second-hand icebox that broke down a week later, and was since used as a bookcase for the almanacs. Father Yerasimo studied the stars. He decided that tomorrow was going to be a cold but dry day.

Because there were more people than chairs in the taverna, extra seats had been brought from the church. The taverner was busy painting his initials on the back of one when Father Yerasimo walked in.

'What are you doing?' he asked sternly.

The taverner jumped.

'Nothing. Just making sure you and I don't mix our property, Father.'

Father Yerasimo picked up the chair and turned it upside down. The seat had the stamp of the church on its underside.

'This will have to wait until after the bishop's visit,' he said.

Soon the place was packed. Everyone was there, including Alexandro the Lame, the oldest man in the village, who came covered in a wool blanket in the wheelchair his brother-in-law had made from old bicycle parts. The chair had four wheels of solid rubber tyres and bent spokes, and, at about chest height, a rubber-bulb horn with a brass bell. The meeting started promptly.

'As you know,' the priest said, 'the bishop is coming tomorrow. I will explain the welcoming ceremony and you should listen carefully. Then you can tell me the things you want to ask His Right Reverence for, as agreed. I will write them down and pass them to him myself, because he will only be here for one hour.'

Father Yerasimo said that he had declared the next day a religious holiday in order for everyone to attend the festivities. It was a meaningless gesture. The people were farmers and public holidays made no difference to their work routine. But on this occasion they did not object to taking the day off, partly because of the priest's promise to forward their requests to the bishop, but also because he had promised them a free banquet afterwards. When the latter was announced, Dr Panteleon, a good physician but without a degree, commented: 'Tomorrow Father Yerasimo will turn water into wine.'

'The taverner would love to get his hands on that recipe,' others added.

Father Yerasimo hit his fist on the table.

'Quiet, gluttonous men and winebibbers! The festivities will not turn into a binge. I'm only going to spare some Communion wine to honour His Right Reverence.'

They all nodded with satisfaction.

'Talking of sinners,' said the doctor. 'A widow called me the other night for her enema, and—'

'I thought you were bound by the Hippocratic oath, doctor,' the priest stopped him.

The other man shrugged.

'It's only valid for paid services. You know I never take money from widows, Father.'

Father Yerasimo felt once again that his was an impossible vocation.

'This is the village of the heathen,' he said. 'I am fortunate no one ever comes to confession, after all. Even if you started tomorrow, I would die of old age before I had finished absolving all your sins.'

In the last year he had only listened, excluding the once interesting but now repetitive ramblings of Alexandro the Lame, to the confessions of two young farmhands, who had attributed their sin to the solitude of the valley. He had forgiven them; but not without first giving them a harsh warning about the dangers of perversion. Still, the truth was that he had been grateful to them: their confession had given him back his sense of purpose. And that was the day when he had vowed at the altar that he would save his congregation even if that meant he would have to sacrifice himself.

Once the details of the visit etiquette were cleared, Father Yerasimo took pencil and paper and waited for the personal requests to the bishop. Someone noted that he was going to be the first official to visit the village since a collaborationist minister had taken refuge there for a few days, and a debate broke out in the taverna.

'The minister was technically a traitor,' agreed Father Yerasimo. 'But don't forget it's because of him we now have a church. Before, mass was said in a goat pen.'

'Still, you didn't have to name the church St Timotheo the Bombed,' said the doctor.

Hiding in a ditch as a Hurricane fighter gunned down his German escort, the minister, whose name was Timotheo, had promised God anything if He would help him make it to the small village in the middle of the valley. God had, and the minister had fulfilled his promise as soon as he had returned to the capital. (Later, when the war ended, that same minister was captured by partisans. Standing on a high stool with a tight rope round his neck he had made a similar promise, but that time God had not listened.)

Father Yerasimo ignored the doctor and started to write. Most people asked for a new well because the water in the existing one was poisoning their intestines. The coffee-shop owner said he had some money for a new icebox, but the trader was driving a hard bargain. Then Maroula the seamstress, a young woman who had arrived in the village as a child with a straw doll and a pedal-operated sewing machine, walked up to the priest. She looked at him with her melancholy eyes and said: 'I want to know what my surname is.'

Twenty years before she had come to the village in a taxi, which also carried her only possessions: a sewing machine and a doll. The people gathered in the square and asked who the girl was. The taxi driver shrugged. 'I only know her name's Maroula.' He refused to say who the woman who had paid the fare was, and he had driven off the same day. Years later, when Maroula had tried to find him, she had been shown a nameless cross in a faraway cemetery built on a promontory being slowly eaten away by the sea. Father Yerasimo nodded sympathetically, and scribbled on his paper. But he advised her that it would be difficult, even with the help of the bishop, and that she should place her faith in God.

'Because whatever happens, don't forget that above any man and woman, He is your true parent, and He'll continue to look after you,' he told Maroula.

'However, when she was dumped here shaking like a scurvy sailor, we had to bring her up ourselves,' whispered the doctor.

Father Yerasimo raised his eyes ready to reply, but unexpectedly saw the face of the butcher in front of him.

Tired, the priest asked, 'What is your request?'

The man leaned forward.

'This is a personal matter, Father,' he whispered.

'Go on.'

'I turned forty last month.'

'Congratulations, of course. Thanks to modern medicine, you may live to be one hundred.'

'And I'm still a bachelor.'

Father Yerasimo slammed his hand on the table.

'Who do you think the bishop is? A matchmaker?'

'I wonder if he knows some suitable brides. I don't mind about looks, Father. As long as she's a virgin.'

'Forget that,' said Dr Panteleon behind him. 'It's easier to find a unicorn these days.'

Father Yerasimo took down the butcher's details, including his political beliefs, his medical record and his physical appearance. He then counted all the requests and added another above the rest: the restoration of the church murals, which had almost been destroyed by the earthquake. After hesitating for a moment, he also scribbled next to this petition, *A matter of great concern among my parishioners, Your Right Reverence.*

It was almost midnight and the meeting in the taverna was coming to an end. The villagers stretched their legs and stood up to smoke one last cigarette before going home. Suddenly, the sound of a horn startled them. It was Alexandro the Lame. They had forgotten about him, thinking he had fallen asleep by the petrol stove where his brother-in-law had pushed him; but now there he was, his bald head emerging from the blanket, wide awake, wheeling himself towards the front where the priest was.

'Your bishop and your God are not worth a cent, priest,' he said aloud, 'if they can't help the sick.'

Alexandro had left for America in his teens with an empty duffel bag over his shoulder, and no one had heard from him for fifty years. Then one Saturday morning the village woke up to find an old man in an armchair in the middle of the square, with a threadbare duffel bag next to him. Alexandro never explained why he had left America, or how he had lost the use of his legs. And when someone had lifted the bag to carry it, packs of hundred-dollar banknotes had fallen out. Alexandro had moved in with his sister and brother-in-law, and the village slowly lost interest in him. Alexandro, thereafter called the Lame, had kept out of sight, leaving his sister's house in the wheelchair only to go to confession. The only person who knew about his past was Father Yerasimo. In the taverna the priest raised his eyes.

'Do not blaspheme, Alexandro,' he said calmly.

'I want to walk again, damn it!'

That was how Alexandro the Lame came to be in the square the next day with the rest of the village. He was in his wheelchair, freshly shaven, wearing his only suit and one of his brother-in-law's ties. As Father Yerasimo had predicted, it was a dry if somewhat windy day. They all stood, waiting, and some time later a cloud of dust arose on the horizon. Because of the condition of the road it took the motorcade another hour to arrive. But when it finally entered the square it proved to be a monumental disappointment.

Not only was the motorcade a procession of rusty cars of unceremonious colours and with backfiring exhausts, but also the bishop's limousine – which must have been black under the thick layer of dust – appeared to be a converted hearse with an extra row of seats. The villagers knew that was true when the door opened and the pacific smell of death overpowered them. First to jump out were the bishop's assistants, and then from the darkness of his limousine the bishop's wearied voice was heard: 'My bowels are minced. That road had more holes than the moon itself.' His breath made the noise of a bicycle pump. Father Yerasimo looked at him as he would have looked at a sunset. The rumours that the bishop was dying were true.

Nevertheless the priest kissed his superior's hand and helped him out of the car.

'It was last paved by a Roman centurion, Your Right Reverence,' Father Yerasimo apologised. 'Apart from being an unrepentant atheist, our mayor is also a worthless politician.'

The bishop's vestments compensated for the defeated impression of his motorcade. He wore a gold-threaded stole with the portraits of all twelve Apostles embroidered on it, a sequinned silk cope and a ruby-studded cross round his neck, and held in his hand a heavy staff. But most impressive of all was his ancient golden mitre, which had been salvaged in the days of the Ottomans by a pious and fast-on-his-feet Christian from the rolling head of a predecessor down the steps of the cathedral.

A group of children dressed in their Sunday clothes gave him flowers, and sang the national anthem accompanied by a glockenspiel. They had started another song, following the priest's orders, when the bishop stopped them by raising his hand.

'I will be sung to enough by the angels soon,' he said. 'Thank you.'

Only then did the elderly bishop notice the red platform.

'Heavens!' he exclaimed, laughing. 'It's the colour of Hell.' He turned to the priest, and asked him light-heartedly: 'Are you suggesting something, Father?'

Father Yerasimo bowed his head, shamefaced.

'It was the only colour available, Your Right Reverence.'

The bishop climbed the platform followed by his entourage. Standing next to the burning stove he stared at the people until they were silent, then after clearing his throat he started the service. Even Dr Panteleon caught himself, with embarrassment, humming the psalms he had once been taught in Sunday school. Towards the end of the liturgy the bishop raised the Communion cup to bless it, and then asked: 'Where is the lame man?'

They moved aside to let Alexandro through. His face had an uncomfortable expression. The bishop left the platform with the cup in his hands and stood in front of him. He made the sign of the cross and said softly: 'Drink, my son.'

There was silence. And then Alexandro the Lame pulled the handbrake of his wheelchair, put his feet one after the other on the ground with slow moves and, refusing the help of his brother-in-law, stood up. The villagers gasped. Then Father Yerasimo started applauding. One after the other the people joined in and a wild celebration started.

For the village it was an undisputed miracle. For Father Yerasimo it was the fulfilment of a vow. His parishioners had been transformed into enthusiastic believers. The musicians ran home and returned with their guitars, their clarinets, their fiddles, and one even brought his tuba, but because he had not played it for twenty-odd years its valves were stuck. Then they started playing all at once, making an impossible noise, while the rest of the village – but not the doctor – rushed to kiss the bishop's hand, bowed their heads, and begged him to cure their arthritis, their lungs – which were lumps of coal from smoking from the cradle – or, better, to give them a clean bill of health altogether.

But there was no time. Followed by the bishop, Father Yerasimo led the way among the crowd, and His Right Reverence was helped back into his limousine. Then his assistants jumped in and the pitiful motorcade drove off. Behind them, the fastest converted Christian congregation in the world waved and cheered, sent wishes which were lost in the wind and congratulated Alexandro the Healed for his unfailing faith. Father Yerasimo sat next to Alexandro and tasted the wine under a WELCOME, YOUR REVERENCE sign.

'You and the bishop will burn in Hell, priest,' murmured Alexandro. 'You're worse than the Mafia.' He looked at his wheelchair, pushed in a corner, with affection. 'I should've never confessed my secrets to you. Imagine! Blackmailing me into performing at your theatre of miracles!'

Father Yerasimo looked at him, and smiled magnanimously. This was the happiest day of his life.

'I absolved you from your sins, Alexandro. And you helped me save the souls of our people in return.' He shaded his eyes with his hand and looked at the cloud of dust in the distance made by the cars. 'Besides, a healthy man shouldn't be in a wheelchair in the first place. He's committing the sin of sloth.'

Alexandro spat with disgust.

'It wasn't that,' he protested. 'By pretending to be sick I finally had someone to look after me.'

Soon the dark shape of the motorcade disappeared over the horizon, carrying to the next stop of their tour His Right Reverence the bishop, his deacons, his subdeacons, his incense bearers, his acolytes and his secretaries.

'Trust in God, my son,' the priest said. 'It's in the next life we reap the rewards.'

Despite the bright sun it was a cold day. He rubbed his hands and put them in the pockets of his cassock to warm them up, and only then did he realise that he still had on him the petition for the restoration of the mural work in the parish church of St Timotheo the Bombed, the request for the new well, the letter concerning the icebox, the other letter about an orphan's enquiry, as well as the butcher's self-addressed envelope to be returned with a list of the virtuous women of the county that were of marrying age.

'Oh well,' Father Yerasimo said with a shrug.

Medical Ethics

D r Panteleon had just started the crossword when the nurse walked in. He had spent all morning looking for his glasses, which he could not find anywhere, so in the end he had to use the magnifying lens. When he heard the door he raised his eyes.

'"Maim",' he said. 'Eight letters.'

He was coming to the end of a career that had lasted over forty years, and which had given him enough satisfaction but little money. He was a physician in a village where people seldom became ill, because they lived on a diet of dandelion and olive oil. The phenomenon was documented in an epidemiological study that Dr Panteleon had authored more than thirty years ago, a report that remained in his drawer after being turned down by every medical journal in the country on the justification that his statistics were not representative.

'Castrate,' replied the nurse. And added: 'You have a patient, doctor.'

The doctor filled in the little squares under the magnifying lens. 'Show him in.'

'It's not a he,' the nurse corrected him.

'If it's a sheep call the veterinarian,' the doctor said impatiently.

The patient was a girl on whom he had performed an appendectomy two years ago. Having left medical school before specialising, Dr Panteleon had no surgical training. But because landslides frequently closed the only road to the county capital where the only hospital was, he often did the operations himself, with the help of the nurse and an illustrated manual ordered by mail.

That girl's operation had been a difficult one. When she had first complained to her mother about cramps and fever, the woman had been misled by the symptoms and tried to shake off her daughter's fears.

'Soon, child,' she'd said tenderly, 'you'll wish this was all the trouble one gets from being a woman.'

Her words had scared the girl even more, but also shamed her, and she had said nothing for another week. Then vomiting and diarrhoea had turned her room into a stagnant swamp overnight, and her stepfather, a callous man whose favourite pastime was capturing sparrows which he fed to his cat, had moved her bed to the veranda so he could sleep in peace. When the doctor had finally seen her, he had estimated that she was two days away from peritonitis.

Dr Panteleon put down the magnifying lens. He looked at the girl like a sculptor inspecting a finished work. She had certainly grown. Her protuberant cheekbones and the tight chest-fit of her otherwise loose shirt were the undeniable signs of maturity. The only reminder of her old misfortune was a yellow tint like the enamel of old coffee cups in her eyes. The doctor was pleased – but living in the country had taught him a terse and modest language without superlatives. 'You look well,' he said.

The girl did not reply. She remained standing, looking at a coloured anatomy atlas posted on the wall which the doctor had put up to cover a patch of flaking plaster. The room aroused in her the sober excitement of a museum visit. On the shelf behind the doctor's desk a row of leather-bound books, with titles she could read but not understand, was kept upright by a yellow skull. To her left, next to the examination table, a red light flashed on the sterilisation oven.

'My stepfather wants you to examine me,' she said.

The doctor shrugged: 'It's been a long time since your operation. You have nothing to worry about.'

'No. He said to do—' The girl stopped and rehearsed the words before saying them: 'A gy-nae-co-lo-gi-cal examination.'

She said the words with such a low voice that they could have been the buzzing of a bluebottle. Dr Panteleon did not hear. He leaned forward. 'What?'

The girl, blushing, repeated her stepfather's instructions. Dr Panteleon regretted having rebuked her. Without further questions he asked her to undress and he washed his hands in the basin at the corner of the room. He conducted the examination in silence, with skilful movements and an inexpressive face, as if he were a mechanic repairing a bicycle. And in actual fact, his mind was all that time occupied with the answers to the crossword he had left unfinished.

'There's nothing wrong with you,' he said, while she dressed again. 'But from now on you should come once a year. It's good practice.'

Dr Panteleon took a new cardboard folder and started writing his report. The girl stood in front of him. She said: 'My stepfather asks if I'm a virgin.'

The doctor looked up. 'You know you are.'

'And can I have children?'

He placed the folder in a cabinet with glass doors. 'I'll need a urine sample to be confident about it, but I don't see why not.'

'My stepfather says, then you have no reason for not wanting to marry me.'

The doctor examined girls for evidence of sexual intercourse so often that he had printed certificates which he would sign, stamp, date and hand out if one were a *virgo intacta*. On the document he would also staple an appendix with the details of the girl's health for the perusal of possible fiancés. It was a practice that violated medical ethics in favour of the ancient unwritten laws of rural seclusion, but one which Dr Panteleon was forced to accept when he started losing his patients to the roving herbalists who sold remedies that guaranteed the conception of male offspring, antidotes for every form of cancer, nettle lotions to cure baldness and other poisons.

The doctor capped his pen and placed it in a chipped mug with pencils and biros. He sat again in his chair with a sigh.

He asked: 'What else does your stepfather want?'

'He says not to ask him for a dowry, because you're already rich.'

The doctor nodded. His eyes wandered around the office. In a corner against the wall leaned the rectangular conference table he had salvaged from the refurbishment of the town hall. He had put tumbrel wheels to it and turned it into a stretcher. Behind the coat hanger was a box of wooden toys. The day before, all the eight-year-olds in the village had come to be immunised against hepatitis. A thought came to his mind then, and he walked over to where a plastic skeleton was hanging from a hook on the wall.

'There you are,' he said.

The skeleton was wearing his glasses. He took them off it.

'How's your mother?' he asked the girl.

'She sends her regards. She says she has to put more calmative in her coffee than sugar because of her back.'

'I will give you some to take to her.' The doctor searched through the medicine cabinet until he found a large brown glass bottle. 'And your stepfather?'

'He's still suffering from constipation. He says the medicines you've given him do him no good, and one of these days he's going to kill you.'

Dr Panteleon fixed a funnel on a small empty bottle and filled it with powder from the other one. 'His haemorrhoids don't get better because he sits around all day reading the papers,' he said calmly. He tapped the funnel and put the lids on the bottles. 'He should get a job,' he added. 'Suppositories don't cure laziness.'

The girl shrugged her shoulders: 'He says, when you come to ask for my hand, bring some more.'

Dr Panteleon wrote something on the label of the small bottle and handed it to the girl. 'Give this to your mother,' he said.

She put it in her pocket without a word. She was waiting for an answer. The doctor studied her.

'Well, I can't marry you,' he said, putting the big bottle and the funnel away. 'I was in the army with your grandfather.'

From the moment she walked in, the girl had been playing with a ribbon she passed from finger to finger, but Dr Panteleon only noticed it now. It could have been a cheap necklace, or a hairband her stepfather had instructed her to take off in order to look more attractive. The doctor searched for his newspaper.

'Besides, I may die soon,' he added casually.

'My mother says men in our town live longer than dictators.'

'Unfortunately I wasn't born here.' Dr Panteleon sat at his desk. He turned to the crossword and picked up his pen again. '"Started by anger – or disgust",' he read out. 'Six letters. What do you think?'

The girl shrugged. She looked at the doctor and played with the ribbon.

'R–e–v–o–l–t,' said the doctor, filling in the boxes. 'An easy one.'

The girl contemplated the office with the nervous gaze of a child who has broken a porcelain vase. Dr Panteleon carried on with his crossword in silence. On a small table by the window was the stack of out-of-date political magazines the barber forwarded to him. Dead flies that had fallen from the sill lay on the covers, which the sun had bleached. It was almost lunchtime and the girl remembered she was supposed to do the shopping before returning home. She spoke up.

'If you can't marry me, then you should at least help me.'

'Help you?'

'My stepfather says I can choose. You or the butcher.'

'Don't you like the butcher?' asked the doctor, without looking up.

'They say he once killed a lamb with a mere look.'

Dr Panteleon shook his head. 'At least he's younger than me.'

'I hate him,' she replied. 'Help me.'

Dr Panteleon still pretended to work on the crossword. In truth he was trying to remember the last time he had been with a woman. It was a long time ago. He realised he could neither remember her name nor her face. Finally, he put down his pen and looked at the girl. His eyes stung as if he had stepped out into the sun from his office. The ribbon was coiled tight round the girl's fingers.

'Tell your stepfather I'll be there at seven,' he said.

The girl showed no emotion. 'Don't forget his medicine,' she reminded him and turned to leave.

'No,' the doctor said. 'Make that eight.'

He sat at his desk for some time and finished the crossword. Then he sent the nurse home and retired to his laboratory.

There he stayed until half past eight preparing half a dozen suppositories, which were twice as big as the instructions said. Apart from the usual ingredients, they also contained the whole of a small vial with a skull-and-crossbones sticker that the doctor had found in the back of the cabinet with the padlock. He put the suppositories in a bottle he plugged with cotton, put the bottle in his patent-leather satchel with the torn handle where he kept his stethoscope and sphygmomanometer, checked the time and left his office in no hurry at all.

Immortality

Then one day a dust devil broke out. It circled the valley for hours like a blind horse, and when the dust had settled we saw her. She was walking on the side of the road towards the village, and at first we assumed she was the antic of an impossible mirage. Only when she had reached the first houses did we suspect that she was real, because in one hand she was holding an open umbrella and in the other a goatskin suitcase with copper studs.

'You will live for ever,' she told us.

She wore a linen jacket and skirt that had been white before the sudden attack of the whirlwind, nylon stockings riddled with bramble as high as we dared to look, a pair of yellow pumps one of which was missing its heel, and over her left eye a rubber patch that gave her face the resolve of a contrite hermit. She put her suitcase down.

'When they told me so, I didn't believe it,' she puffed. 'But this place is truly at the end of the world.'

'You smell of flowers,' we said.

It was afternoon. Lizards crossed the street to hide in the cracks of the opposite walls and the children caught one. The smell of flowers was on her clothes, in her hair; when we pressed our noses on her skin it was there too, and we said it was running in her blood, and was seeping through her pores.

'It's *eau-de-Cologne*,' she explained.

She showed us a glass bottle with a gold cork, shaped to the colonnaded façade of a miniature Parthenon, where naked girls danced around a fountain. It contained the essence of jasmine, she said, and she always carried it with her. There was only one cloud in the sky.

'You walked a long way.'

'Flat tyre,' she said, and pointed her hand in an indeterminate direction. 'An hour away.'

The children played with the lizard. They held it up from its tail and it arched its body to the shape of a hook. We brought her kumquat but she thought there was too much sugar in the syrup, we offered her carob pods but they were too leathery, and she refused the drink we served her because anise gave her nightmares. She sat on her case.

'Give me only water.'

From the goatskin suitcase she took out a pack of wooden rods, and, after we ran our fingers over its lacquered grain, we agreed that the wood was even superior to the oak desk in the town hall. Then, while she assembled the rods with the concentration of a jeweller, more of us came and we all sat and watched her, apart from the younger children who were playing with the lizard.

'Why do they torture that poor thing?' she asked.

'What happened to your eye?' we wanted to know.

From her suitcase she also took out a box and explained that that was a lens at the end of the fabric bellows, that was the focus control, that rubber cable there with the bubble at the end the shutter release, and the purpose of the widow's veil in the back was for the negative not to be burned by light. She screwed the camera on to the tripod and we leaned against the walls with our hands crossed behind our backs. The only thing her equipment reminded us of was the shadow-puppet theatre at the feast of our patron saint. We told her so.

'My other eye is in here,' she said, tapping the camera.

The camera stood on its wooden spider legs. Her perfume made everyone feel as if we had arrived at a foreign place, so much so that our women covered their mouths not to sigh and the children started crying from nostalgia for our village. We men silently agreed then that, as soon as we could save the money, we would buy enough jasmine shrubs to block every street, and pour enough compost and water for them to grow even bigger than the acacias, so that that cruel scent would go on burning our loins for ever.

'Put on your Sunday clothes,' she ordered.

That morning we had shaved with hot water and tallow soap, the women had combed and pomaded their hair, and we had thrashed our children until they had surrendered to their only pair of shoes, which they wore like shackles on the way to church. It *was* Sunday. The sun was hot, and the dark cypresses in the churchyard stood like put-out candlesticks. We blushed. We did not want to admit to her that we were so poor our houses were dirtier inside than out, so much so that we would wipe our shoes on the doormat before stepping out into the street.

'We are wearing them,' we mumbled in the end.

'Oh.'

She told us she had attended coronations and royal weddings, she had been present at the assassination of a famous archduke, and, thanks to her good luck, her camera had also caught the very instant a landing airship had gone up in flames.

'What is an airship?' we asked.

We had never heard any of her extraordinary stories before but we believed her, because in her goatskin case, wrapped in cotton cloth and thick vellum sheets, she had the photographic plates to prove them.

'Is everyone here?'

'Some babies are sleeping.'

'Who's looking after them?'

'The grandmothers look after them.'

'Ask them to bring them over.'

'Yes.'

We did not have to ask her to know that she had come from the capital of the nation. We could tell because our women had demanded nylon stockings like hers before, but we could not find them in the town where we went to buy presents to make them forgive us. The tailors had said that nylon was a stupid idea and whoever came up with it would soon go bankrupt and blow his chickpea brains out, because nylon had no tensile strength whatsoever.

'Where can we buy nylon?' we had asked nevertheless.

'Where fools live: in the capital.'

We wanted our women to forgive us for the time the carriage with the girls passed through the village. It was a four-wheeled carriage drawn by a pair of scrawny mules whose bloated bellies rubbed against each other, and painted on the side were the words EXOTIC FRUIT. The girls on it flapped their legs in our faces, and because they wore nylon stockings their legs sparkled in the sun like hooked fish. Our women never forgave us.

We sent the children to bring the old and the very young. We stood up and she counted us, arranged us in rows, ordered us to button up, and when we thought she was ready she said: 'We need tables.'

If she had asked for the tombstones of our ancestors we would have dug them out too, because her eyepatch had the indisputable authority that tames rabid dogs and turns a charging boar into a rolling porcupine. We rushed to get the tables from the coffee shop.

'I don't have all day,' she scolded us.

Even the children obeyed her commands and lined up in a straight row according to her wishes. The boys held footballs made from ox bladders stuffed with straw, wooden swords whose lethal tips they sharpened every day and cardboard helmets with tufts made from the silken tail of the dead racehorse, while the girls lulled their patchwork dolls with the button eyes. We adults were behind them, one row standing and the second on top of the tables, so that the camera could see everyone. We men straightened our collars one last time and smoothed our cowlicks, while our women manacled their moonlike bosoms under their black cardigans as best as they could, before holding up their babies like trophies, and then we all locked our hands and took a deep breath and held it.

'Keep still.'

She sprinkled powder in a little trough, she raised it above her head, she fired it. It produced a brilliant flash of light that scared the dogs away and a cloud of acrid smoke that gave us tears.

We said: 'We want one too.'

'These plates are expensive.'

It did not matter. She had told us so many times that day that if one did not exist in print one never really existed, and she had seduced us by saying that photography would even bring the dead to life. We searched under our mattresses, ripped open our pillows, dug up the chests with our savings, even broke our children's piggybanks knowing that one day they would forgive our lunatic behaviour, and finally came up with the money.

'Make us live for ever,' we asked.

It took only another minute. Then she packed her camera, the polished hickory tripod, the bottles that contained what she called the developing chemicals, and, opening her umbrella, she asked us to give her a hand with her car. We found it by following the shadow of a scudding cloud, and after we had changed the tyre we watched her drive away. We almost wept again then, not on account of the illuminating powder, but because we could not believe our luck, that we were going to live for ever now, in a photographic plate we would frame and hang on the wall of the coffee shop for everyone to remember. Oh yes, now we were as immortal as the scent of her jasmine perfume.

A Classical
Education

When Nectario first bought the parrot, it could only say one thing and even that was in Portuguese, because it used to belong to a sailor from Porto Alegre until he lost it to the bird-fancier in a decisive game of chequers.

'*Mostre-me o caminho para o bordel mais barato, amigo,*' said the parrot.

Within a month it could say those words in Nectario's language:

'Show me the way to the cheapest whorehouse, friend.'

The parrot was a yellow amazon with a curved bill of mineral strength the size of a derrick's hook, a leathery tongue that perpetually licked its lower mandible and eyes that had the expression of sincere curiosity. Nectario took it home. The bachelor lived in a house more intriguing than the bird's native jungle. There was a sofa which the parrot liked to pluck, a lampshade on a loose floor-stand where it sat and rocked for hours, and an old refrigerator which startled the bird with its noisy motor every time it started. Nectario was delighted. He showed his latest acquisition to his niece, when her parents dropped her off before leaving in the cart for the county capital to sell the corn.

'What do you think?' he asked her.

The little girl looked at the bird indifferently.

'It's like an oversized canary and it doesn't sing,' she declared, and switched on the television.

Nectario was a clerk in the town hall. His job had not only given him myopia, but also kept the scales of his life from tipping on the side of his pathological imagination. His unique state of mind had already cost him dearly: he was lonely. Inevitably, he had embraced the consolation of pets, and tried to fulfil his childhood ambition of becoming an animal-tamer. Once, he had bought two Siamese cats which he taught trapeze acts for months, but they had failed to perform. He took them to the veterinarian in the capital.

'You've been swindled,' the doctor said. 'These cats are deaf.'

Nectario was disappointed, but not for long. Soon he came up with another project. From afar it seemed like an ordinary aquarium, but on closer inspection one could see drawn on its floor a six-lane track with a finishing line. Nectario started training a school of angelfish for the world's first fish race.

'You should've consulted me first,' the veterinarian said. 'Angelfish aren't a competitive species.'

It was during those days of disappointment that the travelling show of exotic birds came to the village. Immediately Nectario saw the parrot he dropped his shopping net. The bird was chained from its leg to a wooden peg and looked back at Nectario with equal fascination. With its thick plumage and large bill, it was out of place among the small, wire cages with finches and canaries. On its breast it had sellotaped a piece of paper which read, REDUCED TO CLEAR BECAUSE IT DRIVES

PATRONS CRAZY. Indeed, when Nectario tried to have a closer look the parrot started repeating the only phrase it knew.

'What does it say?' asked Nectario.

'The first line of a Portuguese prayer,' lied the bird-fancier. And added: 'This parrot is particularly good with languages.'

Then an idea crossed Nectario's mind, and his eyes narrowed down to little slits behind his glasses.

'I want it,' he said firmly.

'You'll need a cage,' the bird-fancier warned him. 'Or you might lose a finger.'

The steel cage was put on the kitchen table with a piece of lettuce wedged between its bars. Nectario would let the parrot out every morning before going to work and put him back in the evening when it was time for its lesson. With the help of a dictionary he translated what was after all not the beginning of a prayer to the Virgin, and in less than a month he had taught the bird to say it. With a sense of pride, the parrot would repeat what it had learned again and again, until Nectario would put a sheet over the cage that sent the bird to sleep.

'His name is Homer,' Nectario informed his niece. 'And soon he will know the classics by heart.'

It was easier said than done, even for a parrot with such rare abilities. Not only was it born in the Amazonian jungle, but Homer had also spent his formative years in the worst slums and ports of the world before arriving at Nectario's adobe house. Its education was going to be a slow process but Nectario was not dispirited. With eyes radiating an unreasonable enthusiasm he read to the parrot every evening from selected works of his classical library. He had bought the books with the tasselled bookmarks in the flea market in the capital, together with a heavy lectern, a footrest, an old dressing gown with a row of medals pinned on it and a pair of corduroy slippers – all because he was advised that that was the only way to appreciate literary texts. But he had barely gone beyond the first book of Apollonius' *Argonautica* when he had lost interest, and the books were then delivered to the oblivion of their shelves where they remained until the arrival of the parrot.

Unlike his owner the bird proved an avid scholar. Long gone were the nights in the company of sailors and publicans; Homer now sat quietly for hours, absorbing every word from Nectario's mellow voice with a knowing nod. It took several days, but finally the parrot could repeat whole sections from a book, and if a page happened to be missing it would have an intimidating fit: a croak it had picked up from a tropical frog followed by a furious flapping of its colourful wings.

'It's speaking in tongues,' said Nectario's niece.

'No,' her uncle corrected her. 'It's Herodotus in the original.'

'Poetry would be more difficult, Uncle.'

Nectario patted Homer on the head.

'It won't be long before he appreciates the dactylic hexameter. You'll see.'

The summer days moved slowly like a train on a hill. All morning Nectario would copy birth certificates and memoranda with one eye on the clock until it was time to go home, where the parrot waited for its epic poetry class, biting off bits of the sofa. Homer's zeal was not purely academic. In order to entice it into further learning, Nectario brought home every afternoon a full paper cone of birdseed, making the boundary between the parrot's thirst for knowledge and its plain gluttony difficult to define. A heatwave had hit the village, and sleeping in the small house was a torture for man and child. In contrast, the weather, as well as the seeds, kept up the parrot's spirits, and many a night were Nectario and his niece awakened by Homer's hearty chuckle echoing from the corridors of the bird's mysterious dreams.

Some days later Nectario received a telegram from his sister saying that the sale of the corn was not going well and that they had to try other towns too. Please look after the child. Kisses.

'We've both been conned,' said his niece. 'You're stuck with me, and I with a philologist parrot.'

Homer had reached Book XXIII of the *Odyssey* the Sunday the yellow wind blew from the direction of the sea, covering the valley by lunchtime with a golden layer of dust.

'Where is it coming from?' the little girl asked her uncle, while cleaning the parrot with the feather duster.

'From the African desert across the sea,' replied Nectario.

Lost in the strange haze, the coach to the capital came and went with its windscreen wipers and headlights on, while those people who ventured into the streets had to wrap scarves round their faces, and hide under their umbrellas and muslin parasols. The air was suffocating. Outside the town hall a vagrant put a cardboard box over his head, cut holes for the eyes and watched the storm lay down heaps of sparkling sand. The storm lasted until the evening. During that time rumours spread across the village that were so impossible even the priest did not believe them. People said, for example, that out in the valley it had suddenly rained fresh dung, followed a few minutes later by three scared camels mounted by Bedouin dressed in black djellabas.

Inside the small house Nectario paid little attention to the phenomenon, concentrating instead on teaching the bird the rules of Greek syntax. Encouraged by his parrot's love of learning, Nectario's ambition had grown too: he wanted now to train the first ever translator parrot. Losing track of time, he worked through the night, managing to keep Homer up with the help of cupfuls of seed. On Monday morning the sandstorm resumed with greater rage.

'The world is about to end!' said the girl in awe. 'Father Yerasimo was right.'

At that moment Nectario was tempting the parrot with another handful of birdseed.

'Not before you finish your milk and toast,' he told her absent-mindedly.

The storm kept uncle and niece from going out. They stayed in for several days, and the girl, ignored by her uncle, watched so many children's programmes on the television that her eyes became square like the black-and-white screen. Occasionally, the parrot, exhausted from recounting Odysseus' adventures, would stop and watch too. Then Nectario would pour more birdseed in the little trough inside its cage and Homer would return to its studies. But it was a futile attempt. The parrot was steadily getting fatter without being able to translate even a word of the ancient text to colloquial speech. Nectario's enthusiasm was failing and his efforts started giving him worse headaches than the smell of Indian ink at work.

The day the sandstorm subsided Nectario's sister and brother-in-law arrived to take the child home. The television was switched off and silence returned to the apartment. That television had been another of Nectario's impulse purchases. He never watched it by himself. He had bought it from the family of a deceased relative in the capital, in order to teach a lamb to bleat every time the President addressed the nation. It had been yet another of his failures.

'Sheep are more independent-minded than people think,' the veterinarian had said, when Nectario had taken the animal to be tested for blindness.

Sitting in his armchair Nectario looked at his reflection on the dark screen. Next to it, Homer was peacefully perching in its cage. Since his niece's departure the house had grown smaller for Nectario. He noticed that if he stretched his arms he could touch both walls and, if he stood up straight, his head would brush against the bulb suspended from the ceiling – both signs that his imagination was drying up. Nectario continued his efforts but with waning enthusiasm. Finally, one evening, the parrot stopped talking and started spitting seeds in its master's face.

'That's it!' Nectario said angrily. 'Tomorrow you are going back where I bought you from. And if they don't want you, I'll stuff you like a Pharaoh myself.'

That night Nectario woke up and found that he had fallen asleep in his armchair. In the dark he saw a pair of eyes lit by the moon. He held his breath and listened. The parrot was talking away.

'It even rhymes!' Nectario mumbled after a while, trembling.

The parrot was reciting a poem for children – one Nectario had never heard before. When it finished that poem, it started another one. After it had said a third, Nectario jumped up from his armchair. He had never taught the parrot any of those. There was only one explanation.

'I don't know how I did it,' Nectario mumbled, 'but I've made something better than a translator out of that parrot: a poet!'

Over the following days, he found out that the parrot had, in fact, composed several poems, and they were all for children.

'He must have been working on them in his time off,' Nectario decided.

He was ecstatic. After years of failure his dreams had come true. He had finally trained an animal to perform what was more than an amazing trick. Now his thoughts were about reaping the rewards of his labour, and many a night he fell asleep at the kitchen table, smiling over his detailed calculations for starting his own little travelling show.

On the day he was going to resign, Nectario awoke to find the parrot in the throes of a bad sickness. The bird was trying to sit on its swing, but its legs appeared to have no strength and every time it would fall headlong on to the dung-covered floor of its cage.

'*Filho da puta!*' it hollered, and tried again without success.

Cold sweat trickled down Nectario's forehead. Hoping it was only parrot fever he rushed the bird to the veterinarian. The doctor lowered the big reflector on his forehead. Homer looked at him with its blurry eyes, and offered the closest a bill can manage to a smile, before singing another poem.

'This bird is stoned,' the veterinarian immediately diagnosed.

It was the hemp seed: Homer becoming a poet was clearly the consequence of overdosing on hallucinogens and the classics, Nectario thought. The veterinarian scratched his head, and looked at Nectario with disbelief.

'What poet? These are nursery rhymes.'

The parrot said a different poem.

'Oh yes,' said the veterinarian. 'My daughter loves that one too.'

Nectario blushed, and suddenly the blindfold of his uncontrollable imagination fell off.

'The television!' he exclaimed.

And the bitter truth dawned on him. He clearly saw, as if before his own eyes, his niece in front of the television watching a programme for children, the parrot keeping an eye and ear on the screen while at the same time reciting Greek with the fluency of a scholar, and himself, Nectario the animal-tamer, with a paper cone of birdseed in one hand and the *Odyssey* in the other nodding approvingly.

He was only a few blocks from the clinic when Nectario stopped and put down the cage. Inside, the parrot was slowly sobering up. Nectario opened the little wire door, got back on his feet and without delay walked away. He was walking fast; the train to the village was leaving soon.

Sins of a
Harvest God

I

From behind the sheet of rain suddenly came the cry of intolerable pain. It was answered by the bark of a dog under the tree in the square, then there was silence again. The rain fell over the village, and the streets and the unpaved square slowly turned into mud. Under the large plane tree the dog squeezed and the sound of the rain through the leaves was like tearing paper. It was a small black dog with a white muzzle. The houses of the village had corrugated roofs, and the water ran down the grooves and on to the concrete verandas with the flowerpots. Because the verandas were badly constructed they were flooded. It was evening, and a big soot-coloured cloud stood above the village and was not moving although a northern wind blew from the sea where the cloud had come from. A flock of swallows travelling south had been caught in the rain and had hidden under the roofs, waiting for the weather to clear. They had been waiting for four hours now and the cloud was still heavy.

A man appeared and started crossing the square. He was walking slowly, limping and holding his belly in both hands. He wore a white suit with a red carnation in the buttonhole, and his shirt and hands were covered in blood. He was walking with his feet well spread out, trying to balance himself. He had passed the wooden platform that stood next to the tree when he fell, when the dog started barking. He tried to stand up again. The dog barked but kept its distance. The man tried to stand, pushing with one hand and with the other he held his belly. His belly was slashed under his jacket, and the jacket was tucked inside his trousers, and his hand held the buckle so that his entrails would not spill out. He spat out little balls of blood in the pools of rain and tried to breathe. He breathed fast and without a rhythm, while it rained and the dog barked and the swallows perched under the corrugated roofs.

The square was dark but for the street-light on the wall of the chandlery. Strings of paper lanterns that the rain had torn to pieces hung from the plane tree. On one side of the square were the chandlery and the taverna, and next to them was the barber's, and all were closed. The wooden door of the coffee shop on the other side of the square was also padlocked, the metallic tables were chained in pairs, one table upside down on top of the other, and the rain rapped against them. All around the square, squeezing themselves under the projecting roofs, the people stood in silence. The barking dog took a careful step towards the man who was still trying to stand up. Someone else appeared from the direction the dying man had come. He whistled. 'Come, boy!'

Immediately, the dog raised its head to smell the air, and saw him. It hesitated between him and the dying one. 'Come!' ordered the man again. The dog ran across the square to him. It shook off the rain from its coat and, wagging its tail, stood on its hind legs so that the man would cuddle it. He patted it on the head. 'Good boy,' he said.

The dying man had managed to stand and he started his unbalanced walk again. His steps were heavier now, and, with both hands holding his belt, he seemed from a distance like a drunk. He walked towards the church on the far side of the square. The wind shook the bell in the steeple and the bell let out a deep, funereal tone. With his head bowed the man followed the sound of the bell, walking in a jagged line towards the church. The villagers watched the dying man in silence.

The bell tolled and its cord, which reached to the ground, swung in the wind. The steeple was about thirty metres high and on top had a cross made from light bulbs that were switched off. Mud from the streets had flooded the tiled churchyard. No sooner had the man walked into the yard than he fell again. The rain carried away the carnation on his lapel while he tried to stand, but his feet slipped on the tiles. He tried several times; in the end he started crawling with an agonising effort towards the church, leaving behind a trail of mud. He used both hands and when his jacket came out from under his belt it was blood that trailed behind him. He reached the door of the church and, seizing both handles, he managed to stand on his feet.

'Help,' he whispered.

The dog on the veranda ran towards him, barking. The church door was locked, and the dying man let go of the handles and started walking in circles with his head down, as if practising the steps of a dance. He slipped again, but managed to grab the swinging cord of the church bell. Dangling from the cord he struggled to stand again, while the bell tolled at every jerk. The man struggled because his feet could not support him any more, and he pulled the cord and the bell tolled. Everyone watched. Men and women and children, they all watched in silence from under the roofs.

'Help me, friends,' pleaded the man again.

But no one moved. As he turned round they saw his entrails hanging from his belly. There was a horizontal gash all the way across his belly from where his entrails were pouring out. But he was not trying to hold them in any more. 'Virgin Mary,' he said, but so quietly now that even he himself hardly heard it. He let go of the bell cord, took a few slow steps back towards the square and fell in a pool of mud and blood.

II

'Mix it with the last of the apricot,' the proprietor of the coffee shop told his sister. 'And they won't be able to tell the difference.'

The woman skimmed the layer of mould in the glass jar with a spoon, and stirred in the contents of the large tin. Then she covered the jar and put it back on to the shelf with the rest of the glazed sweets. The tin she half filled with water, before going out to the back of the coffee shop where a small dog wagged its tail.

'Quince tastes nothing like apricot,' she said, coming back.

She was a middle-aged woman with doleful grey hair kept under a black scarf.

'It's not my fault,' replied her brother, scratching his head. 'I did order apricot. We'll say it's a foreign variety.'

He cut a piece of cardboard, wrote APRICOT – JUST ARRIVED in large letters, and put it on top of the refrigerator where everyone could see it. He was a few years younger than his sister, and like her he had never married. That morning they were sorting the delivery that had come on the train.

It was the day of the celebration. Strings of paper flags stretched from the large plane tree in the middle of the square to the pantiled roofs. A line of coloured light bulbs was wound round the tree trunk, and a row of tables circled the square. A man walked into the shop and took a seat.

'Bring me a coffee,' he said. 'Two sugars.'

He wore black trousers, a waistcoat and a white shirt without a tie. The proprietor brought him the coffee.

'You should have some glazed apricot with that,' he suggested. 'It just arrived this morning.'

The stranger nodded in agreement. As soon as he had tasted the confection he grimaced.

'This is not apricot,' he said. 'It's quince.'

A blush tinted the proprietor's face. He shrugged and put his hands in the pockets of his apron. He was about to say something when he noticed the case under the table.

'It's Austrian,' the stranger said proudly. 'Let me show you.'

Inside the case, on a red velvet cushion, lay an accordion. The proprietor of the coffee shop studied the fine instrument with admiration.

He asked: 'Where's the rest of the band?'

The accordionist pushed away the plate with the quince and washed his mouth with coffee.

'They aren't coming,' he replied. 'But don't worry. The accordion is a band in itself.'

The proprietor received the information with a sigh. He placed the plate with the unfinished quince on his tray and returned behind the counter. Noise was coming from the cellar where his sister was busy.

'Bad news, sister,' he shouted down the trapdoor. 'The band isn't coming.'

'We can't have a celebration without music,' she replied from the dark.

'The celebration was my chance to break even,' the proprietor said, defeated. 'One doesn't get drunk without music.'

On a shelf, between the calendar and the DDT bomb, was the radio. He turned it on and for some time tried to improve the reception by twisting the piece of wire that was its aerial. Finally the crackles subsided, and the proprietor leaned against the counter and listened to the voice coming from its speaker. When it was time for the sports news, he took from his back pocket a football-pools ticket. A moment later he tore it up and threw the pieces into the bin. A voice came from the cellar.

'How did you do, brother?'

The man bent over the trapdoor again.

'The only moment of luck I ever had in this life was when you turned down that suitor,' he shouted.

Many years earlier a salesman of medical encyclopaedias had asked for the woman's hand, but the dowry negotiations had gone on for so long that eventually she had lost patience and declared that she would never marry, passing her savings to her brother to buy the only coffee shop in the village. From the cellar the woman said something in return, but her brother paid no attention because he was listening to the engine of an approaching car. In a moment, a jeep covered in dust appeared in the square and parked under the shadow of the plane tree. A sergeant of the civil guard jumped out and walked towards the coffee shop, brushing his uniform with his cap.

'Coffee without sugar,' he ordered when he entered. 'And three glasses of water.'

'Due to water shortage,' the proprietor informed the sergeant, 'we can only serve one glass per coffee.'

It had not rained for a year and the aqueduct in the valley

carried no water. At night, the wind through its stone arches kept the people awake. The dowsers had failed and the village now relied only on its well, which armed men guarded day and night. The situation was even worse elsewhere, where no christenings were performed because they could not spare the water to fill the baptistery. 'Their skin is dry like kippers,' the driver of the coach that called at every village had recently said. 'One has to see it to believe it.' He was sharing a table with the mayor in the coffee shop, where the coach stopped on its way to the county capital. The mayor felt as if a centipede had crept under his shirt. Immediately, he banned the use of salt in cooking by municipal decree until further notice.

The sergeant sat down and rocked himself in his chair. It creaked as if it were about to break to pieces. He said: 'Then bring me three coffees.'

The annual celebration had been decreed by the prefect to mark the end of the harvest. The fact was that that year there was no reason for celebrations: the drought had completely destroyed the crops. In the parched fields lay the bleached carcasses of runaway animals that had died of thirst, and the valley was plagued by swarms of crows that fed on the rotting flesh. But the prefect had ordered that the tradition should be upheld.

Out in the square the priest was whitewashing the church with a broom tied on to the end of a long stick. Apart from the coffee shop, all other shops were shut for the celebration by order of the prefect. On the balconies national flags flapped on their poles. It was a quiet morning; everyone was at home, getting ready for the festivities. The proprietor asked the sergeant whether he was going to be in charge of the ceremonial squad. The village had a civil guard station manned by a corporal, but he had been taken ill and no replacement was sent.

'There'll be no squad,' he replied. 'I've come alone.'

The proprietor collected the three empty glasses from the table and went to the kitchen. His sister emerged from the cellar with a leg of ham and a chamber pot filled with eggs.

'The squad is not coming this year either,' her brother said.

She carefully put the eggs to boil and started slicing the meat.

'I'm not surprised,' she replied. 'To them the villages are where their meat and eggs come from.'

A girl walked into the coffee shop wearing a dress made from curtain cloth. It was Persa, the mayor's daughter. She was the only child in the village who went to school. Every morning she rode the coach to the county capital carrying a satchel containing a composition book with blue covers and a book of classical literature in the original. She was an avid reader and had a great affection for the tragedies, of which she had watched several at the county theatre. The classical comedies she would also read, but would never go to see them performed. Her teacher had asked her why.

'Because the wooden phalli would make me laugh so much that the ushers would throw me out every time.'

A head emerged from behind a heap of ham and egg sandwiches on the counter.

'Have you seen my father, Whale?' the girl asked.

The proprietor smiled affectionately.

'You are your father's daughter,' he replied. 'If only one of you stood still for a minute, one would see the other pass by.'

Whale persuaded her to wait in the coffee shop. Outside a team of municipal workers was assembling a wooden platform. The celebrations were to start at sunset. On the wall of the coffee shop stood an ivy vine that had been killed by the drought. A moment later the mayor appeared. He was a small man with a round belly and a complacent countenance. At his side he held his umbrella, while tucked into the back of his hat was his handkerchief to protect his nape from the heat.

He immediately asked: 'Where's the music?'

The accordionist had fallen asleep. Whale explained that the rest of the band would not be coming. The mayor's forehead wrinkled to a miserable expression. Then he saw his daughter. A sudden sense of panic overtook him, fearing that she had discovered his plan: that day at the feast he was going to announce her engagement. And no one was going to be more surprised at the news than her.

She was to marry the butcher, a bachelor whose overwhelming desire to father a son increased the older he grew. Once a month he would undertake a two-day journey across the county in his refrigerator van on the pretext of buying livestock from the villagers, but in reality he was after a bride. He was a man of a reasonable appearance; the true reason for his failure was his compulsive tendency to short-change the farmers. His reputation had worsened with the drought, which to him had been a blessing: he had made a fortune by buying everyone's livestock when they could not feed it or water it any more.

'He's the only person in the valley,' Whale had said once, 'to whom the rain would be a curse.'

It was to be a marriage of convenience, commanded by poverty. The prolonged drought had ruined the mayor's crops, and since spring the family had struggled to make ends meet.

'Something had to be done,' the mayor had told his wife, defending his decision. 'We can't live on my salary alone.'

'We could've sold my family heirloom,' said his wife. 'Instead, you traded it for an oak desk for your office.'

The mayor made a dismissive gesture. 'I couldn't sign petitions sitting at a sideboard.'

'My mother gave it to me as a wedding present,' his wife snapped at him. 'In any case, you're a fool if you think our daughter will submit to your machinations. She has the will of a mule.'

As a matter of fact, the mayor had reservations about the engagement too. But he hoped his daughter would understand the urgency of the family's situation. That year they had managed to live off savings, but another two months without rain and there would be no crop next year either. That would mean starvation.

'She wouldn't dare. It'll be in front of the whole village,' the mayor said, referring to the engagement. 'Even your daughter has a sense of shame.'

'My child is sacrificed to the harvest god by her own father,' the woman lamented.

In the coffee shop the mayor relaxed. His daughter still had no idea about the engagement.

'Mother says not to bother with the ice any more,' Persa said, 'because the meat has gone off. Last night she let the cat sleep in the icebox. She says she's been warning you for a week.'

The mayor blushed. 'I had the celebrations to think about,' he mumbled. 'My electorate demands my full commitment.'

'And the worst thing is,' the girl added casually, 'that we're having marrow for lunch. You know how it gives you gas.'

The mayor bit his lip. His aversion to vegetables was an embarrassing subject. At that moment the civil guardsman stood, clicked his heels and gave the military salute. He informed the mayor that there was no squad forthcoming. The mayor acknowledged the news with a bite at his moustache.

'But I was promised a squad of seven men,' he protested meekly. 'In the next village they even get the military band with the sousaphone.'

'There's a shortage of personnel,' replied the sergeant coolly. 'Besides, your village is not going to be a municipality for much longer.'

He was right. A year ago the cartographer had arrived in an old Ministry of Agriculture van, where in place of one of the rear tyres was the wooden wheel of a cart.

'I've been on the road for two years,' he had explained surlily. 'Let's get this over with. I still have half the country to map.'

He asked to be let into the church and a minute later he appeared on the belfry with a pair of binoculars. Only when he came down again and started loading his tripods and surveyor's telescopes back into the van, did the mayor suspect that something was wrong.

'My orders are to report any settlement under thirty houses,' the cartographer informed him. 'You are required by law to resign your post, and the village will come under the jurisdiction of the nearest town council.'

'But we are a substantial community,' the mayor protested. 'And what will I do for a living?'

'I only counted twenty-seven permanent dwellings.'

'It's because of the earthquake. Also, the local stonecutter has recently died. But if you give us a month we'll build the rest.'

The equipment was packed. The cartographer turned the crank and the engine started, spattering oil. He took his seat behind the wheel.

'I'm afraid you will have to wait for the next expedition.'

The mayor breathed again, relieved. 'When will that be?' he asked.

'In fifty years.'

It was an episode that had sentenced the village to oblivion. In the coffee shop, the mayor now squeezed the handle of his umbrella nervously and looked down.

'We are exiles in our own country,' he murmured, remembering the events.

A small cloud passing in front of the sun cast an elusive shadow on to the floor of the coffee shop. Whale dropped the mop and hurried with the mayor to the window. They watched the cloud as if it were an exotic beast. After it had disappeared from their sight, Whale went behind the counter and made a mark on the blackboard underneath a large, childlike inscription that read: METEOROLOGICAL REPORT.

He said: 'Things are looking up, mayor. In August there was only one cloud, but this month there have been four already, and we still have two weeks left.'

The mayor rubbed his moustache; it was the only piece of good news that day. But it could well have been a false alarm. In April there had been eleven clouds but none had brought any rain. For a moment, while the cloud was there, the mayor thought he had experienced an imperceptible coolness, but now the only thing he could feel was his collar soaked in sweat again. Cockroaches were climbing the counter towards the sand-wiches. Whale scared them off with the mop – a bundle of cloth shreds tied round a crooked handle.

'It's because of the freak weather,' he said about the cockroaches. 'Normally they wouldn't stand the winter here. In insect terms, these are octogenarians.'

The sergeant straightened his holster with a perfunctory movement. The air smelled of boot polish and sweat. The mayor wiped his forehead with his handkerchief and checked his watch: there were still several hours until the announcement of the engagement. Suddenly the accordionist yawned and opened his eyes.

'Get some rest, friend,' the mayor said. 'It's not time for the celebrations yet.' He inspected his handkerchief and looked at his daughter with sadness. 'And the sooner they're over this year the better,' he murmured.

III

All afternoon clouds passed over the village with increasing frequency. And while the first cloud, which Whale and the mayor had witnessed, had been small and white, later they steadily grew bigger and heavier and darker. An unhurried wind blew from the direction of the train station and brought the foul smell of its privy to the village. It also shook the dried ivy on the wall of the coffee shop until all its yellow leaves fell off. The wind then scattered them across the square, over the rugs and on to the empty tables and the wooden platform, like discarded circulars.

Every year the mayor received an official envelope with the speech he had to read at the feast, because, after all, the real purpose of the celebration was to advertise the achievements of the government to the peasants. The speech had arrived just in time that very afternoon with the coach. It was going to be the last one he would ever read out. The following week he was going to send his resignation to the county prefect according to the law.

'The funny thing is not that it's still the same communiqué from five years ago,' the mayor said as soon as he broke the wax seal, 'but that what they'd promised us then as imminent is still in the planning stage.'

In front of the full-size mirror in the living room the mayor was trying to fit into his tailcoat and the matching pair of trousers.

'This suit is older than the Bible,' his wife said.

It was his wedding suit, which the mayor wore on every official occasion. His nervousness was increasing every minute. He tried to take his mind off his daughter's engagement.

'Remember when I carried you in the dark all the way from

the church?' he asked his wife affectionately, then took a deep breath before buttoning up. 'Now I can hardly lift the spoon, and I need a searchlight in either hand to find the outhouse at night.'

His wife smiled for the first time that day.

'It doesn't matter. You're still the man in my dreams.'

The mayor inspected himself in the mirror. There were holes in his waistcoat.

'Damn moths,' he said. 'They would drill through steel. Nothing can stop them.'

His wife fished a white pellet from his pocket and smelled it.

'Old fool,' she said. 'I always told you that the naphthalene was the box on the bottom shelf. You've been feeding the bugs mints.'

At that moment the doorbell rang. It was the butcher. He was wearing a white suit with a red carnation in the buttonhole of his lapel, and a shirt with buttoned-up collar but no tie. His hair was plastered across his forehead and he held his carbine. He looked worried.

'What are you doing with that?' the mayor asked.

'I was on sentry-go at the well.'

The mayor had forgotten. Every man in the village was taking part in guarding the well around the clock. Tonight the butcher had to swap places with another man in order to attend the feast where his engagement would be announced.

'Bastard,' grunted the butcher. 'He demanded half a mutton.'

The mayor looked into the feverish eyes of his future son-in-law. He wondered once again whether he had made the right decision. But it was too late now, and he whisked his thoughts off like bothering flies.

'Here, friend,' he said. 'Have a mint.'

'Have you told her yet?'

The mayor signalled him to be quiet.

'At the celebration,' he whispered, looking behind his back. And he added, with a great deal of uncertainty, while sending the butcher away: 'It will be the most pleasant surprise.'

The butcher went off to the coffee shop carrying the carbine over his shoulder. Whale brought him a glass and the brandy bottle. The sergeant looked at the rifle and asked the butcher whether he had a permit for it. The butcher looked back and grinned like a child caught stealing.

'It has no lock,' he lied. 'It's my father's. He jammed it after my mother had threatened to kill him.'

A rolled-up newspaper was on the windowsill and he took it.

'You won't read anything new in that one,' Whale informed him. 'It's only there to scare the flies off.'

Indeed, the paper disintegrated as the butcher leafed through the yellowed pages. In the square the lanterns were lit and people started arriving for the feast. Across from the coffee shop was a little shed with a handwritten sign above the door that read, THE DISTINGUISHED GENTLEMEN'S BARBER. The barber's shop had only one chair and a mirror broken by the earthquake which was of little use, so the barber often took the chair out and served his customers in the square. The butcher felt the stubble on his chin.

'Go get me the barber,' he ordered Whale.

The barber was a small man with the nervous habit of looking behind his back as if he were being followed. He was the mayor's political adversary, but in the elections he would never receive more than five votes, so the news of the mayor's dismissal had exhilarated him. On the coat-stand a mynah perched. He spread a towel on the table and arranged his tools in rows. One of the combs was broken and most of its teeth were missing. The butcher picked it up.

'That one is for bald customers,' the barber explained, and tied a towel round the butcher's neck. He mixed some lather and applied it to the sitting man's cheeks. The butcher offered his throat to the razor.

'Women used to avoid me like the plague,' he said after a moment. 'But I never stopped believing that somewhere there was someone who'd be right for me.'

'You should always give your hands a scrub before leaving the abattoir,' the barber said, concentrating on his job. 'Women are attracted to beautiful hands.'

'And shoes,' added Whale.

'The funny thing is,' the butcher continued, 'that my bride was closer than I thought.'

The razor stopped halfway down the butcher's cheek. The barber and Whale looked at each other. The butcher still stared at the ceiling.

'I shook hands with her father. He says she's crazy for me, but too shy to tell me herself.'

At first they did not believe him, because in his own village the butcher was not popular. They could think of no man who would give him his daughter. But they also knew that the drought had made many people desperate.

Whale asked: 'Who is she?'

'You'll know soon enough.'

The barber dipped his razor in the bowl and continued.

'Whoever it is,' he said, 'her family must be eating their shit from hunger.'

The feast started in a sombre mood. The priest said an abbreviated mass from the platform. It was interrupted twice by sudden salvos of the church bells, because the bell-ringer had been drinking since morning and misinterpreted two of the priest's pauses as the end of the service.

'This is such a sign of bad luck,' said the mayor's wife, 'that it is not even mentioned in the almanacs.'

The mass ended with a long prayer for rain. The mayor was restless. 'We prayed so much for rain,' he commented, 'that if it works we'll have to build an ark.'

Finally, stuck in his formal suit, the mayor walked up the steps to the platform to deliver his valedictory speech. No one paid any attention to it. Instead, the villagers' eyes turned one moment in the direction of the clouds and the next to the roast boars on the tables, which they studied with reverence.

' "... and I can assure you," ' the mayor read, ' "that we are going to find the answer to the water question before the year is out!" '

The crowd broke into a wearied applause. They knew the end of the speech by heart. The mayor asked the crowd to stand and nodded towards the accordionist. As soon as the music started everyone guffawed.

'Not a waltz, friend,' the mayor said, annoyed. 'Play the national anthem.'

The accordionist obeyed. The civil guardsman stood to attention and raised his arm in a military salute. On the platform, looking at his people whom the drought had reduced to sleepwalkers, the mayor felt like the captain of a sinking ship. The anthem ended. The moment to announce the engagement had arrived.

'My fellow citizens,' the mayor said, trembling. 'May I have your attention.'

Suddenly a drop fell on the official communiqué that he was still holding in his hand. The mayor looked at the blotched typescript with amazement.

'We are . . .' More drops landed on the speech. '. . . blessed!' he mumbled. Then, raising the megaphone to his mouth, instead of announcing his daughter's engagement, he shouted: 'The rain, the rain!'

It was the moment everyone had dreamed of in their feverish

sleep. The men took off their shirts, the women rolled up their sleeves; their skin was so dry that the rain at first burned like acid. Within moments the autumnal shower grew heavier. The accordionist took refuge under the plane tree, but the crowd dragged him out and ordered him to play the rumba, the tango, carnival music – anything as long as it was loud enough to hear over the thunder of the God-sent storm. A dance broke out across the square.

The butcher did not join in.

Standing alone in the middle of the crowd he felt as if someone had hung a cowbell around his neck. The rain soaked his hair and the black shoe polish he used to cover his greying temples trickled on to his white suit. His yellow eyes looked beyond the dancing crowd and over the red roof tiles, in the direction of the villages where women at doorsteps spat whenever they saw him and children threw stones at his van. Then the mayor touched him on the shoulder. He said that the engagement was cancelled.

'Thank you for offering to help my family,' the mayor said. 'But the rain will look after us now.'

'We shook hands,' the butcher mumbled.

The mayor replied with a shrug. No sooner had he turned his back than the butcher recovered from the stupor of his humiliation.

'A promise is a promise, mayor,' he said. 'One expects it to be kept. This gun, for example,' he continued, unslinging his carbine, 'promises that if I shoot it will send you to Hell.' He raised the gun and clenched his teeth. 'And I hope it will not let me down the way you did.'

He fired at point-blank range. The crack travelled out to the valley, and its echo mixed with the music and the laughter of the villagers.

'Father!' cried Persa.

The butcher ran into a side street. In the mud, the mayor lay on his back with the carbine next to him.

'I'm a mess, child,' he replied with shame.

The crowd made a circle round him and craned their necks. Women sobbed but the mayor could not see them. He smiled at the fading shadows. The crowd searched for the civil guardsman.

'My gun is empty,' the sergeant said, embarrassed. 'They don't issue bullets for routine assignments. Otherwise—'

The mayor sighed: 'This place sends more people sooner to the next world than a battlefield.'

Whale's dog walked up to the mayor and licked his hand. The mayor patted it on the head before the priest bent down next to him.

'Is there anything you would like to say, my son?' he asked quietly.

'Yes,' the mayor replied. 'I forgive everyone who didn't vote for me in the last election.'

Those were his last words. A carving knife was stuck in the flank of a roast on the table. Whale pulled it out and wiped its greasy blade on his apron. Lightning cracked. People and dog went silent. The rain built up and the wind made it fall at an angle. The dog crouched under the platform and the crowd backed under the corrugated-iron eaves all around the square, leaving Persa and her mother alone with the dead man. The rain fell over them, on the laid tables, the clay plates, the roast that lay intact, the bowls of dried fruit. The earth was already turning to mud when Whale walked away from the lit, silent square.

Sacrifice

Father and son had finished and they were washing the knives in the watering trough. The sun was going down. The killing had been going on all afternoon. They washed the twelve-inch knife with the wooden handle tied with string, and the other one with the nine-inch blade that was for carving. Both knives had blunt points because they were very old. The water in the trough was dirty with fodder and flies. An hour earlier the boy had gone back into the house to fetch the bayonet his grandfather had brought back from the war, and now he was washing that too. The bayonet had a serrated edge and on its handle was a little silver skull. Both edges of the blade were sharpened. The boy washed the bayonet carefully. The sun shone one last time on the blades and the water, and went down.

'I'll change the water,' the boy said.

'You're a good boy.'

The boy left the knives on the table on the veranda and

pulled the plug in the bottom of the trough to drain it. While
the trough drained he went to the well and brought water in the
bucket.

'You're a good boy,' said Dionysio. He then went and sat in
his chair under the vine on the veranda. It was a rocking chair
but he didn't rock in it; he sat and watched his son. There was
still some light coming from behind the hills.

The boy did everything meticulously. He scrubbed the
trough with the steel brush, then put the plug back and poured
in the water. He was whistling; it was as if it were the beginning
of their working day. But it was evening and his father could
hardly see him.

'Turn a light on, son,' Dionysio asked, when the boy had
finished with the trough.

The boy went into the house and the naked bulb that hung
from the vine on the veranda went on. Immediately, mosqui-
toes and gnats circled it. Under the light the three knives lay on
the table, arranged in size. The bayonet was the smallest. There
was still a little blood on its steel handle, and it slowly dripped
on to the oilcloth that covered the table. The boy came back
with two beers.

'Here, Father,' he said, and sat on the stool.

He took a long swig and let out a sigh of satisfaction. The
father looked at the boy.

'Did he hurt you?' he asked.

'Not at all.'

He leaned over. 'Let me have a look.'

'It's nothing really,' the boy said, and rolled down his sleeve.

They both had old work clothes on, bloodied at the front.
Their shirts were stained from the collar to the cuffs, and their
trousers too. Dionysio looked at the boy.

'Wash your face,' he said.

The boy ran his hand over his cheeks and then looked at his

188

fingers. There was blood on them. He put the bottle on the table with the knives and went to the trough.

'You're a good boy,' his father said.

A cockroach flew to the light. As soon as it touched the bulb it fell on to the table. It walked over the knives for a while and then took flight again. A cicada had begun to drone when the boy returned.

'We did it,' the boy said. 'It wasn't easy, but we did it, Father.'

'Yes, we did.' Dionysio took a sip from his beer.

'He fought as if he had a chance.'

Not too far away, two small circles of light moved up and down in the dark. The boy finished his beer.

'The neighbour's coming,' he said. 'You want another, Father?'

'You shouldn't drink.'

'I'll bring one for the neighbour too.'

The father said: 'I didn't know you drank.'

'I'll get the beers.'

'Not for me.' The father took a little sip and passed the back of his hand over his lips. 'You're too young to drink,' he said, raising his voice so that the boy could hear him from inside the house.

The car arrived. It was an old pickup truck without bumpers and rear window. A man jumped out and dusted his clothes. He slowly climbed the steps to the veranda.

'You ought to get a new one,' the father said.

The neighbour turned and looked at his truck.

'She's fine,' he said with a modest smile, and sat on the stool. 'I'd rather get a new woman.'

The boy returned with three beers. He gave the neighbour one and put one on the table. The neighbour looked at the knives.

'He had to go, neighbour,' the boy said, and took a long swig.

'You killed him?' the neighbour asked Dionysio, surprised.

'*We* killed him,' the boy replied. 'I helped too. Father?'

'You're a good boy, son.'

'Are you feeling all right?' the neighbour asked the father.

'He had to go,' the boy said.

The boy leaned against the railing of the veranda and drank with his hand hooked on his belt. He faced the farm, but it was dark now and he couldn't see anything. He turned to the neighbour.

'He stabbed me,' he said. 'You want to see?'

'Did he hurt you?' The neighbour stood up.

The boy rolled up his sleeve. There was a wound halfway up his forearm, where the blood had dried.

'You see?' he asked. 'He fought it.'

The neighbour felt the wound with his finger, carefully. The boy smiled.

'Are you all right now, son?' his father asked.

The boy said: 'Two men weren't enough.'

'Are you all right?' Dionysio asked again.

'My arm hurts.'

'Put some iodine on it,' suggested the neighbour.

'No, I mean the muscles.' The boy finished his second beer. 'He wouldn't go down, neighbour. You had to see it. We wrestled.'

The neighbour shook his head. He sat down again, and picked up his beer.

'He fought as if he had a chance,' the boy said.

'You drink too much, son,' Dionysio said quietly. He was looking at the dark beyond.

It was quiet on the veranda, but for the sound of the insects circling the light. The boy took the other bottle from the table.

'He was a breeder,' he said. 'He wasn't expecting it. It's not in their blood, neighbour. The others just look at you with their stupid eyes. They know. It's in their blood. But they never kill breeders. He was confident.'

'He was a fine beast,' the neighbour said.

'It doesn't matter,' Dionysio said.

'He was a Hereford,' said the boy. 'Father saved for five years.'

'It doesn't matter now,' his father said.

'Do you need anything, Dionysio?' the neighbour asked.

'He saw us coming and didn't move,' said the boy, and drank: talking was making him thirsty. 'He just looked. He thought he could handle us.' He paused to spit, and then continued. 'The carver did nothing. The twelve inch cut his tongue and he swallowed it.'

'Go and change your clothes, son,' his father said.

'Can you believe it, neighbour? He ate his own tongue and then was angry. He knew what was coming then.'

'Right,' said the neighbour.

'Then I remembered Grandfather's bayonet. Never used it before. But I've kept it always sharp. You want to see?'

The boy took the bayonet from the table and held it under the neighbour's eyes. The silver skull shone in the yellow light from the bulb. It was a heavy knife.

'Very fine indeed,' the neighbour said.

'Look at the blade.'

'Very fine.'

'See the teeth? Normally, they don't allow those in the army.'

'Right.'

'But then it was war,' explained the boy. 'In war everything goes, neighbour.'

'Of course.'

The boy held the knife in both hands. The neighbour looked away.

'Son, go and change,' Dionysio said tiredly.

'He fought as if he had a chance,' the boy said. 'He was big. That's what gave him confidence.'

'Go and change now.'

'When he took the bayonet he cried like a wolf. He knew what was coming then.'

The boy drank beer. The bitch walked out of the dark and wagged her tail. The boy bent down and rubbed her head.

'I killed him, girl,' he said. 'I killed him, all right.'

He turned to the father. 'I'll carve a crucifix from his horns. What'd you think, Father?'

Dionysio looked down. Slowly, he started crying.

'She was my baby.'

'I'm sorry, Dionysio,' the neighbour said.

'She was a little baby.'

'I'm sorry for your loss.' The neighbour rested his hand on Dionysio's shoulder.

'She was the light of my eyes.'

Dionysio cried. His shoulders shook as he cried. The boy watched him, biting his lips.

'I'm here, Father,' the boy said.

'You're a good boy,' his father said, sniffing.

'I'm sorry,' the neighbour said again.

'Thank you, friend.' Dionysio wiped his eyes on his shirt.

'I can lend you some money,' the neighbour said awkwardly.

'It doesn't matter.'

'I'll ask the priest for a collection.'

'He had to go,' the boy said. 'He killed my sister.'

The father looked out at the dark again. Some blood was round his eyes, from his shirt.

'I told Father he had to go,' the boy said. 'He was a killer.'

'Go and start the fire, son. We have to burn our clothes. You can't wash those.'

'He fought it, neighbour. My hand was in his throat down to the elbow and he still fought it.'

'Go and change, son.'

'His blood was hot. I didn't know blood's so hot. I mean, it was steaming, neighbour.'

'Go and change now,' Dionysio repeated.

'My sister liked him. She trusted him.'

The neighbour shrugged his shoulders. 'You can't trust a beast.'

'I told her, don't go near him. Look at his eyes, I said. Those aren't the eyes of an angel.'

The neighbour drank from his beer. The boy had finished his. The neighbour looked at Dionysio.

'You have a shotgun,' he said.

'No cartridges,' said the boy. 'I checked everywhere.'

'I thought we had some,' Dionysio said to the visitor. 'I don't use it much.'

His son rubbed his nose.

'No,' he insisted. 'There weren't any, I swear. I looked. It had to be the knife.'

'It'd have been easier that way,' said Dionysio. He looked at the boy. 'I'm sorry you had to do it, son.'

'It had to be the knife, Father. No cartridges. It'd be very easy otherwise.'

'He wore me out. I'm old. I'm sorry.'

'I'll look after you, Father. And the farm.' The boy turned to the neighbour. 'I'm taking a correspondence course in book-keeping. I'm good. But I like the outdoors. I do the course because I have to, but it's the outdoors.'

He gestured towards the dark. The neighbour nodded.

The boy continued: 'He cost us a fortune, but he had to go. He knew what he'd done.'

'He was a beast,' said the neighbour.

'He killed her and then carried on grazing as if nothing—' said the boy.

The father started crying again in silence. 'My sweet baby.'

The boy tried to hug his father but the old man brushed his arm away.

'Don't, Father. I love you. Tell me what to do. Anything.' Dionysio cried.

'Are you proud of me, Father?' said the boy.

'I'm sorry, friend,' said the neighbour.

'When we drove back from town in the afternoon, Father thought it was a calf lying there.'

'I'm sorry for your loss.'

The tears washed the blood from the father's face as he cried. The knives lay on the table. The neighbour looked at them.

'There were no cartridges, you see. I swear to you neighbour,' the boy said, and rubbed his hands together, nervously. 'It had to be the knife. You believe me, don't you?'

The Hunters
in Winter

We were lost; that was how we ended up in the village. We had been on the road for many hours when the storm caught up with us and we missed the crossroads. It was a storm like no other. The snow covered the windscreen, burying the wipers under it, and we could see no further than the edge of the bonnet. Everything was white. 'We are driving through the clouds,' the driver said. It was true. The clouds had come down over the hills and they were heavy with snow. 'I tell you now; we may be heading for the cliffs.' Because the road was almost as rough and uneven as the rest of the terrain, we could not tell whether we were still on it. We could not see the road posts. We crossed ourselves, we prayed, we drove on.

Later, we could tell the road was descending because our ears hurt.

'Slow down,' we told the driver. 'You're going too fast.'

'It's worse. Whenever I brake the tyres slide on the ice.'

The jeep was old. Flakes of rust were falling off its doors and the spare wheel was fixed on the bonnet with rope.

'We'll take it,' we had said. 'We are going on a hunt.'

That was a month earlier. We had thought we would be back in a week. We did not know the hunt would go on for so long. We had promised to pay for it when we returned with the money from the kill. It was big enough to carry ourselves, the guns, the tents, the food. The kill we would carry on the roof. We do not know what happened to the man who sold us the jeep. When we left, he was waving at us. 'Have a good hunt,' he was saying. 'See you soon!' We had waved back. That was the last we saw of him.

But it was a bad hunt. The winter was warm, and the deer had moved higher, where there were no roads and no tracks. We had to leave the jeep and walk for days, stalking the animals. Then one day the weather turned. First the rain, then a hail hard like glass, then snow. We had returned to the jeep and run away, but the storm caught up with us. That was how we ended up in that village.

In the jeep we had three carbines, two double-barrelled shotguns, five knives, two pistols. The pistols we had for protection. We had heard about the brigands in the mountains.

'They'll cut off your fingers one by one, friends,' they told us.

'We carry guns,' we replied.

'They are devils. Bullets don't kill them.'

'We also have knives.'

'They'll use them to gouge out your eyeballs, friends.'

'We are not afraid.'

We heard other stories about them too, but we never saw those men. If they ever existed they must have moved on. We only saw deer, but we could not kill any. There are big deer in those mountains, but we were wasting our time because of the weather.

When the weather cleared we saw the valley. We did not know there was a valley. Like we said, we came from far away. We came for the hunt. We were happy we had escaped the storm, and we were happy because in the bottom of the valley we saw a village. Its houses were small and white as dice, and smoke was coming from the chimneys. 'They'll give us food,' we said. 'We are fortunate. Step on it, driver.'

Then it happened.

We were coming out of a bend when the driver slammed on the brakes. The jeep skidded sideways and finally stopped a mere foot from the edge of the precipice.

'Look,' the driver said.

In the middle of the bulldozed road two peacocks perched. 'What are they doing here?' we asked each other. 'How did they survive the storm?' We did not know. We drove on. Hawks flew out of the briars and circled the jeep. We drove over potholes and ditches filled with water. We passed a herd of goats. We were driving fast. We did not see the herdsman's mongrel until it was too late. We stopped and shot it, so that it would not suffer. It had no chance anyway. We apologised to the herdsman; it was only a dog.

'We are sorry,' we said. 'We come from far away.'

'It was a good dog.'

'We are sorry. We are hungry and tired.'

'Go back where you came from.'

He was an old man. He was angry. He raised his stick to hit us. We fired in the air to scare him.

We reached the village at dusk. In the streets were donkeys laden with baskets, in the coffee shop old villagers playing cards. The street lights had blown. A dog in the square bit the ticks off its belly. We parked. A crowd was walking round the large tree in the middle of the square. There was a lorry whose headlamps lit a sign that read, THE BEST ROVING SHOW OF EXOTIC BIRDS – HALF A DRACHMA ONLY. When the people saw us they stopped; they were silent.

'Where can we spend the night?' we asked.

'Who are you?'

We said we were hungry and tired. 'And we want to get drunk,' we added.

'What are you doing here?'

We pointed to the lorry: 'Is that show any good?'

'They have a parrot that sings both verses of the national anthem. What do you want?'

We said we wanted to see the showman. He was in his caravan, painting a cockatoo with a brush. He explained: 'One of the lovebirds died. And those bastards won't perform unless they have a mate.' He finished with the cockatoo and then put it close to a fan to dry. He rubbed his hands with cotton daubed in turpentine.

'So?'

'We found a pair of peacocks; they almost killed us.'

He shrugged. 'They're not mine. They belong to the dead.'

'The dead?'

'The dead. They live at the cemetery. The villagers are feeding them. So that they might shit on their mothers' graves,' he joked.

In an iron cage was a large owl. We played with it.

'Leave her alone!' the showman shouted at us. 'She doesn't like strangers. Who are you anyway?'

After a moment he said: 'I apologise.'

We decided to stay a while because we liked the people. They were honest, and we were glad we had come. There was a *pension* in the village and we took rooms there.

'How long are you staying for?' the landlady asked.

'A few days. Until we fix the jeep and the weather improves.'

'The weather will be fine tomorrow. Why the guns?'

'We are hunters.'

'There's no game in winter.'

'There are deer.'

She looked out. She said: 'Tomorrow will be fine. The sky is clear. Don't you see the stars?'

'We don't trust the stars.'

There was a Virgin-and-Child icon in every room. We slept well. The next morning we woke up late. In the lounge the air smelled of tobacco. We ducked the strips of flypaper and sat at the tables. The landlady had seen us, but still leafed through a book without covers.

'If people learned from books,' we said, 'libraries would be closed to the public.'

'I need the rooms,' she said. 'I'm afraid you'll have to go.'

'Bring us breakfast, lady.'

'There are travellers coming tonight I had forgotten about. You don't have to pay, of course.'

'We are hungry, lady.'

We had shaved, we wore our hats, we smelled of lavender. We lit our cigarettes, while the food cooked. We ate in silence. Then we tried to call the garage in the county capital, but the phone was down.

'The phones went down yesterday, before you came,' the woman said. 'We don't know when they will be up again.'

'Where can we find the mayor?'

'This place has no mayor.'

We fed the cat.

'Don't feed her,' the landlady said. 'Or she won't be chasing rats.'

'Is there a civil guard station here?'

'It's closed. The corporal is away in the hospital.'

We left the *pension*. It was a fine day. We said we would trust the stars from then on. The civil guardsman had had an appendectomy, and someone had killed the mayor with a carbine. The driver went to try and fix the jeep. We had hit a ditch on our way to the village, and the axle was bent. We had to straighten it or else it would wear out the bearings in no time.

'There's a blacksmith,' they told us. 'He'll help you.'

'Thanks.'

'I can do it in no time,' the blacksmith said. 'If you give me a hand.'

We were tired. We could not help him.

'I will ask someone else,' the blacksmith said. 'No problem.'

'Take your time, friend,' we said.

'It's no problem,' he insisted.

'We are not in a hurry, friend.'

'No, really.'

'We'll stay for a while, friend.'

'As you wish.'

Some of us needed a shave, others also a haircut. We had plenty of time to spare. That was why we went to the barber's shop. A man with brilliantined hair was in the chair when we entered. He got down, paid and left. The barber was sweeping with his back to the door. 'Have a seat.'

Then he turned round.

'Who sent you?' he asked.

'We are hunters,' we explained. 'We got lost in the storm.'

'What storm?'

The barber was dressed in a white shirt, cotton trousers with braces, an apron made from an old bed sheet. He also wore black shoes with white vamps, carefully polished.

'That road over the mountains is only good for oxen,' we said. 'Nice shoes.'

'We are poor people,' he said.

'We are poor too, barber,' we assured him.

We liked him. Most people in the village were kind to us. There was a crow on the coat-stand. The bird did not like us. It was a strange bird.

'It's a mynah,' the barber said. 'I bought it from a bird-fancier some time ago.'

The bird could talk: 'Bastards,' it said. 'One of these days.'

'Shut up, Solon,' said the barber.

'One of these days!'

We said that if he could teach a bird to talk then he could also teach it manners. The barber looked at our guns. Some we had put against the wall, some we kept on our laps. They were expensive guns. They were not loaded in case there was an accident. We were careful. But they were valuable and we could not trust the lady in the *pension* with them.

'I apologise,' said the barber.

A man pulling a mule came to the door. He could not see us in the dark. He was an old man, and his hands were shaking.

'I came for my shave, barber.'

'Not now, Fanourio.'

'I look like a thief, barber.'

'I am sorry, Fanourio.'

'But I have an appointment.'

'The barber is busy,' we said. 'You'll live longer with a beard.'

He left. One of us sat in the barber's chair. It was an old chair made from plumbing pipes welded together. We asked the barber about it.

'The blacksmith made it,' he said. 'The same man who's fixing your jeep.'

'He'd better do a better job with the axle,' we said.

'He will, friends.'

It was a fine morning. We would have left after the haircut and the shave, but the jeep was not ready. Also, there were crows in the square, pecking the dust. We were told it was a sign that the storm had not passed. We were told the storm was sly like a snake. That was what they told us: like a snake. The barber finished shaving the last of us.

'Rub in some cologne, barber. Our faces look like steaks.'

'Of course, friends.'

We stood up to leave. He said: 'This razor here belonged to a pasha back in the days of the Ottomans. It has an ivory handle. Keep it as a present, friends.'

'Pashas didn't shave,' we said. 'They had beards.'

The barber washed his other tools and dried them with his apron.

'My combs were used by odalisques. My scissors are sterling silver. I want you to have them. Who sent you?'

We said that we were hunters.

He said: 'Thank you for calling.'

The cur we did not kill for fun. It was in the square, grunting and chasing its tail when we came out. There was froth coming out of its mouth and it tried to snap at our legs. We did those people a favour. We poked the dog with our shotguns for a while and then we fired. We cleaned the gun barrels on our clothes.

A woman said: 'Murderers.'

'It was rabid. We did you a favour.'

'Murderers.'

If we had not shot it in the head we could have shown her the frothy mouth and the bitten tongue. We explained as best we could.

Later the woman spat at us: 'Animals.'

'Our mouths are dry like coal.'

The waiter brought drinks. We were in the coffee shop. He
was a gentle giant of a person. We had three brandies each. The
giant kept them coming.

'On the house, friends.'

'Thank you.'

'Where do you come from, friends?'

'Afar.'

'We have nothing here.'

'Right.'

'Why did you come?'

'We got lost in the storm.' We drank more brandy. It was still
on the house. We said: 'You are very hospitable people.'

The wind pushed the door open.

'I only have that television.'

It was on a shelf facing the tables. It was new.

'Soon every house will have one,' we said.

'Take it.'

'Why?'

'Please.'

A cat walked in, miaowing. We threw a glass of water at her
and she ran away. 'You are crazy,' we told the giant. We left.
Across the street, someone came to his veranda with a crank. It
was a concrete veranda so badly made it sloped from one end to
the other. Its canvas awning was rolled out. The wind was
growing and he had to roll in the awning.

'Come here, friend,' we said over the wind.

'One moment, friends.'

'We need your help.'

'One moment.'

We asked: 'Why didn't you come when we asked you,
friend?'

'I am sorry.'

He stood up and brushed his clothes with his hands, he wiped the blood from his lips and nose.

'Where is everyone?' we asked.

'Home.'

'Go and get them.'

'Yes.'

'Ask them to come here – the children and the old too.'

'Yes.'

'And to leave their doors unlocked.'

'Yes.'

'Do you understand, friend?'

'Yes.'

It was snowing when they came. We were standing under a roof. We had our guns under our arms to shelter them from the snow. The wind had died down. It snowed quietly, like a merry Christmas. We wore our coats, gloves, boots, hats and scarves. It was cold.

'Not all of you are here,' we said.

They looked at each other. Some old people were missing.

'They can't walk.'

'Carry them.'

'What do you want?'

'We are hunters,' we said.

'What do you want?'

The snow had covered their ankles. They stood naked in the square, and it still snowed. The clothes were one big heap behind them. Their clothes were rags and their bodies were withered. We asked them once again: 'Who are you going to tell?'

'No one.'

It was a beautiful snowfall, unlike the storm that had brought us to the village. We stood and watched it for a while, rubbing our gloved hands together. Then some went into the houses.

The snow covered the roofs, the trees, the electricity wires. The air was so thick, our ears felt as if plugged with cotton.

'What are you going to do to us?'

We pushed a barrel to where we stood and lit a fire with their clothes. It warmed us up until it was our turn to go into the houses. The stoves were lit there, the food was cooked, there was wine. Those people were poor, but we still wished we had beds like theirs to lie in every now and then.

'Please, don't,' the mothers cried. 'They're only little girls.'

It was cold outside, but in the houses the fires burned. We were in no hurry. All that time the people stood in the square, covered in snow, shivering, weeping.

Later we said: 'We are going now.'

We loaded the jeep, we drove off. It took us hours to find our way back. Like we said, we were lost. That was how we ended up in the village.

Applied Aeronautics

Nectario was outside the butcher's shop when he took out the bundle of banknotes from his pocket. One, stuck to an old piece of chewing gum, dragged out the lining and sent a handful of coins to the pavement. Nectario looked at them, as if they were pieces on a chequerboard, before bending down to collect them. On the other side of the glass the boy turned and glanced at him while bringing down the cleaver on a leg of veal. The blade cut the bone in two and also took a thin slice off the boy's thumb.

It was mid-December. In the shop window hung a row of plucked turkeys among plastic garlands and coloured bulbs. A sign read: IF YOU THINK OUR TURKEYS ARE SMALL WHY NOT BUY AN OSTRICH THIS CHRISTMAS. When the drizzle started again Nectario hurried into the shop. There were no other customers. The boy was sucking his thumb.

'You have the feathers?' Nectario asked.

'You're a jinx,' the boy replied, examining his thumb.

'Quite the opposite. I've just had a good omen. Seven coins fell from my pocket.'

The boy gave him a blank look. Nectario explained.

'Don't you see? Seven sages, seven wonders of the world—'

'I too had a sign from the cleaver,' interrupted the boy. 'An inch to the left and I could be feeding my thumb to the rats.'

The man bent over the counter and looked at the bleeding finger.

'Just as I thought!' he exclaimed. 'A very long nail. Liable to fall into evil through seeking strange pleasures.'

The boy put the meat on display in the window and wiped his hands on his apron. It was closing time. He cleaned and put away the cleaver, the heavy brass tenderiser and a plumber's hacksaw he had for parting the veal ribcages. Last, he wiped a set of carving knives with black handles and hung them on the wall.

'The boss said today that if business carries on like this, I'll have to get a job as a knife-thrower in the circus.'

'You'll also need a suicidal assistant,' Nectario said.

In the chandlery across the street the lights went off. A moment later its steel shutters came down. While the boy locked up from inside, Nectario put the money on the counter.

'I can always get a job in the slaughterhouse,' said the boy.

'Forget it. People loathe slaughterers.'

'I don't have to tell anyone.'

'It doesn't matter. After a week there, even the whites of your eyes will be red.'

Nectario counted the money again and put a note from the pile back in his pocket. The boy saw him.

'Put that back.'

'Why?'

'Seasonal increase.'

The refrigerator turned itself off the moment the man put the note on the Formica. Outside the coach driver sounded his horn one last time before leaving for the capital.

'I can be a musician,' the boy said, scooping the money into the pocket of his apron without counting it. 'I used to play the xylophone.'

'Oh, yes. In the Royal Brass Band.'

'Exactly.'

He left through the back door and reappeared a minute later with a hemp sack over his shoulder. Even though it was large and seemed full, he carried it without effort. He put it down and grinned: his yellow canines were long and sharp. Nectario looked at them, and at the boy's dark hands and long nails.

'A sack of turkey feathers,' the boy said. 'As agreed.'

'You're turning into a dog,' Nectario said. 'From eating raw meat.'

'I haven't had a cooked meal since my mother left us for an impresario of trapeze tigers.'

Nectario curled his lips. 'Is that a fact?'

'That's what my father wrote in his last letter, before his tanker disappeared in the Bermuda Triangle.' He crossed himself with reverence. 'God rest his soul.'

'Last time you told me you grew up in an orphanage for the offspring of executed villains.'

'That was my blood brother.'

The boy took off his apron and hung it on the door. Nectario picked up the sack and they left through the back door. They had only taken a few steps when it started to rain again and they found shelter under a balcony. Nectario took off his jacket and covered the sack. Left only with his shirt, he was soon shaking from the cold and his teeth rattled like a telegraph transmission. Every time the rain seemed to wane he made false starts, asking the boy to follow him. But the boy remained against the wall, smoking, his hands in his pockets.

'I'd ask you for one,' Nectario said after the fourth attempt to escape the rain, 'but tonight I need clean air in my lungs.' The boy looked at him. 'I also haven't eaten anything for two days,' continued Nectario. 'I have to be light.'

They stayed there watching the rain. When it finally stopped, Nectario's hair was wet and his shirt was stuck to his skin. With his fragile constitution he gave the impression that had he fallen in the torrent of rainwater he would have been carried away like a paper boat. Shaking he put his jacket on, picked up the sack and the two of them set off again.

'Weather reports are as reliable as horoscopes,' the boy said, with his head in his jacket.

'When were you born?'

The boy told him.

'A Scorpio,' said Nectario earnestly. 'Of course. Seeing more of people's deepest motivations than others do, you have a tendency to be cynical.'

The boy lit his last cigarette and threw away the empty pack. As they walked on, the torrent flooded the street and carried the pack off. A street light illuminated the drizzle. 'Interesting,' commented the man, and studied the rain with curiosity. 'It's as if it's raining light bulbs.' Suddenly, he stopped and put down his load. 'Damn!' he remembered. 'We need glue!'

At that time of night it was impossible to find any. The chandlery was closed. They found the kiosk in the train station open, but the closest thing to glue it sold was jars of thyme honey. 'It could work,' said Nectario. 'The problem is that honey attracts insects. We'll use wax instead.'

They remembered the candle-maker. Light was coming from behind the lowered blinds of the workshop, and they knocked at the door. A woman opened and looked at them with surprise.

'We are on our way to a wake,' lied the boy. 'We need candlesticks.'

The woman looked at them suspiciously.

'Who's dying?'

'Anastasio.'

'God bless him. It's because of people like him that we are still in business,' said the woman.

'We have to go,' the boy said. 'In the dark even the widow might fall asleep.'

'Isn't there electricity in the house?'

'Of course.' The boy put his arm around the woman and spoke softly. 'But you see, the deceased had a horrible accident with the harvester.'

'Poor man.'

'And since they couldn't find all the pieces, they switched him with an unclaimed body from the morgue in the capital.'

'Jesus!' exclaimed the woman, and crossed herself.

The boy calmed her down.

'As long as the lights are off even the widow won't be able to tell.'

They bought enough funeral candlesticks and left in a hurry. Because they looked as if they were part of a procession they stopped in the first alley, threw away the mauve fabric bows and tinfoil decorations of the candles, and walked on. At that time only a few villagers were in the pool hall. The pavement slabs had sunk as the ground beneath softened from the rain and a pool of water had formed. Nectario contemplated the situation. Eventually he took off his shoes and socks, rolled up his trousers and waded through it.

'Where are we going?' the boy asked, watching Nectario put his shoes back on.

'You'll see,' replied Nectario. He was silent for a while, and then said: 'Give me your left hand.' The boy did so. Nectario took it in his hands and looked at the palm while they walked. 'Excellent,' he said. 'Your mount of Mercury denotes a great interest in science. I knew you were the right person to help me.'

They were almost there. Once in the churchyard, Nectario put the sack down to catch his breath. Suddenly, a light went on in the small house next to the church and a man in a gown and nightcap appeared in the window.

'Who goes there?'

It was Father Yerasimo. He rested the oil lamp he carried on the sill and put on his glasses.

'It's only us,' Nectario said. 'We felt like praying to St Timotheo before going home.'

'That will be the day,' murmured the priest, recognising them. He was about to go back to bed when he noticed the sack and the candles. 'What are those?'

'Christmas decorations,' explained the boy.

Father Yerasimo looked at them from inside the house for a while, and then closed the window, shaking his head in disapproval. Quietly, Nectario and the boy entered the church and took the steps to the steeple.

The belfry was Nectario's workshop. There was a carpenter's bench, where a hacksaw, a plane and a small mallet lay. The floor underneath was sprinkled with sawdust. Nectario had been working there for months. The boy closed the trapdoor behind them.

'How come no one has found you out?'

'No one comes up here. The bell-ringer has developed a fear of heights,' Nectario said. 'He now rings the bells with a rope from the ground. Pass me the candles.'

Nectario started the fire under a pot and put in the candlesticks. 'If only the priest knew what we were doing,' he said. He then shone a light in a corner of the belfry. Against the wall stood several wooden frames with pieces of patterned fabric stretched over them. 'It's bed linen,' Nectario said. 'Be careful.'

Only when he had assembled everything on the bench did the boy speak: 'It looks like a kite.'

From above, the contraption had the shape of a cross as long as it was wide, with a span twice that of a man's extended arms. The transverse frames were connected to the top end of the vertical frame by steel hinges, and each transverse frame had a handle underneath. A pair of braces was nailed near the top end of the contraption.

'It's the best one I've built so far,' Nectario explained. 'It's based on the anatomy of birds and the early monoplanes.' He touched one of the wings. 'Unlike monoplanes, the wings are not braced to the fuselage. By flapping them up and down I will be able to control elevation. And because I can control them individually, there is no need for a rudder.' He moved the wing and the hinges creaked. 'I used door hinges. A bit heavy, but I compensate by having given up meat for a month.' The boy looked on, biting his lip. 'Those braces were my only pair,' added the man. He pulled up his shirt: his trousers were kept in place by pieces of rope. 'I tested their tensile limit by hanging from the balcony for over an hour.' He patted the boy on the shoulder. 'It is a perfect design. I double-checked my calculations and weighed everything three times.'

He took the pot with the melted wax off the fire. 'However, there is one thing missing,' he said. 'The turkey feathers.' He found the sack they had carried that evening. 'Now,' he instructed. 'Dip their quills in the wax and stick them on to the fabric like this.' He took a feather and, after dipping it into the pot, quickly pressed it on to the taut fabric, so that the feather pointed towards the rear of the machine. 'The feathers will reduce drag,' he said, checking after a moment to see whether it was firmly glued.

'It will take us all night,' protested the boy.

'You'll be paid by the hour.'

They started work. At dawn they sat on the sofa and inspected the flying machine.

'I'm ready to try it.'

'You'd better pay me first,' said the boy.

Nectario fetched his wallet and gave the boy a few notes.

'Keep the change,' he said. 'You did as good a job as any Scorpio would.'

The time had come. Nectario climbed on the window. The belfry was facing the churchyard. It was a rectangular yard, with a row of cypresses around it and islands of geranium pots on its cement floor. Nectario stood on the ledge; the first light showed on the horizon. Behind him the boy rubbed his arms to warm up. After a night of intermittent rain, a clear day was dawning. There was no wind. From the distance came the sound of sheep bells. Lights went on inside houses.

Standing on the ledge with the boy's help, Nectario removed his shoes and tightened the braces of the flying machine over his shoulders. He took hold of the wings and tried their operation. Apart from the creak of their dry hinges, they worked perfectly. 'Remember to oil these later,' he instructed the boy. 'I don't want to be late for my appointment with my destiny.' Then he breathed in and out several times, spread out his arms and leaped forward.

It was the sound of the crash that brought the villagers out that morning. 'Nectario again,' they sighed. 'Get someone to call the doctor.' They removed the broken pieces of wood from his shoulders, they wiped the blood off his face with clean rags, then gave Nectario brandy to drink. While they waited for the doctor, they started piecing together the remains of the flying machine. Scratching their heads, they could not suppress their admiration for its complexity. Then someone pointed out the feathers and they all shook their heads.

'What a fool,' they said with a single voice, and looked at Nectario bleeding on the tiles. 'Didn't he know that turkeys can't fly.'

On the First
Day of Lent

I

The moment he raised his eyes the warden felt as if he had stepped into a ransacked mausoleum. Of the festoons that decorated the walls there only remained a few plaster-of-Paris leaves under several layers of cobweb. From a nail hung a torn geopolitical map whose colours were bleached by the sun; red pins were stuck over certain provincial towns. Behind the desk was a national flag strung not on a proper mast but a coat rack, and on the floor, where it had fallen during the earthquake three years earlier, lay the portrait of the President in a pile of broken glass. Across the room a camp bed with a hollow mattress occupied most of the space, together with a still warm iron stove and a neatly arranged woodpile. The warden closed the glass door behind him and buttoned up his flies. It was the first Monday of Lent. He puffed his cheeks and dried his hands on his trousers.

'Sergeant!' he shouted.

A young man with mournful eyes entered and saluted.

'One washroom towel,' the warden said. 'Absent without leave.'

'The cleaner, warden.'

The warden eyed his subordinate with suspicion. 'The cleaner died three years ago, sergeant. Did she not?'

'Three years and seven months, warden.'

'Well?'

'A new cleaning lady started. Once a week.'

'She should first bring a clean towel before removing the old one.'

'Yes, warden.'

The sergeant saluted again and turned to leave.

'Sergeant.'

'Warden?'

'A brown one – as before. The dirt doesn't show on brown. More hygienic, you see. Understood?'

'It was white, warden.'

The warden dismissed the sergeant with an abrupt gesture. 'Brown. Go.'

For a while he studied the map on the wall. The pins indicated his tour of duty that had culminated in his present appointment many years earlier. Since then his head had lost most of its hair, except for a few grey tufts round the sides like a wreath of dusty laurel, and – at about the same time – his career had lost its steam. The French windows to the balcony were open and a little draught carried in the smell of cooked okra: lunch was being served in the refectory across the courtyard. It was a bright afternoon, but the watchtower's shadow had crept over the office. The warden switched on the lights, sat in his chair and wheeled himself in front of his old Remington. He fed three letterheads with carbon paper in between through the rubber cylinder and lit a cigarette.

He had written little when he started cursing.

'Sergeant!'

The door opened again.

'One oil can,' said the warden. 'Missing in action.'

On his desk were stacks of unfinished paperwork, a rack with rubber stamps, pencils with broken tips, an empty inkpot, a black-and-white photograph of an old couple framed in sterling silver and a fan that scattered sheets on to the floor with every pass. On the wall was a Law School diploma. The sergeant searched the room until he finally found the oil can under a disused roll-top bureau with a stuck shutter. He passed it to his superior and brushed the dust off his knees.

The warden said: 'Dismissed.'

He lost his appetite for work as soon as he had lubricated the typewriter's ratchet. He propelled himself to the other end of his desk and took the black-and-white photograph in his hands. He breathed on the silver frame, polished it with his cuff, then put it back on his desk with reverence and walked out to the balcony. It faced the courtyard of the penitentiary. It was a large unpaved courtyard with buildings on three of its sides, while on the fourth was a brick wall with barbed wire and sharp glass. As soon as he saw him, the sentry on the watchtower threw away his cigarette, slung his gun over his shoulder and stood to attention. On top of his box the flag was not raised – the warden made a mental note to reprimand him later. The refectory was a single-storey building with a tiled roof, a tin chimney and a row of windows without panes. Inside the prisoners sat in rows and ate quietly, while two guards leaned against the door frame with carbines in their arms. Apart from the administration block there were two other buildings in the compound. Those had arched galleries and housed the prison cells. In the hills were the mines of the penitentiary, and not far away passed a railway line which then descended towards the valley. The warden walked in from the balcony. As soon as he dropped into his armchair with a sigh he heard a knock on his door.

'What?' he yelled.

The door opened.

'He is waiting, warden,' said the sergeant.

The warden tried to remember. 'Of course,' he finally said. 'Bring him in.'

The sergeant left and returned with a prisoner. He was a big man with sleeves rolled up above the elbow, and he breathed heavily from the effort of climbing the stairs. He had his hands in his pockets, tattoos on both forearms and in his eyes a permanent expression of mistrust. Behind him the sergeant carried a bouzouki in one hand and a hacksaw with a long rusty blade in the other. The warden took the instrument from him and nodded appreciatively. He walked up and down the office; more than pensive it was a tired and defeated walk – he looked like someone waiting for a delayed bus.

'Are you familiar with the works of Beethoven, Velisario?' he asked.

The prisoner scratched his unshaven cheeks. 'Who?'

'Ludwig van Beethoven. The greatest composer of all times.'

The prisoner shrugged.

'Never mind,' the warden said. 'Let's see what you can do.'

'Do?'

'Play something.'

He handed the bouzouki to the prisoner. The big man hesitated before removing his hands from his pockets and receiving it like a piece of porcelain.

'You have a plectrum?' asked the warden.

'A what?'

'A – forget it. Play.'

Velisario was a bricklayer sentenced to three years for involuntary manslaughter when a chimney he had built collapsed and killed a man during the earthquake: the subsequent investigation had exposed poor workmanship. He strummed the strings with his thumb and the bouzouki produced an artless sound.

'Sorry, warden,' he mumbled. 'Out of practice.'

'Not at all, Velisario; it's the acoustics of your instrument. We need to improve them somehow.'

He snapped his fingers and the sergeant passed him the hacksaw. He then rested the bouzouki on his desk and sawed its body in two. Under the soundboard were hidden several small paper packets.

'Hashish,' the warden confirmed, and ordered: 'Two weeks in isolation.'

The sergeant clicked his heels and the prisoner made a disgruntled sound.

'And no dinner during the same period,' said the warden, augmenting his decision. 'Understood?'

'As you wish, warden,' replied the sergeant, and took the prisoner out.

The warden massaged his eyebrows. He had not trimmed them for some time now. He also had a moustache that disappeared every third month – whereupon he invariably regretted having shaved it off and immediately grew it again. He had tried to compensate for his baldness by growing the hair at his temples and combing it over his smooth patch but the result had embarrassed him. As far as his apparel was concerned, he wore clothes that most often agreed neither with his mourning tie nor with the sobriety of the penitentiary. In winter he wore a grass-green three-piece suit, turquoise silk shirts with button-down collars and handmade boots with square caps, while his bald patch he hid under an astrakhan cap. In summer it was one of his two white linen jackets, a striped shirt, a pair of cream trousers and two-colour suede moccasins. His clothes were always pressed; he did it himself, for that habit gave him the satisfaction of attending upon someone. His outfits had raised many an eyebrow among the guards – the warden had noticed.

The next time his aide came to the door he did not knock. He quietly opened it and looked inside.

'You're pestering me, sergeant,' the warden said. 'Like a gadfly.'

'About the transfer, warden.'

'What transfer?'

The sergeant looked down. 'Mine, warden.'

His superior had not forgotten.

'Right. What about it?'

'Today's the deadline, warden.'

The warden sank into his armchair, and his expression softened to a concerned father's. The young man was standing in the middle of the office. He wore his cap straight, his buttons and boots were polished, and he was even shaved – a daily habit he shared with none of his colleagues. Until the sergeant had applied for a transfer the warden had paid little attention to him. He crumpled the sheets in his typewriter, nervously.

'Why the prison service in the first place, sergeant?'

The sergeant had not yet replied when the warden asked the next question.

'What do you think of life here, son?'

'It's like working on a farm.'

The warden did not react to the impulsive comment; he had grown accustomed to the resignation of his staff. In fact, he had started feeling a little like that himself. That was why he secretly hoped for an appointment at the Ministry. He fed a clean sheet into the typewriter, put on his glasses and started writing the recommendation without thinking.

'A career demands sacrifices, sergeant,' he said without taking his eyes from the typewriter.

'My family needs me, warden.'

'A woman?'

The sergeant blushed. 'No. My father, warden. He's unwell.'

The only sound in the office was coming from the typewriter. Suddenly the young man said, referring to the likelihood of an affair: 'How could I, sir? So far from everywhere . . .'

The warden nodded while typing. 'Of course. So far.'

The shadow of the watchtower moved and the sun shone again in the office. It illuminated the dust that covered the desks, the chairs, the filing cabinets. There were old newspapers under the furniture and traps with stale cheese the mice never touched. A little noise was coming from outside: lunch was over, and the prisoners were out in the courtyard, idling away in groups of two or three, or kicking a deflated football. With his back to them the sentry on the watchtower was smoking. Back in the office the sergeant thought of the day he would be leaving the penitentiary like a hostage contemplating the moment of his release.

'Done.' The warden signed the letter and gave it to the young man. He checked his watch. 'Bring me Aristo in thirty minutes,' he said.

The sergeant saluted and left. The warden followed the smoke on his desk and discovered his cigarette. Next he wheeled himself to the balcony door where the sun wormed its way into his bones. He drew on his cigarette several times before sighing.

'The guards are more desperate to escape this place than the prisoners,' he declared.

He had woken that morning with a sense of sadness after a long, uneasy sleep. On one occasion he had opened his eyes only to see in the dark what he had first thought was his father's ghost, and, even though he had soon realised it was only the coat rack with the national flag, he could not stop shivering; so much so, that he had to light the stove and wrap himself in his aide's tunic he had found in the ante-room. Not long after, and while in a brief but deep sleep, he had heard the siren. Jumping out of bed, he had run to the window in panic and watched the prisoners escape the penitentiary through open gates; with them the guards were also fleeing. Such was the authority of his nightmare that the first thing he did when he truly awakened that morning was to dash to the balcony: the bulletproof gates were in place and shut.

It was mainly caffeine that had caused his endless nightly torments and turned him into a barbiturate addict. Some of the pills he took to treat his insomnia, others in order to prevent his nightmares, and a few simply because he liked their taste.

He had joined the prison service upon his discharge from the army where he had been conscripted after university. Not long after that he had become deputy warden in a reformatory and his talents started showing themselves. He would teach callisthenics every morning come rain (when his aide would stand behind him with the umbrella) or shine, hold Bible readings in the refectory after lunch invariably pointing his damning forefinger at a slumbering youth, and, in the evenings, conduct the prisoners' choir in songs of redemption he had composed himself. Soon his indefatigable efforts had been rewarded. His promotions resembled a journey without a map: he was sent to the posts furthest from the capital, posts none of his colleagues wanted. But no sooner had he settled in a new job than he was ordered to move to another assignment at the opposite end of the country. He had done stints in various correctional facilities, and more recently in a camp for political dissidents which did not feature in his curriculum vitae because the government denied not just its existence but also that of the island it was built on. After all those years his reputation had yet to reach the capital, and the Bronze Cross for Distinguished Services to the Nation had become for the warden, as for many of his dozing colleagues in the prison service, a middle-aged hallucination.

In the courtyard a game of football started among the inmates. Through the balcony railing the warden watched the bare-chested men run the length of the pitch that was marked out with quicklime lines, and a feeling of embarrassment stirred in him as if he were spying through a keyhole. Watching he slowly fell asleep in his leather chair; when he opened his eyes again the yard was empty. Without getting up he swivelled round and as his eyes adapted to the dimness of his office he made out the shape of a standing man.

It was Aristo. He had his thumbs hooked in his pockets, and he was shifting his weight from one leg to the other impatiently.

'Warden,' he greeted him.

'I'll be right there, Aristo.'

The casters of his chair let out a rusty sound as he slowly pushed himself across the wooden floor towards his desk. He did not follow a straight course because he had to avoid the nails coming out of the floorboards.

'Sergeant!' he shouted as soon as he docked behind his desk.

The young man came to the door immediately.

'Cup,' said the warden. 'Land and refuel.'

The sergeant returned a moment later with the coffee pot and filled the empty cup. The warden took a sip, then ordered: 'Dismissed.' He leaned back and examined the prisoner with an expression whose aim was to intimidate. But Aristo showed no sign of distress.

'So,' the warden said. 'Your mother's memorial service.'

Aristo wore trousers that barely reached his ankles and a T-shirt with holes in the armpits (there was no standard uniform in the prison; the inmates wore the clothes they had arrived in or those sent by relatives). He had a short moustache, messy jet hair, a pointing nose, and the whites of his eyes were yellow from jaundice, which gave his stare a sinister intent. Although he had recovered from the hepatitis he had contracted upon his arrival at the penitentiary, he was still kept off the mine shift by order of the warden. He scratched his sideburn and hooked his thumb again on his pocket. He had a strange way of moving the oar-like arms he kept close to his body, like someone confined inside a telephone box. He was drenched with sweat from playing football.

'It is, warden.'

'Tomorrow?'

'Yes.'

'I see.' The warden nodded. 'How long ago did she die?'

'A year, warden.'

'Recent. My condolences.'

'Thank you.'

'How old again?'

'Eighty-one, warden.'

'Eighty-one,' repeated the warden thoughtfully. 'A good age. Your father alive?'

'Never met him,' the prisoner said.

'A shame. I see why you have to be there.'

'Yes, warden.'

'Do you have a woman, Aristo?' the warden asked unexpectedly. He pretended to search for the right words. 'Is there someone out there that makes you maudlin just by thinking of her?'

The prisoner pushed his hands into his pockets nervously. He said: 'No, warden.'

226

'Naturally. Besides, you spend far too much time with us; there's simply no time for that sort of relationship.'

'I guess there isn't.'

Flies circled the steam rising from the coffee cup. While the warden had been asleep the afternoon shift had departed for the mine and the rest of the prisoners had returned to their cells – apart from the cleaning detail. He could hear them scrubbing the mess tins with steel brushes in the refectory, making a noise that resembled the drone of cicadas. The warden said nothing for a while, and looked at the prisoner with an expression that indicated austerity – or defiance.

He said: 'Relationships are very important, Aristo. Don't you think?'

The prisoner replied with a curl of his lip.

'You're wrong, Aristo,' said the warden. 'Look here.' He picked up the framed picture on his desk. 'These are my parents.'

The prisoner gave the photograph an indifferent look.

'Until they died I never felt truly alone. Even when I wouldn't see them for months.'

The warden looked at the photograph in silence: a cross-legged man with a moustache on a wooden chair with a straw seat, and a woman in a headscarf standing behind him and resting her hand on his shoulder. They both stared somewhere high and to their left with an intense and rigid gaze. The warden put the frame back on his desk and checked his watch.

'You will be back by three o'clock tomorrow, Aristo.'

'Of course, warden.'

The warden pleated his lips and gave the prisoner a sharp look.

'Fifteen hundred hours. Tomorrow.'

'Yes, warden.'

'If you haven't entered that gate by one minute past three,' he said pointing somewhere outside the balcony door, 'I'll unleash the dogs, and when they bring you in I'll crush you like a louse. Understood?'

Once more Aristo nodded in agreement.

'Now go. Happy Lent.'

But the prisoner did not move. 'Warden,' he said, 'I have no clothes for the service.'

The warden bit his moustache and sized up the prisoner for what seemed a long time. Suddenly, he jumped up from his seat and walked to a listing wardrobe across the room. He tried to open it but it was locked. Annoyed, he searched the drawers of his desk for the keys and tried them all before admitting defeat.

'Sergeant!' he shouted.

Eventually his subordinate had to break down the wardrobe door with the butt of a shotgun. After removing the broken boards and clearing the sharp splinters, he stood to attention with the shotgun on his side and saluted.

'Very well, sergeant,' said the warden.

Several dark suits hung on the rail. The warden looked at a few without taking them out, before deciding. The cellophane hid a deep blue, cashmere and cotton suit of herringbone twill in perfect condition. He took it down together with its wooden hanger. 'It was my father's,' he explained. The prisoner nodded, and the sergeant watched with silent jealousy. The warden continued. 'He had worn it only once – at his golden wedding.' He ran his fingers along its lapel. 'He died only days after.'

The prisoner asked: 'Is it my size, warden?'

'My father – God rest his soul – was considerably taller than I am. Try it.'

He passed the jacket to the prisoner. It was an exquisite garment but out of fashion, and for that reason it emitted a haunting ambience. The prisoner buttoned it up and stretched his arms: it was short in the sleeves.

'It fits like a glove,' said the warden, and brushed the dust off the shoulders. 'Now the waistcoat and the trousers.'

The prisoner put on those too. The trousers were short as well, but the dead man must have had the belly of a horse. The warden rubbed his chin and found a pair of leather braces in the wardrobe. He also discovered a white cotton shirt and a pair of brown shoes which, after he had stuffed them with several sheets of typing paper, fitted perfectly.

'You can keep everything,' he said. 'But take good care of them. They're family keepsakes.'

'By all means, warden.'

'Go now.'

The prisoner turned to leave, but once again he had to stop at the door.

'Aristo.'

'Warden?'

The warden raised his hand slowly. 'Like a louse, Aristo,' he said calmly and squeezed the tips of his thumb and forefinger together. 'Remember.'

II

When the earthquake had hit the work camp for miscreants, the earth had cracked open to swallow one sentry box (the guard had awoken just in time to run for dear life), sixty yards of the perimeter barbed wire and the water tower, as well as the camp's coop with all the chickens and the armoured jalopy for inmate transport. If only the destruction had stopped there. Ten minutes later the tiled roof of the prisoners' block had caved in and its adobe walls crumbled to dust, while inmates and guards had watched in terror and hugged each other in the middle of the courtyard. The same evening, the chain gang had walked all the way to the penitentiary more than fifteen miles away, whose concrete buildings had weathered the earthquake undamaged.

'Shut up,' the guards escorting the prisoners had repeated during the march. 'It's only an interim solution.'

Three years later miscreants were still brought to the penitentiary where, apart from being kept in a separate block, they were treated no differently from felons: they ate along with everyone else in the refectory, did shifts in the mine, were allowed visitors only once a month and temporary releases were out of the question.

Aristo was serving two years for petty larceny. It was not his first time in prison – he had become involved in crime at an early age with an enthusiasm disproportionate to its returns. He was only eleven when he stole the postman's bicycle, and had neither escaped the long arm of the law – although that first time he was sent home with only a caution – nor, more painfully, his mother's leather belt. Any form of punishment would prove futile. When one night a year later a policeman had surprised him as he was coming out of the church with the miracle-working icon of St Polycarp under one arm and a silver oil lamp under the other, Aristo had mumbled that he was taking them to his mother to cure her sleeplessness. Dragging the boy by the collar, the policeman had not yet climbed the steps to Aristo's veranda when he heard the woman's snoring through the open windows; he turned round at once and carried Aristo to the station where the boy spent the next two days in a cell.

Later Aristo left his home town for the country. But wherever he went he found only villages of whitewashed walls and tiled roofs, with coops put together from sheets of corrugated iron, small vegetable gardens and churches with cracked bells. Those places offered him a pitiful booty of bent candlesticks, shaved sheepskins dyed to resemble leopard hides, brooches made not from sterling silver but burnished aluminium, and strings of plastic pearls.

'I'm not a proper thief, judge,' he would argue whenever brought to court. 'I'm essentially a rag-and-bone man.'

The trivial value of his loot meant that when caught he was always charged merely with a misdemeanour.

The triviality of his successes had in no way curbed his devotion. In a small country where word of mouth travelled faster than a telegram, Aristo had to master the art of disguise. He learned to wear shiny rings and chain necklaces, put on fake gold teeth and smear his face with boot polish to imitate a gypsy; he had an infantry uniform with honorary ribbons on the breast for the days he was a credible Korean veteran; and a barrel organ he had found at a coach depot allowed him to travel as – his favourite identity – an unsuspected itinerant musician.

His most recent victim had been Stella. An improbable spinster who had surrendered to the complacency of chores out of a lack of courage to face the world rather than a sincere preference for solitude, she had been easy to trick out of her jewellery. His loot had surprised even himself: he only had to take a look to realise that those rubies and violet amethysts were true minerals, the heavy bracelets were not electroplated iron but twenty-four-carat gold, and damn his mother if he could not smell the ocean in the white pearls of those interminable strings. It was his best job yet. And he would have walked scot-free if it were not for the priest. Not only had he lost his treasure and been sent to prison, but as soon as he had arrived at the penitentiary he had also contracted hepatitis. For six whole months the scythe of Death hung over his head, and to this day he had still not shaken off jaundice.

The priest's name was Father Yerasimo, he had learned.

Aristo had served eleven months and seven days when he went to see the warden and requested a seventy-two-hour release.

'A what, Aristo?'

'On the strength of good behaviour, warden.'

'I'd sooner play Russian roulette.'

'It's a personal matter of great importance, warden.'

The warden had taken off his glasses. 'And what would that be?'

Aristo had explained about the memorial service. The warden had wiped his glasses with his handkerchief and looked at the lenses against the light as if perusing precious stones. 'I can tell you outright to forget the seventy-two hours, Aristo. But I will consider twenty-four. Go.'

The cell was a converted corridor. There were fifteen beds on either side with very little space in between, pushed against the wall and covered with moth-eaten blankets and pillows without cases. Above each bed were crosses and religious icons, posters of naked women, calendars, the photograph of a girlfriend or a child. The floor was laid with stone-dash which the cleaning detail mopped once a week, the doors at either end of the cell had iron bars, and there were also vertical bars over the windows. Dressed in the borrowed suit and carrying his old clothes over his shoulder, Aristo entered and went straight to his bed where he collapsed with a deep sigh. He started rubbing his neck, his arms and thighs, which were stiff from the football game.

'I feel like after ten hours in the mine,' he announced, even though he had never done any work in the penitentiary on account of his sickness. 'I'm certain my condition is chronic.'

The man in the next bed did not understand. 'That's very

bad, Aristo,' he said, and nodded sympathetically. His name was Manouso. 'Let's hope at least it doesn't linger.'

'My stomach feels as if a snake is moving inside,' Aristo complained next.

'I've stolen some hardtack from the kitchen,' the other suggested.

'Birdfeed,' said Aristo with an expression of distaste. He wore the cashmere suit. He took out a crushed cigarette packet from the pair of old trousers he had over his shoulder, then threw them on the floor. He smoked lying on his back, looking at the ceiling where large pieces of plaster hung like bats among the cobwebs. It was cool and quiet in the cell – it reminded him of a coffee shop when everyone else was having their afternoon rest. The other prisoner sat up. He wore shorts and a soiled vest.

'This is a good one,' he said. 'Do you want to read it when I'm finished, Aristo?'

He had a crumbled comic in his hand. The title read: *Donald Duck and the Hidden Treasure of the Conquistadors*.

'You're wasting your time, Manouso. You should be studying the encyclopaedia instead.'

A leather-bound tome was gathering dust under Aristo's bed. It was a concise world encyclopaedia in a single volume, a present from a Christian society, in the translucent pages of which Aristo had read about hepatitis.

Manouso's ears turned red; he was illiterate but would not admit it.

'You know I would if only I had my glasses, Aristo.' And he swiftly changed the subject. 'What's with the suit, friend?'

Aristo explained it was a present from the warden. He raised his head slightly and looked left and right. 'Where's Velisario?'

'Isolation,' replied the other, solemnly. 'What do you mean a present?'

'Stupid pachyderm,' Aristo said about the absent prisoner. 'How long for?'

'Pachy what?' asked Manouso knitting his brows. 'Two weeks.'

'I told him to try with a violin.'

'But there's more room in a bouzouki, Aristo.'

'A bird in the hand,' said Aristo.

Manouso was disconcerted. 'What bird, Aristo? I said bouzouki.'

Aristo puffed his cheeks. 'Less room, yes, but they wouldn't have found him out if he had used a violin. Violins sound like a throttled chicken even in the hands of virtuosi.'

'Who's Virtuosi?' asked Manouso.

Aristo blew a ring of smoke and watched it rise in the air. 'You wouldn't know him, my friend. He's from Italy.'

The other man took out a string of worry beads and thought about Italy while playing. But his mind was too weak for such a journey. He was a peasant serving one year combined – trespassing and damage of private property – for having cut out the tongue of his neighbour's donkey.

'You had to hear it to believe it, Aristo,' he said, having forgotten already their previous conversation. 'That beast's braying was worse than a bee trapped inside your head.'

Across the cell men dozed in their beds, played cards or read magazines in silence. There was the stench of sweat and unwashed feet.

'At least it's quiet here,' Manouso added. He then reached out and felt the fabric of Aristo's suit with his eyes shut as if stroking a cat – it was that smooth, he thought. 'Excellent,' he said. 'Very excellent.'

He turned the breast inside out to look at the lining; it was made from crimson satin.

'Exactly like the inside of my uncle's coffin,' Manouso said sincerely. 'Red and shiny. Very excellent, Aristo.'

He sat back. Outside the change of guard took place on the watchtower. The relieved watch handed over his bullets, climbed down from the tower and walked across the earthen courtyard towards the guards' mess. As he passed near a crow pecking he kicked the dust and the bird took flight with a cry.

Manouso asked: 'How much, Aristo?'

'Twenty-four hours,' Aristo replied slyly.

Manouso started scratching his back under his vest. The mattresses, the blankets and pillows were infested with lice. No matter how often they fumigated the cells the lice were always there. Manouso brought his hand close to his face and, clenching his teeth, he squeezed the bug caught in his fingertips.

'I can't believe you got leave. No one has ever got leave – not to mention a suit.'

Aristo grinned conceitedly. On the wall above Manouso's bed was a crude cross carved from olive bark. A blue charm against the evil eye was tied on the cross with a piece of fishing line.

'And when are you going, Aristo?'

Manouso was wearing a watch. Aristo caught his wrist, checked the time, then said: 'In an hour.'

Aristo's wall was covered with football posters. There was a line-up in green-and-white strip, several black-and-white photographs of players, a threadbare team scarf nailed diagonally. The decorations gave the impression of a domestic shrine. Aristo searched for his cigarettes.

'When your team plays in the yard the warden is always at the window. He never misses a game,' Manouso said in a low voice. 'I guess he likes football.'

Aristo ignored him. Manouso studied his new shoes, and

shook his head from side to side. 'Twenty-four hours,' he said gloomily. 'First-time offender but not an hour's release for me, because the warden thinks I represent a serious hazard to the public.' He started scratching again and asked casually: 'How old was your mother, Aristo?'

Aristo lit a cigarette and tried to remember what he had told the warden. 'Eighty-three,' he guessed with confidence, wrongly.

It was time to get ready. He put out his cigarette on the floor, and took down a tablecloth drying on the window which he spread over his bed. Then from a shoebox he removed a razor, a lathering brush, a plastic comb and a fresh packet of cigarettes. Watching him Manouso crushed another bug and wiped his fingers on his shorts.

'You're not going to a memorial service,' he whispered meekly.

Aristo stretched his lips to a smile. He had a perfect set, but stained with nicotine. He folded the tablecloth and removed the laces from the old pair of shoes he was leaving behind. He tied the laces together and then round the tablecloth in a double bow.

'Hmm?'

'You're going to get even with that priest.'

Aristo lifted his mattress. A crowd of cockroaches underneath ran rapidly in every direction. He dug his hand into a hole in the mattress and took out a thick roll of banknotes. It was all his savings and he put it in his pocket. He then opened a tin of brilliantine, scooped out an excessive amount and combed his hair back with his fingers, until he could feel it was flat – mirrors were not allowed in the cells. He finished by wiping his oily fingers on his moustache.

'What priest?'

'The priest who sent you here, Aristo.'

Aristo chortled. It was a half-hearted, nervous reaction. He looked all round and said: 'You'll get me into trouble, friend.'

'I worry about you, Aristo.'

'Thank you, friend.'

The other man looked down, embarrassed. 'As long as you don't do anything foolish.'

'You're the fool,' said Aristo. 'With a mouth bigger than a crocodile's.' He put down his bundle. 'Do you know what a crocodile looks like, Manouso?'

Looking at the floor Manouso shrugged and scratched his neck where the lice tormented him.

'Have you ever seen any Tarzan films, Manouso?'

Manouso said that he had.

'Remember the animal that swims in the river?'

Manouso remembered of course. 'In the water,' he said. 'Like . . . a lizard?'

'Yes, a reptile,' Aristo said. His eyes had almost lost their yellow tint now; they were white and invincible. 'An amphibious reptile.'

Manouso nodded. If he knew about something it was about Tarzan films; he had watched them all many times over. While Manouso thought about Tarzan and the crocodile, Aristo stood up, threw the bundle over his shoulder and walked towards the door. Manouso followed him with his eyes.

'And Tarzan knifes one in every episode,' Aristo said in a teacher's voice, and knocked on the bars with his knuckles.

Behind him Manouso shrugged and scratched his neck. His face was red now.

'That is a very excellent suit you're wearing, Aristo,' he finally mumbled as the heavy door opened. 'Very excellent, friend.'

III

Stella, the woman who had lost her life's savings to the itinerant musician, ran a small *pension* less than an hour's drive from the penitentiary. The extension of the coach route had meant that the *pension* was one of the few businesses that delivered a modest profit in a village of otherwise inclement poverty. Furthermore, her vegetable garden doubled her income, which since the death of her parents went almost intact under the mattress because she neither had a husband nor children nor distant relatives. Every other month Stella hung the CLOSED sign on her door and travelled to the capital, where she stayed for two days before coming back with a little treasure in her vinyl handbag. No one knew about it; she had persuaded her fellow villagers that her regular journey was nothing but the fulfilment of one of her mother's vows. The lie went like this: after her husband's death Stella's mother had prayed to join him as soon as possible and without pain, in return for a five-foot wax candle lit in the capital's cathedral six times a year.

'And why do you have to stay overnight?' the villagers had asked Stella, rubbing their chins.

'Because, since I'm in the capital,' she had replied, 'I might as well pay the cinema a visit.'

And because she knew those people did not forget, she always remembered to buy the programme from the cinema near her hotel. She never watched the film: the moving image made her seasick.

It had been only a day before Aristo's afternoon call when Stella had returned from the capital. In her handbag she had a pair of antique earrings whose pendants the jeweller had insisted were the solidified tears of angels, and also, according to her plan of deception, the programme from *Attack of Atomic Spiders from Outer Space* to show her neighbours.

'We live like animals here,' they had sighed, once they had read the film synopsis for the second time. 'Civilisation starts and ends in the capital.'

Posing as the itinerant barrel organist Aristo had stolen those earrings too. He had left the *pension* through her bedroom window, which faced away from the street, and had headed straight for the train station. It was an unfortunate coincidence that Father Yerasimo had also been out that afternoon. Certain that Stella was asleep, he was cutting flowers from her azalea for the vases in the sacristy. With the pair of scissors and the flowers in his hands the priest had looked the thief in the eye and faced an insoluble dilemma: should he raise the alarm and expose at the same time his no matter how trivial impropriety to the same people he struggled to teach the obstinacy of virtue? In the event he decided otherwise, and watched the thief wink at him in silence and walk away.

From Stella's *pension* Aristo had hurried to the train station. At that time of day the only person there was the stationmaster who sat facing the single railway line, dressed in shorts, an unbuttoned shirt that exposed his belly and a pair of rubber flip-flops that belonged to his wife. He was sitting on the bench under the wall clock, in the shadow, his cap and signalling flag next to him, scratching his chest and staring at the distance with eyes glazed over. Aristo approached with his barrel organ under one arm and a bundled tablecloth that hid his loot under the other.

'Good afternoon,' he said.

The stationmaster jumped. 'Who are you?' he asked sharply.

Aristo put down his baggage and pretended a deep sigh, as if he were a wayfarer. 'Give me a ticket for the first train.'

The stationmaster muttered with annoyance for the violation

of his equilibrium. Nevertheless, he dragged his flip-flops towards the ticket office, unhooked a handwritten chart from the wall and sat at the desk.

'Destination,' he demanded wearily.

From the other side of the counter Aristo shrugged. 'The capital?' he suggested.

'County or state?' the railway official queried with annoyance.

Aristo asked the fare for each.

'Single or return?'

It was to be a single journey.

'Compartment or economy?'

Aristo asked for an economy seat. The stationmaster ran his finger across the chart and read out a price on which he had secretly added half a drachma to compensate for his disturbed afternoon. Aristo handed over the contents of his pockets.

'County,' the stationmaster confirmed, having counted the money.

'What time?' Aristo asked.

The stationmaster checked his watch and consulted the timetable.

'17.03,' he announced. 'Estimated. The express via the penitentiary.'

The station clock showed almost quarter to five. Aristo nodded with satisfaction and looked at the road with the blossoming tamarisks he had come from. It was the only route to the village and was empty. The stationmaster returned to the platform, flung his cap at a noisy cicada on the wall he could not reach otherwise, and dropped back on the wooden bench. Soon he was asleep.

Had the train arrived on time Aristo would be sleeping in the best hotels in the capital and not in a flea-ridden bed in the penitentiary. But a whole hour and fifteen minutes had to pass before he would finally hear a whistle and see smoke in the distance. No sooner had he gathered his bundle and slung his organ over his shoulder than he had heard a voice behind his back: 'That's him!'

It had been the damn priest. Once he had arranged the azalea flowers in the vases of the sacristy he had notified the civil guardsman, a nervous corporal armed with a revolver who was now with him. Aristo started walking slowly towards the railway line. If only he could cross before the train arrived, he thought.

'Halt!' shouted the civil guardsman. 'In the name of the Law!'

Aristo made another step, and heard the cocking of the pistol behind his back.

'It's loaded,' the corporal informed him in a quivering voice.

Aristo listened to the steam blasts of the locomotive, still too far away. He let his baggage fall on the platform and turned round with his hands up. The priest hurried to bring the baggage to the guardsman. At the same time the noise of the approaching train awakened the stationmaster. He sat up, surprised, and buttoned up his shirt. 'What's the story?' he asked.

The priest explained that he had chanced upon a burglar while picking camomile; yes, that was the culprit. While the priest talked, the corporal, pointing the revolver at the stranger, searched the tablecloth bundle.

'Well,' he said, fishing out a silver brooch. 'What do we have here?'

'A magpie's loot,' the priest answered animatedly. 'We caught a magpie. What did I tell you, corporal? A little thieving magpie.' He fondled the wattle under his white beard with a triumphant smile and bent down to study the stolen items himself. 'Look what this little bird has gathered,' he said again. 'A real pirate's booty.'

The stranger said: 'They're my woman's.'

'They're his woman's,' repeated the priest, and the corporal grinned with disbelief.

At that moment the train entered the station. As soon as it came to a stop the engineer leaned out of the cab and looked at the men on the platform.

'What's the story, friends?'

'There's enough for a felony here,' said the priest, raising his voice above the noise of the locomotive.

'What's he done?'

'It's a misunderstanding,' Aristo said.

'A felony,' insisted the priest. 'What do you think, corporal?'

'I was taking them to the pawnbroker,' mumbled Aristo. 'They were given to me.'

'Who gave them to you?' asked the train engineer.

'I ask the questions,' said the guardsman.

'Are you going to charge him with a felony, corporal?' asked the priest.

'That's the public prosecutor's business,' explained the corporal. 'I only conduct the arrests.'

'This is enough for a felony, though.'

'I wouldn't be surprised,' the civil guardsman said. 'Don't tamper with the evidence now, Father.'

'I bet my beard he's wanted by the metropolitan police.'

'That wouldn't surprise me.'

'Is he dangerous?' the train engineer asked.

'He's public enemy number one,' replied the priest.

'I wouldn't be surprised if he were,' said the guardsman.

He took out a piece of rope from his pocket. His revolver was still pointed at the stranger, its barrel shaking.

'Tie him up, Father. Tight. He might well be the pension raise I've been dreaming of.'

'Certainly,' the priest said. 'You'd deserve every drachma.'

He hesitated, then asked: 'Do you think it's likely there's a reward, corporal?'

'Is there a reward?' asked the engineer too.

'I wouldn't be surprised if there was one, Father.'

'For assisting the authorities?'

'Yes, Father.'

The priest tied the man's hands behind his back meticulously. 'Because the church is in need, my son.'

'Of course. Thank you, Father,' said the guardsman. 'Now let's get going.'

The sun had set when they knocked on Stella's door. After a hibernating sleep that had continued all through the afternoon and well into the evening, she had awakened cured once and for all of the fiendish nightmares that had been tormenting her for years. She had celebrated the fact with a thorough wash of her carpet-long hair, straightened it and adorned it with a white camellia behind her ear. When she opened her door the priest curled his lip and forgot the reason for their visit.

'*If a woman have long hair, it is a glory to her,*' he recited. '*For her hair is given her for a covering.*' He raised his finger to catechise on the sin of vanity some more.

'We're here to conduct a police inquiry, Father,' the guardsman interrupted him.

The priest said that as far as he was concerned Christian indoctrination was never untimely, but he always complied with the wishes of the secular laws. The corporal thanked him and turned to Stella.

'This is a serious matter,' he began, taking out of his pocket a notebook and pencil. 'A matter of public order. Now. Are you acquainted with the individual in custody?'

She made a positive nod. The corporal licked the tip of his pencil and wrote down. 'Under what circumstances?'

For months after that evening Stella could not explain what

had happened inside her head on her doorstep. For she had had only to look at the stranger with the moustache, the neatly combed hair and the eyes whose whites were more brilliant than a porcelain she had once almost bought, to forgive him unconditionally. She remained silent for some time; she could not come up with a credible lie to save him.

'Well?' the corporal asked.

Suddenly Stella remembered a passage from the synopsis of *A Bullet for the Silent Inspector, Part II: Day of Reckoning*. 'All I can say,' she announced, 'is that he's a haunting memory from my darkest past.'

The priest brought his hand over his mouth and goggled his eyes in a reflex reaction. But the guardsman bit his pencil, and eyed the woman with disbelief.

'I can't write that in the deposition,' he said. 'You need to be more specific.'

Aristo stepped in: 'Tell him you gave me the jewels to pay my gambling debts. Tell him we're together. Tell—'

The corporal slapped him across the face with the notebook to quieten him.

'It is true,' said Stella solemnly.

'This place is Babylon!' the priest shouted, and shook his head in despair. '*Mother of harlots and abominations of the earth.*'

The woman bowed her head as if from the weight of her shame. It only encouraged the priest.

'Even spinsters have made pacts with the Devil!' he said, losing his composure. 'Have· you committed fornication, woman? I demand to know!'

Her silence only confirmed every question he asked her. Finally, the priest shook his head and said contemptuously: 'Soon there won't be enough names in our language to christen all the bastards in this village.'

It was the guardsman's turn, who was sensing the arrival of a headache. The fantasy of a celebrated arrest had evaporated, and with it the chances of a decent pension. He turned to Stella.

'I therefore assume you do not wish to bring charges.'

'Correct.'

Aristo demanded to be released. Disheartened, the corporal put his notebook in his pocket and started untying the rope. But the priest did not intend to give up yet.

'One moment,' he said. 'In the name of God.'

Going down on his knees he rummaged through the stranger's baggage, and soon his obsessive search proved fruitful: under the barrel organ's mechanism he found five apricot compote tins Aristo had stolen from the village chandlery earlier that day.

'Aha!' he exclaimed, beaming with pleasure. 'I bet my sacred stole these aren't canned music, corporal.'

The goods constituted only a misdemeanour, but Aristo was given the maximum sentence of two years' incarceration when the magistrate found out that it had only been eleven months since the defendant's previous arrest.

Father Yerasimo had testified in court; that was how Aristo had discovered his name.

IV

Aristo walked across the football pitch towards the penitentiary gates, trying to take his mind off the events of his arrest; but his memory was like a stray dog which once stroked could not be shaken off. He kicked a stone angrily at one of the empty petrol drums that were the goalposts; the metal made a deep, reverberating sound. Holes were worn in the earthen pitch and stones dug out whose long afternoon shadows looked like rats.

In the deserted courtyard Aristo listened with satisfaction to the creak of his new leather shoes. With the sun behind his back the sentry with the rifle appeared as lean as a flagstaff. When he opened his eyes and saw Aristo he immediately stood to attention – until he realised the man in the blue suit was not the warden, and went back to sleep. Aristo puffed; the formal evening suit was making him hot. He wiped his forehead with the back of his hand, and his hand on his tablecloth bundle.

Suddenly, as he was reaching the halfway line of the football pitch, a sharp pain lanced his liver. He was not surprised – like jaundice it was a legacy from hepatitis; but the attack robbed him of all his optimism. He passed his hand under the cashmere waistcoat and rubbed his hollow abdomen. He walked on, avoiding the holes and the stones while nursing his pain, and before he had crossed the goal line he had forgotten the priest and instead was thinking of the woman. Through the spyglass of his memory he saw Stella in the courtroom, witness for the defence, in a dress with cyclamen made from the pink marquisette of her redundant mosquito canopy. The dress had made the magistrate frown; it was most inappropriate for a court of law; she was not attending the carnival; he could hold her in contempt. The stenographer had smirked; the defence attorney had bitten his lip and objected feebly – he had been overruled.

Sparrows sat on the barbed wire of the perimeter wall, small like clothes pegs. Aristo took from his pocket one of those marquisette cyclamens. He held the creased artificial flower as if he was holding a butterfly and looked at it briefly, with a hint of embarrassment, then put it back. It was enough to restore his determination: he was going to go ahead with his plan.

The French windows to the balcony of the administration building were shut. A motionless shadow could be seen behind the pane: was it the warden or the coat rack? Aristo had reached the gate. A guard sitting on an empty fruit pallet in the shade played with a string of amber beads. He looked at Aristo's brilliantined hair with a sullen expression in his blue eyes, and then indicated the suit with a move of his eyebrows.

'Hey, Great Casanova,' he asked sarcastically, 'where did you find that? Eh?'

Aristo put down his bundle and buttoned up his jacket. His hair shone under the sun and it smelled of roses.

'My property,' he replied.

The guard snorted. 'You, Casanova,' he said slowly, 'can't afford to dress a scarecrow.' He played with his string of beads. 'You'd better not have borrowed it without asking. Did you borrow it? Did you, Casanova?'

Aristo grinned in defiance. 'A present from the warden. You can check with him.'

The blue-eyed guard went silent and his fingers stopped fondling the worry beads. He looked at the prisoner for a moment, enough for his eyes to travel from the fine jacket to the trousers with the sharp crease to the expensive shoes. On the wall behind him was a Bakelite telephone without a dial. He picked up the heavy handset, tapped the hook a couple times and said something. When he put the handset down again his sullen expression had changed to one of enmity.

'Permit,' he demanded.

The official document was in order. It was signed by both the warden and his assistant, it was rubber-stamped at the bottom and over the prisoner's photograph, and the duty stamps were of the correct amount. The guard gave back the permit, but suddenly spat between Aristo's shoes.

'To get one day's furlough I had to break my toe with my rifle butt,' he said. 'You, Casanova, had only to play football with your shirt off.' He licked his lips slyly. 'Or did you have to do something else too? Eh? What else did you have to do, Casanova? Tell me.'

Aristo replied with a contemptuous stare.

The guard knocked at the steel gate. It opened from outside and another guard came and stood across it. He was also a non-commissioned officer but, unlike the other, a recent recruit.

'What is it?' he asked, touching his revolver instinctively.

The blue-eyed guard said: 'Let the gentleman through.'

The second guard looked at the prisoner. 'What for?'

'The gentleman has decided on a holiday.'

'What holiday?'

'The climate here is bad for his health, you see. Look at his eyes.'

'What's wrong with his eyes?'

'Yellow like yolks. Can't you see?'

Aristo looked away with anger. The second guard took a step back.

'Has he got yellow fever?'

'No. Pee for tears.'

'What did you say?'

'Let him out.'

'What did you say? I was told the inmates are never issued leaves.'

'Well, this gentleman is making history.'

'What do you mean? Does he have papers?'

The other nodded affirmatively. 'I've checked them personally.'

'You have exceeded your authority, guard. It's the duty officer's responsibility to validate permits.'

'Let him through, eh?' the other said wearily.

'I'm not letting anyone through without papers,' said the second guard. 'I'm the duty officer.'

The blue-eyed guard snatched the permit from Aristo's hands and gave it to his colleague; he looked at it suspiciously.

'The papers have to be in order,' the second guard addressed the first one, apologetically. 'There's the procedure. Don't you know the procedure?'

He studied the permit in silence. When he was satisfied of its authenticity, he verified the time on his wristwatch, signed the document, returned it and stepped aside for Aristo to exit. He then closed the gate with a loud bang, slid back its heavy bolt and padlocked it.

From behind his window the warden watched until Aristo had disappeared down the path that led to the county road. The penitentiary was built on a low, cinnamon-coloured hill sculpted by the rains to the shape of a snail's shell. The road that passed at the end of the path was paved only recently, but its asphalt and concrete mileposts ended abruptly five miles ahead when the contractor had run out of gravel. From that point onwards the county road was an uneven track of clay dust, slowly flattened by the tyres of the coach to and from the county capital.

The warden leaned against the frame of the French windows and bit his moustache until he could taste the cigarette tar on his whiskers. He wished he could lie in bed and sleep until the following day. His neck was stiff, a gurgling sound was coming from his chest every time he breathed out, and he was hungry. He lit a cigarette. While thinking about Aristo a deep blush crept towards his cheeks, as if someone could hear his thoughts. Suddenly the door opened. The warden dropped his cigarette, startled.

'The inmate has left the compound, warden,' the sergeant reported.

The warden could feel his heart beat against his breastbone. 'Very well,' he mumbled.

The sergeant looked at his superior with curiosity. He said:

'A certain other inmate has requested a brief conference, warden.'

'Who's that?'

'Manouso. A miscreant.'

The warden made an expression of misery: he knew very well the man who had been tirelessly applying for leave since his first day in the penitentiary.

'Later,' he said, and attempted to recover his composure with one of his stock commands: 'Now retreat in orderly fashion, sergeant.'

Only when he heard the bolt click behind him did the warden breathe again. Annoyed for having left, as he believed, the door to his soul ajar, he paced up and down his office without taking his cigarette from his lips. Gradually his heart slowed down under the weight of its recurrent morbidity. The torn map, the flag on the coat rack, the broken portrait of the President on the floor, the heavy typewriter made the warden feel like a shipwrecked captain surrounded by the flotsam of his sunken ship. He could hear his assistant's typewriter in the ante-room. He thought of Aristo again, and other feelings seized him like constrictor snakes: first came self-loathing, then depression. Little by little he fell asleep in his armchair.

That afternoon he experienced his worst ever nightmare. He was visiting the doctor in the nearby village because he had chest pains. Dr Panteleon had asked him to stand behind the fluoroscope, and he had only had to glimpse at the screen to diagnose the problem. 'Your heart is missing, warden,' he had said matter-of-factly. With the help of a mirror the warden had looked at the screen too, and had seen that where his heart should have been a medal was now dangling from a ribbon: the Bronze Cross for Distinguished Services to the Nation.

The warden suddenly woke and rushed to the balcony and vomited over the side. He then drank the rest of his cold coffee, but it did not put out the flames in his mind either. He had no idea how long he had been asleep, but it was still light outside.

'Sergeant!' he shouted.

His assistant entered.

The warden said: 'Manouso.'

'Still waiting. Says it's urgent, warden.'

'Send him in.'

Manouso walked in with a reverent smile, rubbing his hands together: his mood was the complete opposite to the man's behind the desk. The warden sighed.

'Nice afternoon, warden,' said the prisoner amiably. 'First day of Lent.'

The warden sank into his armchair. 'Make it quick. I'm busy.'

The prisoner hesitated. He had yet to say a word when the warden started talking instead.

'My answer is no. I cannot allow a cut-throat to walk the streets until he's realised the full benefits of his just incarceration.'

Manouso immediately dropped his mask of friendly disposition.

'I'm no murderer. It was only a donkey, warden,' he protested. 'And its braying was worse than a bee inside one's head. If you—'

'No.'

The prisoner collapsed on a chair without asking permission; the warden raised an eyebrow but said nothing.

'This place suffocates me, warden,' Manouso said, his eyes filled with tears.

'Good. That's the whole idea.'

Because the French windows were shut Manouso's sweat quickly saturated the air in the room. The stench added to the warden's depression. Pinching his nose he opened the windows and breathed deeply several times, as if he were doing morning exercises. Behind his back Manouso's eyes narrowed.

'This place stinks,' he said with venom. 'Some convicts are not only given permits but also suits.'

The warden turned round; no one had contested his decisions before. He opened his mouth to call the sergeant but realised to his surprise that he was more exhausted than infuriated.

'This conference is over,' he said. Then, almost imploringly: 'Go.'

'I can be of use to you, warden,' the prisoner said earnestly.

'Go – if you have no desire to spend the whole Lent in isolation.'

'But I can save you from embarrassment, warden. You have made a wrong decision.'

'Sergeant!' shouted the warden. 'Alert!'

His aide burst in with a wooden truncheon in hand. Without delay he pushed the prisoner against the wall and held him there.

'He had you fooled, warden!' squeaked Manouso, as the truncheon pressed against his throat. 'It's not a memorial service Aristo is going to.' He swallowed with difficulty. 'But where he's going, warden, it's very likely there'll be a funeral after he's left.'

The coach slowed down with a screech of its brakes. Aristo kept his hand stretched out in a hitchhiker's signal until it came to a stop. His bundle was at his feet. He raised his hands to his collar, instinctively, to fix his tie and only then did he realise that he had forgotten to ask the warden for one. He buttoned down the starched collar with irritation: only peasants wore a formal shirt without a tie. Then he walked up to the open door of the coach and grinned. The conductor returned him a hostile look: the penitentiary was the most likely place the stranger could have come from. Aristo asked for a ticket to the next village. He was told the fare.

It was too expensive for such a short trip, he thought. He would need his savings later.

'You pay more to go on a merry-go-round,' said the conductor.

Aristo appealed for a discount. He said he was a conscript on leave to see his mother but had unfortunately forgotten his documents in the barracks. The conductor sniggered.

'Anyone with such a suit ought to have enough even for a taxi,' he retorted. 'Are you sure its pockets aren't torn and you've dropped your money, friend?'

He pulled the door shut and the driver revved up the engine. Aristo swore at them, but his voice was lost in the noise and the fumes from the torn exhaust. As the coach drove off he stepped into the middle of the road and made an obscene gesture in its direction. Then he looked down and saw that he had stepped into a pothole filled with mud.

He shielded his eyes and surveyed the landscape around him. Not far away he noticed a landfill site where a bulldozer was turning the earth. He saw a little whirlwind start there and come towards him with a hiss, raising the dust and shaking the olive trees of a neat orchard. He closed his eyes until it had passed, leaving behind the smell of rotten garbage. The sign at the coach stop creaked on its post, and a crow with dusty wings landed near it and pecked at a hole. In the distance another vehicle approached.

It was a dump truck. Only the driver was in the cab, while another man was standing in the back holding on to its side. The back shook and banged from the potholes, causing the man almost to fall off, but the driver did not slow down. Aristo saw the truck approach with a feeling of hopeful anticipation. Then the moment he raised his hand to flag it down he heard its engine make a choking noise and die. The truck rolled a few more yards and came to a halt where Aristo stood. The driver jumped out, raised the bonnet and stood staring at the engine and scratching his cheek. Like the man in the back he was dressed in smelly overalls and rubber boots. Aristo came and looked at the engine too. The driver ignored him; both men stood there looking under the bonnet with a vacant expression. The driver lit a cigarette and continued staring, but attempted to touch nothing.

The man in the back leaned over the side. 'What's the problem, boss?'

'It's dead,' the driver said after a while. 'Dead and gone.'

'Dead and gone,' repeated the other. And, satisfied with the diagnosis, he squatted down in the back.

Now, as it happened, not long ago Aristo had read in the penitentiary an illustrated article on car mechanics. He had found it in the concise world encyclopaedia.

'Try the air intake,' he suggested. 'In some models it's narrower than a chicken's throat.'

The driver looked at him sideways. 'A chicken's throat, eh?' he scoffed.

The voice from the back queried, 'Did we run over a chicken, boss?'

'Likely the storm blocked it,' Aristo continued.

The driver looked at the engine with disgust: it was covered in oil and grease.

'Are you sure?' he asked.

'I'd sooner stick my hand in a brazier,' the voice from the back declared. And proposed, lazily: 'Wait. Someone will drive by.'

'Narrow piping is a common problem in older cars,' Aristo explained.

'This one's a dump truck, friend,' said the voice from the back.

'But are you sure it's the pipes?' the driver insisted. 'As night follows day?'

Aristo shrugged. 'It's very likely.'

'Boss, he's not sure,' surmised the voice from the back.

In the end Aristo repaired the damage himself. When he had finished, in addition to his shoes being covered in mud from the pothole earlier on, there was now grease under his fingernails and an oil blotch on the starched cuff of his shirt. But he had earned himself a free ride. He threw the pipe wrench in the back and sat next to the driver with optimism. A crucifix was suspended from the rear-view mirror together with a tin bell.

The driver told Aristo that they were contractors who hauled garbage from the villages to the landfill site.

'Collection, transport, burial,' he explained. 'We offer a full service. A rewarding job sometimes – but mostly boring and tiring.' He sighed. 'All in a day's work.' Aristo's clothes caught his eye. He stretched his hand and fingered the fabric. His soiled fingers left a dirty mark on the waistcoat. 'Cashmere,' he concluded, returning his hand to the steering wheel. 'Expensive?'

Aristo inspected the stain with annoyance.

'It cost a fortune,' he replied.

'And why not?' the driver approved. 'There are no pockets in shrouds.'

Aristo rubbed the stain with his thumb. In vain: it would never go. He gave up. 'It is imperative for a man to have at least one good, well-pressed suit,' he said.

'Naturally. Cleanliness is next to godliness.'

Ahead, a fox was crossing the road. The driver shifted down a gear and sped up. But the truck was so slow that the animal merely gave it a look and carried on at the same leisurely pace, until it vanished into the briars on the other side.

'Damned animal,' the man in the back said through the hatch. 'There goes seven drachma fifty, boss.'

Aristo was intrigued.

'The fox is a pitiless bandit, my friend,' explained the driver. 'The Ministry has put a price on its head.'

Aristo closed his eyes and rested his head against the door. Soon he was dreaming of Stella's jewellery. It had passed through his hands as fleetingly as running water but he could still describe every single piece of it in minute detail: the collection was a little treasure. Aristo smiled in his sleep, and then his mind led him through the rooms of the *pension* to its garden. But no sooner had he stepped out on to the veranda than he saw that the tomatoes, the gourds, every pot of mint and basil, even the grapevine and the palm tree were not real but cut-outs made from pink marquisette. He woke with a haunting tingle, abruptly, and presumed they had arrived. Instead, the truck was pulling in to a coffee shop on the roadside.

'I hope you're not in a hurry, friend,' said the driver.

There was a cemetery not far away, where the weeds had grown thick and tall round the listing wooden crosses. One could easily mistake it for a vineyard, Aristo thought, and jumped out to stretch his legs.

'That's fine,' he let slip. 'No one knows I'm coming.'

V

Resting his elbows on the mahogany counter, the pawnbroker looked at his reflection in its glass while picking his nose with surgical attention. On the other side of the display were trinkets arranged in rows on red velveteen, each with a piece of paper next to it that read, PRICE ON REQUEST. The pawnbroker was bored; no customer had called in for many days and that was the reason he was open this first day of Lent which was normally a public holiday. Still, he was in good spirits because thanks to the carnival he had finally offloaded almost the complete wardrobe he had acquired from the closure of the county theatre. The only items that remained on the rail were a satin Pierrot dress with enormous buttons, its matching pair of bell-bottom trousers and lacquered-silk pointed cap, and, of course, the white Marie Antoinette dress and its unsaleable accessories: the folding corkwood guillotine and the polystyrene head with the spring-operated eject mechanism.

The pawnbroker puffed with contentment. Buying the theatrical costumes had seemed a good idea at the time but, as it had turned out, it almost ruined his business. Several times had he lowered the blinds and locked the door just as the bailiff was arriving at the village with the writ of seizure in his folder. The pawnbroker quivered from the memory. But the carnival had changed all that. He rubbed his hands together and renewed his promise to St Timotheo of a sterling lamp for his altarpiece icon.

Through the door crack a bad smell crept in. The street had been littered with garbage since the morning after the carnival: confetti and paper garlands mixed with dried mud, plastic whistles and broken masks, rotting fruit and the bones of barbecued meat. The villagers had been expecting the refuse truck for over a week, during which a needle-sharp rain had torn down the strings of decorations left hanging. Finally, that morning, the sun had mediated – but it had come all too late. The pawnbroker heard a lorry engine and raised his eyes absent-mindedly. He started. There was a customer in the shop. He removed his finger from his nostril and wiped it on his trousers. Aristo was looking at the Pierrot suit.

'It's silk,' the pawnbroker said. 'Very fine weave, sir. Feel it.'

Aristo did not touch it. He moved on and scrutinised the Marie Antoinette dress.

'Cotton,' Aristo said. 'Are these the only dresses you have?'

'Only a week earlier,' the pawnbroker replied and counted out with his fingers, 'we had one gorilla, one Grim Reaper, two complete suits of armour, a Drac—'

'Are there any real clothes in this junk shop?'

The pawnbroker frowned. 'These are the only ones – but I'll do you a good price.'

The Marie Antoinette was expensive.

Aristo said: 'The carnival isn't for another year.'

'So? A French royal dress never goes out of fashion.'

Aristo rapped his fingers on the counter for a moment. Then he deliberated: 'Wrap it up – but leave out the paraphernalia.'

From the counter the pawnbroker offered a victorious smile and pulled out a sheet of wrapping paper. Aristo wandered round the shop with his hands clasped behind his back, stopping now and then to look at a piece of cheap bric-à-brac. Behind his back the pawnbroker noticed the expensive suit with admiration, and then saw that his customer had a beautiful but also sallow and angular profile like a weathered rock.

'We also stock certified medication,' he said. 'By appointment of the King – before being exiled, of course. In particular, we offer a syrup with edelweiss extract – excellent for contagious diseases. There's only one bottle left. It retails at half a drachma and three-quarters.'

Aristo did not reply. He walked up to a grandfather clock.

'An exquisite timepiece,' the pawnbroker said from the counter; he had trouble wrapping up the baleen stays of the costume. 'It never misses a minute.'

According to the electric clock behind the counter the antique one was almost one hour slow.

'It just came in from abroad,' the pawnbroker improvised. 'It tells Paris time.'

Aristo moved on to a framed collection of pistols.

'In actual fact,' said the pawnbroker cunningly, 'only ten minutes earlier a certain customer expressed an interest in that very clock.'

'Is that a fact?' murmured Aristo inattentively.

'He was standing where you are now. He said he'll be back on Ash Wednesday.'

Aristo froze. 'What day is it?' he asked.

The other man removed the string he was wrapping the dress with from his mouth. 'Monday,' he said matter-of-factly.

Immediately Aristo snapped his fingers. 'It's Lent!' he exclaimed. 'How could've I forgotten!'

'First day of Lent,' confirmed the pawnbroker. 'Yes. We fast until Easter.'

'Damn,' Aristo repeated thoughtfully.

The pawnbroker shrugged. 'It comes round once a year, friend, and it's only forty days. It's not the end of the world.'

Aristo did not move; he seemed as if weighed down by his thoughts. He raised his eyes and they fell again upon the cheap frame with the brass tag that read, HISTORIC HANDGUNS. Under the glass was a flintlock pistol with a broken wooden handle studded with gems, next to it was a rusty revolver without a cock, and the third one was a flat semi-automatic. Aristo smiled.

'That frame would look great on your mantelpiece,' suggested the pawnbroker.

Aristo pointed to the flat pistol.

'It's a Luger,' said the pawnbroker. 'It belonged to the butcher, who used it in the slaughterhouse – of course I've had it decommissioned since.'

'How much for it?'

The pawnbroker collected the mothballs that had fallen from

the Marie Antoinette costume and put them in a glass jar labelled COUGH LOZENGES. Finally he decided.

'I couldn't possibly sell only that one. They come in a set that places them together in their proper historical context, you see.'

'Their historical context,' repeated Aristo, and eyed the shopkeeper with mild irritation.

'Yes.'

Aristo was broke. There was only one way. He said: 'You can have my waistcoat.'

'It's soiled.'

'You can dry-clean it. In any case, it probably cost more than half the junk in here combined.'

The pawnbroker came from behind the counter and touched the garment.

'The material is exquisite,' he admitted. 'But who needs a waistcoat on its own?'

'You can sell it to any card sharp,' suggested Aristo. 'In films they always wear waistcoats but no jackets.'

The pawnbroker thought about it and his mouth watered.

'Not a bad idea, friend,' he said.

Aristo removed his waistcoat, and the other man took down the framed pistols and presented them to his customer. Without warning, Aristo threw the frame to the floor, stepped on it, removed the inoperable Luger from among the shards and hid it in his pocket. Next he picked up the bundle with his personal items, then the enormous parcel that contained the theatrical costume, and went without a goodbye, leaving the door open.

'Happy Lent,' said the pawnbroker behind him on his way to fetch the broom. 'And remember: the fast lasts only forty days. A grown man ought to stand it; it's good for one's soul.'

A motorcycle was set against the front wall of the civil guard station. Both tyres were flat, the headlight hung down from its electric wires and the exhaust was ripped. A man in uniform squatted in front of it with a toolbox next to him. Even though he had his back to the street Aristo recognised him instantly: he was the corporal who had arrested him almost a year earlier. A bitter taste reached his palate; he raised the manila-paper packet that contained the theatrical costume to his shoulder and hid his face behind it. Only a moment later the corporal turned round.

'Careful, friend!' he shouted from the other side of the road. 'You're about to trip over.'

In the middle of the street lay a torn bass drum left behind by the brass band that had played without stop all through the carnival Sunday. Aristo waved his thanks, walked round it and quickly disappeared into the shadows of the first alley. Still looking behind his back, he headed for the *pension*.

The day was losing its light. In the *pension* Stella collected the bedding airing on the windowsills. She folded the sheets and bedspreads, then plumped up the pillows chilled by the evening wind and finally closed the windows. In the rooms the mattresses lay bare on the bedsteads. They were old and hollow, each with several holes in their striped fabric, from where coarse grey wool came out. Whistling, Stella made the beds. At the kitchen sink she worked the handpump and filled the coffee pot and a large kettle. The jars with coffee and sugar were next to the stove, on either side of a flaking tin of Ceylon tea. The matchbox was empty; Stella stood on her heels and reached for the wholesale pack on top of the cupboard. Waiting for the kettle to boil she drank two cups of coffee, put her cup upside down on to its saucer to read the dregs later, and poured the fava beans into a bowl and let them soak. She performed her domestic tasks with pleasure. A fly landed on a strip of flypaper that hung from the ceiling. Stella watched the insect's struggle with fascination, while trimming her hangnails, and then it was time to tame her mane into a tight bun and wrap it in a towel the size of a blanket. In the bathroom there was merely enough space for the basin, the toilet bowl, the tin washtub and the plastic watering can. Suddenly, while she was showering with the watering can, there was a knock on the door.

No sooner did Stella see Aristo's face than the towel wrapped round her head slipped off and her flushed face was instantly covered with raven waves of hair. Aristo cleared his throat.

'Please let me sit down,' he said. 'My feet have more blisters than the moon.'

Through the open door the *pension* filled with flies. Still dripping lather under her wet dress Stella picked up the swatter; her hand was trembling.

'Have you noticed how flies never seem to go out the way they come in?' she said with equal awkwardness.

Several minutes passed while she chased flies and before it occurred to her to let him in. Aristo collapsed on a chair and laid his packet under the kitchen table.

'You're wearing a suit,' Stella said.

Aristo stretched his arms shyly. 'It's short.'

He sighed mechanically and looked around the room. Flies whizzed above his head and flew straight on to the flypaper. Stella spoke up.

'Men are taller these days,' she mused.

Another silence ensued. It was several minutes later when she noticed the paper packet under her table. Aristo caught her looking at it.

'It's for you,' he said.

The Marie Antoinette costume smelled of naphthalene.

'For me?' Stella asked, and touched it without lifting it up.

Then Aristo took a deep breath and said it.

'You can't marry without a wedding dress.'

Ever since Aristo's arrest Stella had lived with the memories of his trial and his Christmas card. It was the card he had proposed to her with, and to which she had replied with a single word: *Yes.*

'But it's Lent,' she mumbled.

Aristo's ears turned red, and he nodded. He had managed to get a suit for himself and a white dress for the bride, and Stella could provide rings from her jewellery box, but in his excitement he had forgotten that weddings were not performed during the fasting season. He had finally remembered in the pawnshop. It had been a difficult moment; Aristo knew it would be impossible to get another leave from the penitentiary, and the wedding would have to be delayed until after his release. But he could not possibly wait that long; in the pawnshop he had found the solution. With a mischievous grin he removed the pistol from his pocket. Stella took a step back.

'Don't worry,' he said. 'It's even less lethal than a feather duster.'

But Stella refused to touch it.

'Women,' Aristo sighed with a masculine air. 'They're even afraid of shadows.'

He finally persuaded her, and Stella went to the garden to make herself a bouquet from the gardenias.

Not far away, Father Yerasimo parted the shade at his window and observed the pair of men shovelling the garbage into the dump truck. The torn, filthy carnival decorations reminded him of the story from Exodus about Moses and the golden calf.

'*These pagans have sinned a great sin,*' he recited, '*and have made them gods of gold.*'

Over the previous week his mood had gradually recovered from the abysmal despair induced by the pagan celebrations of the carnival to a good humour due to the approaching Passion, when his spiritual faculties would be deployed into that most important of the annual Christian observances. Such was his buoyancy that it was not until the third time the brass knocker chipped his door that he finally noticed it.

'Hallowed be Thy name!' he exclaimed with an electric reaction as soon as he opened up. 'The . . . the . . .'

'The magpie,' completed Aristo.

Stella was behind him, dressed in the flamboyant white dress, and her face was as determined as Aristo's.

'Come to the church, priest,' Aristo said. 'You're blessing a marriage today.'

Father Yerasimo let out a nervous chuckle. 'You're both out of your mind,' he said. 'Lent is a time for fasting and penance. Not sexual union.'

'But he was granted a leave so we could get married,' explained Stella. 'It's our only chance or we'll have to wait for another year.'

The priest shook his head in refusal.

'He's even borrowed a fine suit, Father,' she pleaded.

'First, you will have to complete your punishment,' Father Yerasimo addressed Aristo with austerity. 'Then, confess your sins and take up catechism. And a couple of years after that I might think about it.'

It was the right moment for Aristo to demonstrate the persuasive skills of the pistol. Father Yerasimo looked at the barrel of the Luger. Believing in the afterlife is one thing, he thought. Rushing to it, another.

'Let me get my stole, son,' he said with craftiness, walking towards the bedroom where he hoped to escape through the window. 'We have to do this properly.'

His plan was too obvious to work on a professional swindler; Aristo raised the pistol. 'Open that door, priest,' he said with a convincing threat, 'and I promise you it'll lead you straight to Heaven.'

★

Five shadows stirred behind the plane tree. One was the corporal's and the others belonged to the men who made up the prison party: the warden, the sergeant, Manouso and the blue-eyed guard who carried a sub-machine gun in mint condition. After taking the party to Father Yerasimo's house the corporal had brought them to the church where they had finally tracked Aristo down.

'He's armed!' the sergeant uttered. 'Take cover!'

The men ducked behind the enormous trunk. The guard with the sub-machine gun hooked his finger in the trigger nervously. He said: 'Forget that Bronze Cross now, warden. Most likely to nail you on a wooden one.'

'Guard,' the sergeant reprimanded him.

'He signed the permit, didn't he?'

Aristo stood at the church door. In his hand he held the pistol with an air of insolence. Tangling with the plane leaves, a swarm of sparrows chirped. The men underneath held their breath.

'Warden?' the sergeant asked for orders.

His superior signalled him to be quiet. But then Stella appeared at the threshold of the church: the warden felt like a husband returning home to find a stranger wearing his pyjamas.

'A . . . a woman,' he muttered.

'What is she in a carnival suit for?' the blue-eyed guard asked.

The warden felt a sharp pain in his chest. 'It's her . . . like a wedding dress. She's . . . his bride.'

'In a minute she'll be his widow,' the guard said, raising his gun.

'We should offer him the chance to surrender,' suggested the sergeant.

'What for?' the guard whispered. 'He won't. He's done the priest in, remember?'

The sergeant wiped the sweat off his forehead with the back

of his hand, and tried to maintain his sanity. 'We don't know that.'

At the entrance to the church Aristo kissed Stella. The sun was setting and her white theatrical costume had turned a honey-like colour.

The warden mumbled: 'He's not in love ... with that woman. He isn't.' The pain in his chest increased.

'Why doesn't Father Yerasimo come out?' the corporal asked.

They could not have known that the priest had locked himself in the sacristy after the ceremony.

'Oh, he did him in all right,' Manouso said authoritatively. 'I can tell from his face.'

The guard raised his head above the low stone wall that ran round the trunk of the plane tree. 'Look at that pee-coloured face,' he said. 'He's almost laughing.'

'Where's Father Yerasimo?' asked the corporal again.

The warden lowered his head and shut the others out of his thoughts. He whispered with a sense of self-pity: 'I even gave him my father's suit.' The pain in his chest felt as if his heart was being torn out and he immediately recalled his medical dream earlier that day. He raised his eyes again. 'Where's my waistcoat?' he wondered in a daze. 'He's lost my father's waistcoat — or sold it.'

'We should wait,' the sergeant insisted.

'What for?' asked the guard with the sub-machine gun. 'We don't want to lose the element of surprise.'

'Poor Father Yerasimo,' mused the corporal. 'He wasn't all that bad.'

'Warden?' asked the sergeant.

'A little tap on this trigger and the Great Casanova will have more holes than all the cheese in Switzerland,' the guard said with bravado.

'Quieter,' whispered Manouso. 'We'll lose the element of surprise.'

The guard took another look from behind the tree. 'He has no waistcoat and no tie. A true gentleman ought to wear at least a tie at his wedding.'

'What?' asked the sergeant.

'But the judge will surely give him a fine necktie to go with the suit,' the blue-eyed guard added. 'Made of hemp.'

'A hemp necktie?' Manouso asked, and scratched his head. 'Of course.' He chuckled. 'Hemp necktie! Ho ho. It's the—'

'Shut up,' the sergeant ordered.

'It's true,' the guard defended the prisoner. 'There's a stiff noose awaiting Mr Casanova whether he gives himself up or not.'

'Warden?' asked the sergeant again.

But the warden remained silent.

The blue-eyed guard pushed his cap higher and took aim. 'On your signal, warden,' he whispered and licked his lips.

The corporal plugged his ears with trembling fingers. Taking Stella by the hand, Aristo started slowly across the square. In his other hand he carried the empty pistol.

'Let him have it,' Manouso hissed.

'Warden?' asked the sergeant with urgency.

'They're coming right at us,' whispered the corporal.

The sergeant took his revolver from its holster. 'Warden?'

He turned and looked at his superior: he saw him on his knees, his head buried in his hands, drowning in a pool of tears. The sergeant laid his hand on the warden's shoulder with embarrassment. The blue-eyed guard fixed Aristo in his sight.

'On your signal, warden,' he almost pleaded with a trembling, impatient voice. 'He'll spot us soon.'

But again he received no order. Across the square Aristo was coming towards them at a slow, untroubled pace. He wore a marquisette flower in his buttonhole, and he still insisted on waving the pistol. The guard turned and looked at the warden with puzzlement.

'Sergeant?' he asked in desperation.

'Let him have it,' Manouso answered instead.

The Legend
of Atlantis

T he meeting ended with a thump of the prefect's fist on the conference table; it overturned the crystal decanter and the sherry lees spilled over the polished surface, the official memoranda and the surveyor's maps, before the blood-coloured liquor trickled towards a tie that lay on the varnished surface like a coiled snake (it was blue, silk, with yellow stripes arranged diagonally, and the prefect had removed it from around his neck an hour earlier when the meeting was reaching one of its operatic climaxes).

'It was my favourite,' the prefect mourned, as the silk soaked up the sherry. He regained his composure, stood up and hissed with clenched teeth: 'Morons . . . You'll pay for this.'

At the other side of the rectangular table the three members of the village delegation received the adjournment of the emergency audience with a miserable expression: they had failed irrevocably. Their sherry-stained petition with the signatures of all the villagers was thrown into the wastebasket, and their gifts of a demijohn of home-made brandy and a hard dry cheese the size of a tractor wheel were returned without even being tried. Then the secretary opened the door and bowed in the direction of his boss. Leaving the room that smelled of sweat the prefect turned and delivered his Parthian shot:

'You have seven days. Exactly.'

And before the three villagers had even put on their caps, he and his attendants disappeared in the catacombs that were the corridors of the county hall.

'Turd,' said the chandler.

His comment reverberated in the empty room. On the wall was a row of framed and labelled posters that showed the grandest public works built by the present government: a narrow asphalt motorway passing through a dynamited gorge, a concrete bridge reaching across a dry riverbed, a provincial airfield where a portable cabin with flowerpots outside was its terminus. Last among the posters was an empty frame simply labelled, HYDROELECTRIC DAM. The stationmaster, one of the village delegates, looked at it with the eyes of someone coming across the portrait of a late relative.

He sighed. 'It is over, friends. In a week we'll be living worse than the gypsies.'

His companions nodded their heads under a circle of buzzing flies that had smelled their cheese. Outside the traffic sent clouds of fumes through the open window, while the sound of revving buses made the steel blinds rattle. The three men paced round the enormous conference table with their hands clasped behind their backs: they were dreading the moment they would arrive home and announce the news to their fellow villagers.

They had not volunteered for the task. When everyone had signed the petition – including the dead in the cemetery for whom their surviving descendants had acted as proxy – every man wrote his name on a little card and put it in an empty feta barrel which was twirled well before Father Yerasimo drew the three lots.

'Turd,' the chandler had muttered. 'Steamy donkey turd.'

'Hell,' the stationmaster had said. 'Hell and fallen angels.'

'Bitch,' the taverner had grumbled. 'Mongrel bitch with dry teats.'

The rest of the men had sighed with relief.

'Silence, blasphemers,' Father Yerasimo had told the three delegates appointed by chance. 'Bear your cross like our Saviour.'

And so they had gone to the county town – taking with them the cheese and the brandy, peace offerings to the mercurial county prefect. Pacing round the conference table the three men now remembered the day many years earlier when the government surveyors had come to the village to announce the construction of the dam across the entrance to the valley. At first the villagers had misunderstood.

'It'd be good for business,' the taverner had said. 'All those tourists coming to photograph the dam.'

The surveyors had guffawed. 'That is correct,' they had said. 'The only problem is that by then your village will have met the fate of Atlantis.'

However, for years after the only reminder of that haunting encounter was a steel sign that read, HYDROELECTRIC DAM SITE – CONSTRUCTION IMMINENT. Little by little the rains stripped off the paint, the metal started rusting, and the bare sign seemed even more pitiful after being perforated by the thick shot from the villagers' guns. Then, when everyone in the village had forgotten about the dam, the bulldozers had arrived.

It took two years to build it and then the engineers had started the construction of the hydroelectric plant. For the past eight months they had also been working on diverting the waters from two rivers into the valley. The contractor was a German firm.

'At six hundred hours on Friday the engineers will blast the dykes and inundate the valley,' the prefect had delivered his Caesarean ultimatum. 'In accordance with the project timetable. And you are warned for the last time.'

The stubbornness of the villagers meant that they now had only a week to relocate to the designated area in the middle of a vast and arid land more than a hundred miles away. Their efforts to be granted a better location and brick houses rather than the canvas army tents of the temporary encampment had yielded only nebulous promises – it was imperative that the project was completed before the announcement of the general election. No matter how many times the three delegates circled the conference table their mood did not change.

'It's starvation,' said the taverner. 'Pure and simple. Without good earth the village is doomed.'

The stationmaster shrugged. His uniform was brushed and ironed and its buttons sewn on. His cap was stuffed with newspapers to recover its shape and its badge shone after having been immersed for twenty minutes in boiling vinegar the previous evening. His wife had spared no effort to confer decency on her husband on that most important mission.

He said: 'The farmers will be indemnified, of course . . .'

The taverner dismissed the other man's optimism.

'Indemnification is like trading one's stove for a roast sheep. One eats well for a while, but sooner or later the meat runs out. And where would one cook one's beans then?'

'You are correct,' the stationmaster replied. 'But at least the farmers will get some square meals. Whereas my early retirement means a reduced pension . . . Or, in your terms, taking the stove to give me not meat but a bag of beans to start with.'

The taverner puffed his cheeks.

'If only the mayor were alive,' he contemplated.

The three comrades nodded with mutual and unbearable melancholy: the world had become a vast sea of injustice in which their village floated like a slowly disintegrating raft. Increasingly the air in the conference room was infused with the smell of garbage. The chandler walked to the window. His eyes wandered across the concrete landscape. A refuse lorry was making its way up the street, stopping for the dustmen to collect bins from the pavement. Suddenly the chandler goggled.

'The Germans,' he lamented, 'are taking over our country.'

Across the street, where once was a colleague's shop, he had seen that the signboard read, DELICATESSEN. He immediately backed away from the window, imagining that inside the shop a man with a handlebar moustache, a starched apron and a spiked helmet was standing at the counter slicing a leg of ham with a conqueror's smile. The thought enhanced his depression. In a corner of the conference room was a bucket of sand for putting out cigarettes; no sooner had the chandler spat in it than he resented the triviality of his politeness in the adverse circumstances. He kicked the brass bucket with disgust and it rolled across the room, spilling sand and cigarette ends. The stationmaster checked his watch.

'We have a coach to catch,' he suggested wearily.

They were outside the room when the taverner returned in a hurry, and from the conference table he picked up the prefect's tie and shoved it in his pocket with a sly smile. Then the three delegates walked across the long corridors of authority, down the spiral marble staircase and, leaving behind the cool darkness of the tiled foyer with its wooden benches, stepped into the boisterous sunshine of a September afternoon in the county town.

In the coach they maintained a grieving silence. They had taken over the last row of seats, and throughout the return journey they passed the cheese and the knife to each other with assembly-line frequency and took turns at the demijohn. In between they would glance out of the window. On the flat roofs of concrete two-storey houses billboards rose above the forests of television aerials, while from the railings of the balconies underneath hung clothes to dry. When the coach reached the town border they saw the construction sites, where graders levelled the earth of stripped olive groves whose trees now lay along the side of the motorway. Dump trucks loaded with sand and gravel overtook the coach and raised the dust off the tarmac; the conductor instructed the passengers to shut the windows. The coach slowly drove on, and for a long time the three men could see nothing but endless lines of uprooted trees awaiting transport – until finally the glass misted over from the vapour of their sweat. Progress was advancing across the country like an occupying army. The three appointed delegates drank more brandy.

They had finished the cheese when the coach entered the village, and they quickly swigged down the last drops of brandy. Outside the coffee shop the whole village had been waiting for more than two hours. Immediately they heard the horn they sprang to their feet. In contrast, the delegates themselves were too drunk to stand; they asked for chairs to be brought from the coffee shop before they retired in turn behind the plane tree to urinate, and then sat down under the shade in the middle of the square and asked for cold water to drink. Only after having three glasses each did they break the news.

At first the crowd showed no emotion. But their feelings were in such a precarious balance that it only took one person to start crying for the rest to follow suit, and soon the square was flooded with tears. The sobs of the people were taken up by the dogs and their whining was carried across the village and scared the sheep. The sun was going down when the wailing finally dried up. It was then that the houses started bleeding. From the balconies, the verandas, the windowsills a red fluid trickled down the whitewash as if an old wound had reopened – only in the crumbling town hall with its balcony decapitated by the earthquake and the boarded-up shutters did nothing appear to happen.

It was not blood of course, but a ceremonial libation: in their desperation the villagers had remembered the customs of old.

'You are wasting your wine,' said Father Yerasimo, raising his voice. 'Your pagan gods can't help you now.'

The crowd almost ignored him. But they did drink some of the wine before pouring the rest over their walls, and they did not stop until the plaster was the colour of blood. When they finished there was so much alcohol everywhere that one could get drunk simply by sniffing the air. Also, because it was now twilight, the entire village seemed as if it had descended into Hell. It was time to start laying the blame.

'My mynah would've done a better job representing us,' the barber said, wiping his tears.

The chandler hiccuped from so much brandy and wine.

'There was nothing more anyone could have told them, friend.'

The taverner belched and, recalling the speech the prefect had given them that afternoon, backed his comrade: 'It's a matter of national policy.'

'Exactly,' added the chandler, and quoted from the same speech: 'The hydroelectric plant is a spoke in the wheel of progress.'

Zacharias the lawyer rubbed his chin. 'But how can they flood the valley when the train is still running?' he asked.

The stationmaster shifted on his chair nervously.

'In actual fact, lawyer,' he said, 'train services have been suspended since last week.'

'The day before yesterday you told me I'd just missed the express!' uttered the barber. 'After selling me a ticket.'

The stationmaster was now shamefaced. His wife came and stood next to him and took his hand in hers.

'One has to make a living, friend,' the stationmaster apologised. 'The truth is that our station has been redundant for some time. The diesel locomotive does not need to stop to take on water every half an hour – unlike that old kettle on wheels.'

'But how are we supposed to travel?'

'By coach. Under the plans for express transportation the size of our village did not justify its own station.'

There was silence. The stationmaster removed his cap and while he emptied out the folded newspapers his wife caressed his balding head with affection.

'This is all academic now, of course . . .' he added, and puffed with helplessness before turning to the coffee-shop proprietor. 'Bring me a cup, please. Coffee, two spoons, lots of sugar.'

Standing at the gas stove and thinking about progress, Whale instead put four spoonfuls of coffee in the pewter pot. He returned with the tray.

He said: 'The stationmaster is right. It'd be easier to stop a steamroller with bare hands than fight progress.'

The stationmaster tried his coffee, and spat it out immediately.

'Even Whale has got it,' he said. 'It's no use talking about it any more.'

They had all barely bowed their heads to his words of surrender when Maroula the seamstress walked into the middle of the gathering. She swallowed such a big mouthful of air that she appeared to increase in size. 'There was nothing for me to talk about in the first place,' she announced. 'Because I'm going to go nowhere.'

Not only was her only treasure a pedal-operated sewing

machine whose leather drive-belt was about to snap, but also she was an orphan who had failed to trace her parents: there was neither a fortune to be lost nor one person in the world to miss her.

'We should stand our ground until they build us a proper village,' Maroula added. 'With brick houses and arable land.'

It did not take long for everyone to be in agreement – the first time in the village's history. And before the stars had come out the stationmaster had already telegraphed their decision to the county town, and – in anticipation of the prefect's answer the following morning no doubt – the villagers returned to their homes under the influence of a warm and heavily alcoholic breeze.

'Everyone out!'

They could not see who was talking but the authority of the voices was enough to force them out of their beds and into the street in their nightdresses. Dawn was only just beginning and the night was still in the air and there was dew on the leaves. Rubbing their arms over their patched-up nightdresses the villagers stood, shifting their weight from one leg to the other: they were barefooted and the cobblestones were cold. The smaller children cried. Then, when their eyes became used to the light, they saw they were surrounded by a squad of civil guardsmen carrying truncheons. After lining up the villagers in rows the guardsmen stood aside and an officer appeared, dressed in fatigues. At first the villagers could not see his face, as it was hidden behind a large handkerchief. But once he had blown his nose and put the handkerchief in his pocket they saw that he was a feverish major with a shoe-brush moustache and sleepy eyes. Sniffing repeatedly, he walked up and down the line-up.

'So, here are our rebels,' he said. 'And what a fine gang it is.'

He stopped to attack his runny nose again with his

handkerchief. 'Quite a ruthless lot!' he exclaimed with the voice of someone pinching his nostrils.

In the hills across the valley that was soon to become a lake the sun was about to rise.

'Poets think there're only a handful of moments more glorious than a sunrise,' the major said. With a loud noise he summoned the phlegm in his throat and spat it to the ground. 'Me, I'd rather stay in bed.'

The villagers looked at him with a defenceless, embarrassed expression. Some of the men were only in vests and long johns.

'Because, as the proverb goes, sleeping is as good as eating, friends,' continued the major. He paused to admire the diamond of the sun as it emerged from behind the hillcrest, then said: 'I detest going hungry.' And, without taking his sleepy eyes from the hills, he raised his arm in a signal. 'Load that herd of sheep into the trucks,' he ordered.

The journey, which lasted for three hours, felt to the villagers like the route to Calvary. At first they drove on the motorway, but soon they turned on to a dust road that carved its way across a quiet, yellow plain that had once been cultivated fields but had been abandoned when the earth was exhausted. They drove past the windmills of dry water pumps where crows had made their nests, and past abandoned farmhouses that stood with their doors open. Later, they reached their destination. The encampment was set in a hollow depression. Green tents were pitched in round rows outwards from an open area in the centre, and up the sandy hillocks in the fashion of an ancient amphitheatre. In the centre of the camp, canned food and jerrycans of water were stacked under a stretched tarpaulin, together with an army radio telegraph.

'Home sweet home,' the major said. He explained: 'The wireless is to be used by its authorised operator only. Where is he?'

The stationmaster came forward with his cap in his hands.

'Good. The prefect sends his warmest wishes. He wants you to know that work has already started to canalise water from the dam into your fields. It should not take long; after all, the site of your settlement has been carefully selected by the surveyors for its favourable geological features.'

The major checked his watch, spat more phlegm to the ground, and climbed back into the truck.

'Also, it cost next to nothing to expropriate.'

For the rest of the day the trucks travelled back and forth between the village and the camp carrying everyone's belongings and animals. The operation continued into the evening under lights powered by a diesel generator, and when it ended the settlement resembled a flea market. There were chintz curtains still on their railings and chamber pots the guardsmen had not bothered to empty, portraits which had been mixed up in the trucks and no one could tell whose grandfathers those moustachioed men were, and icon lamps broken during transport. There were stacks of mattresses ten feet high, chiffoniers missing drawers and censers that filled the air with the smoke of olibanum. And there were also the animals: chickens that from their fear had laid eggs without shells, a cage where two cocks had been locked together by mistake and were giving each other deadly pecks – a group of guardsmen watched and betted on them – turkeys wandering free among the dusty furniture, dogs sleeping in enamel bathtubs and rats coming out of cupboards.

Only when the trucks with the civil guardsmen had gone away and the clamour of arguments about the ownership of things subsided, was the full weight of their misfortune felt by the villagers: they were nothing but a band of unwanted refugees. It was only then that they felt shame for the way they had treated the gypsies passing through the village over the years. But even more so they felt shame for themselves, when they considered the pettiness of arguing among themselves since time immemorial. And that in turn made them feel a loneliness like that of seafarers stranded on an island that is not on any map. It was with those things in mind that it happened. In an agreement of crying eyes that needed no vocal affirmation the villagers washed off the dust that was making them look like eerie sleepwalkers, changed from their nightgowns, pyjamas, camisoles and long underpants to clean and decent clothes, and within hours of the civil guardsmen's departure they started back in the direction of the village.

Their march lasted six days. They arrived home exhausted, carrying what they could from the camp, and were followed by an endless and motley herd of loud sheep, dogs, poultry and calves.

'Tomorrow we'll vote for another delegation,' the people agreed, before retiring to their empty homes.

That night they slept better than ever because their sense of pride was their bedfellow, and they had that little understanding they had managed about themselves. They slept for many hours, exhausted from the odyssey of their journey, some breathing with loud wolf-like howls and others hissing not unlike snakes, until at dawn they suddenly awoke to the sound of thunder – but they thought they had dreamed it because the sky was as clear and blue as a September sea.

They went back to sleep only to hear some time later the dogs yelp and bite their ropes, the donkeys neigh, the horses trample their hoofs, the hens cackle as if a fox had sneaked into the coop. They had forgotten what day it was. The men had merely managed to put on their boots and the women take the babies in their arms when the tide reached the village, carrying on its crest wooden sheds and goat pens, while caught in its torrent were the stones of the ancient aqueduct, several miles of lethal barbed wire and the watchtower of the abandoned penitentiary.

Under the covers Father Yerasimo turned his head and, seeing the spume of oblivion, reached for the cross hanging from the bedpost. He had barely touched it when the current carried off the small house like driftwood.

When the waters had reached the dam, their rush slowed down and the level across the valley began to rise, until it reached the ridge of the roof of the tallest houses, the marble cornice of the town hall, the tiled dome of St Timotheo and eventually stopped a few feet from the belfry. Whatever was not tied down or weighed down came up to the surface one after the other: the tables and the cues of the pool hall, the icons of the Apostles and other parts of the torn altarpiece, a small cage with a dead canary, a lacquered box of a barrel organ, the cetacean mass of the coffee-shop proprietor who had slept through it all and drowned without knowing it.

Later, a flotilla of torn pages of books appeared, drifting among the dreary flotsam. The water had smudged the ink on all of them but one, where a lonely word of faint letters was written: 'ΤΕΛΟΣ' – which means, THE END.